A Wicked Yarn

A Craft Fair Knitters Mystery

Emmie Caldwell

BERKLEY PRIME CRIME
New York

BERKLEY PRIME CRIME
Published by Berkley
An imprint of Penguin Random House LLC
penguinrandomhouse.com

Copyright © 2020 by Mary Ellen Hughes
Excerpt from *Stitched in Crime* by Emmie Caldwell copyright © 2020
by Mary Ellen Hughes

BERKLEY and the BERKLEY & B colophon are registered trademarks and
BERKLEY PRIME CRIME is a trademark of Penguin Random House LLC.

ISBN: 9780593101681

First Edition: December 2020

Printed in the United States of America
1 3 5 7 9 10 8 6 4 2

Cover art by Mary Ann Lasher
Cover design by Judith Lagerman
Book design by George Towne

For Christopher Gawronski, the top reader—
and probably writer—of the bunch of us

Chapter 1

Lia surveyed the scene before her with contentment, a feeling that not so long ago she doubted she would experience again but which she now savored. Her gaze wandered over the vendors who lined the huge barn, readying their booths for the start of the Crandalsburg Craft Fair: quilts, pottery, jewelry, suncatchers, and so much more, along with her own knitted goods. It was a beehive of activity and amazing colors as the craftsmen set out their wares, and she was so glad to be a part of it. She knew Tom would be proud of how she'd pulled her life back together after losing him. It had been hard, and required plenty of help, but she'd done it. Not the same as her old life—and never would be—but fine. She scolded herself. It was more than fine. Her new life was good!

Lia turned to her booth. Was it ready? Cabled crewnecks hung at the back, along with lightweight summer cardigans. Baby blankets, sweaters, and pink-and-blue-ribboned caps lay at one end of her front counter, knitted place mats, coasters, and two afghans neatly folded at the other.

Her stocktaking was interrupted by sharp, attention-getting claps. Belinda Peebles, the craft fair's manager, marched through the center of the barn, her strident voice carrying to the rafters. "Come on, people! It's almost ten! Enough with the dawdling. Get yourselves together!"

Dawdling? Lia's eyelids twitched. She hadn't noticed any dawdling. She saw vendors reacting to the unwarranted scolding with annoyed looks or ducking out of view. Lia knew Belinda was often edgy before the beginning of a fair weekend, but this seemed more than usual. She caught Belinda's eye as she circled Lia's way and pulled her over with a subtle head motion.

"You okay?" Lia asked.

"I would be if this group would get its act together!" The fair manager impatiently brushed back a strand of dark brown hair that had dared to slip out of her bun. "This is a big weekend. Mother's Day!"

"Everyone knows that, Belinda," Lia said gently. "They're probably on pins and needles themselves. A little pep talk would go a long way, I'd say. Remember Miss Jenkins revving up our soccer team before a game and what a difference that always made?" Lia was glad to see a smile creep across Belinda's face and added, "You know we all appreciate the work you put in for the craft fair."

Belinda stared into Lia's blue-gray eyes a moment before nodding briskly. She gave a determined tug to straighten the knit tunic that hugged her sturdy frame and took a few steps back from the booth.

"Good luck, everyone! We have a large crowd already gathering out there. I know it's going to be a great weekend!"

Faces cleared, and Lia heard a few mild cheers. She gave Belinda a thumbs-up as the manager walked by, heading toward her office and looking less tense, though still not happy. That concerned Lia, who owed a lot to her old friend. She knew that Belinda came across to many as difficult and overbearing, but Lia knew about her softer side.

It was because of this considerate friend that Lia had made the move from York to Crandalsburg, a wrenching but ultimately healthy change for her after Tom died so suddenly. Belinda recognized how painful it had been for Lia to be surrounded by daily reminders of what she had lost and brought her to the small town where she lived, beginning with short visits. Those visits eased Lia into making it a permanent stay.

And it was Belinda's craft fair that now gave Lia a new and exciting purpose: managing a booth filled with hand-knitted items, both her own and those of her knitting circle back in York. She and the group had long run out of people to knit for and ached for new challenges and outlets for their skills. Knitting for the craft fair connected delighted buyers with their lovingly made items and gave joy to all. A win-win, they all agreed, with Lia taking a modest percentage of the total sales to compensate for her time and efforts.

When Bill Landry, who worked security for the fair, opened the doors of the Crandalsburg Craft Fair at precisely ten o'clock, Lia focused on the surge of shoppers, all looking excited and eager—a very good sign. They fanned out, some turning to the booths at each side of the entrance, while others made beelines for particular booths. Lia was delighted to see a pair of women heading her way.

"This is it, Carrie," the older of the two said to her

companion. "This is where I bought those place mats. Ninth Street Knits."

Lia smiled at the mention of the name she and her knitter friends had chosen. Ninth Street was the location of Jen Beasley's home, just outside of York, where they'd met weekly for so many years.

"Hello again," Lia greeted the auburn-haired woman. "You bought the light green place mats a couple of weeks ago, didn't you?"

"Yes!" The woman looked pleased to be remembered, and Lia blessed her ability to recall faces, though names were a different thing. "They went great with my kitchen colors, and Carrie, here, loved the little daisies knitted into the corners."

"Do you have them in yellow?" Carrie asked.

"Let's see." Lia quickly found one set of yellow place mats and pulled them from the pile.

But Carrie's face fell. "There's no daisies," she said, which was true. These were flower-free, though Lia had worked in thin stripes of white.

"Look, there's daisies on these blue ones." Carrie's friend found a set in navy blue. "The dark color really sets off the white flowers."

"But I wanted yellow, to set off my new dishes." She looked over to Lia. "Can I order them?"

"Absolutely." Though Lia had knitted the blue place mats, she was currently in the middle of an ambitious, multicolored afghan. But she knew her fellow Ninth Street Knitter Maureen Evert had the daisy pattern and would have the time. She gave Carrie a form to fill out and an estimated time frame for the finished product, then collected the deposit. By the time they were done, new customers had arrived to browse.

Lia was kept pleasantly busy for several minutes. When there was a lull she sat on her folding chair and pulled out the burgundy-colored square that would eventually be part of the afghan. As she knitted, she observed the action and the atmosphere of the craft fair. Booths were filled with a mind-boggling array of wares in all sizes, shapes, and colors, as well as media: wood, leather, glass, metal, fabric, and clay. Then there were the canvas and paper paintings of Joan Fowler and framed photographs of Mark Simmons. Most vendors were artists in one way or another, in addition to her booth neighbor Olivia Byrd, who made herbal soaps, and Zach Goodwin, who brought in honey from his hives. Where Lia fit in, she wasn't sure. Somewhere in the middle worked for her.

A glance at Olivia showed her to be a bit frazzled, which was ironic since one of the things she sold, besides her handmade soap, was an essential oil that promoted calm. She had lip balms, too, and herbal bath salts that sent lovely aromas wafting over to Lia, who was sure the wonderful scents affected her customers in a positive way as they fingered her items, putting them in the best mood to buy.

Olivia's stress appeared to come from her struggle to find a particular lip balm among the many for an impatient customer. Lia was glad when Olivia finally found it. It was a small sale, but satisfying every customer was important, especially when your business was slow, as it had been for Olivia lately. When the woman left with her purchase, Lia caught Olivia's eye and smiled encouragingly.

She was about to say something, too, when she heard her name called and turned her head. Belinda leaned over the side of Lia's booth that edged the walkway leading to the office.

"When you get a chance, would you come back for a minute? I need to talk."

"Sure." *What about?* rose to Lia's lips, but she'd have to wait to find out. Belinda had already turned away. Lia continued to work at her afghan square until a new customer appeared at her booth. She stood to help the young man decide on a Mother's Day gift of cozy knitted slippers, but part of her mind remained on Belinda and what she wanted to discuss. It was clear something was bothering her friend.

Chapter 2

"Alfred is selling the barn," Belinda stated flatly as soon as Lia took a seat in front of her desk.

Lia's mind went blank. Alfred? Then it came to her. "Alfred Schumacher?" Lia had heard about the Schumachers, how they'd owned the barn for generations, gradually selling off farmland but managing to hold on to a few acres surrounding the large barn. The craft fair used the empty fields for parking and to accommodate booths outdoors during milder months.

"Why?" Lia asked. "Rather, why now? After all these years."

"Alfred says he's getting too old to deal with it. I think the offer was too good to turn down." Belinda sank her head into her hands, a rare show of emotion other than impatience.

"I'm sorry," Lia said. "What does this mean for the craft fair? Will the new owner let it go on?"

Belinda lifted her head slightly and shook it. "The new owner—assuming the sale goes through—is Darren." Her eyes hardened. "There's nothing he'd like better than to destroy me and everything I've worked for. Once he gets his hands on the property, the craft fair is done for."

"Oh!" Lia had met Darren but didn't know him well. He and Belinda had been married briefly. It was during a busy time in Lia's life, when she was working as a surgical nurse while also guiding their daughter, Hayley, through the turbulent teens. The busyness of both couples, in fact, had limited their opportunities to socialize. Lia remembered finding the man pleasant and charming, at least at first. She remembered Tom commenting that he'd met used-car salesmen who were more sincere than Darren.

"Darren's a businessman, Belinda." Lia had tapped into her memory and come up with the fact that he was a real estate developer. "Surely he wouldn't sink money into a property simply to hurt you, would he?"

Belinda laughed grimly. "You think not? You don't know him. He never wanted the divorce, you know." She grimaced. "Not because he cared anything about me, but because it disrupted his life. It made him look bad, and he hated that. *Really* hated it. This is a man who'll get his revenge, no matter how long it takes or what it costs him."

Lia knew that Belinda and Darren's divorce had been a bitter one, but Belinda always kept the details to herself. It didn't appear she'd come out terribly well, financially. She put in long hours managing the craft fair as well as other events at the barn and wasn't living in luxury.

"What will you do if you lose access to the barn? Can you move the fair somewhere else?"

"No," Belinda said. "This is it. The Crandalsburg Craft

Fair thrives in great part because of its proximity to Gettysburg. We're within reach of tourists and day-trippers who come to see the historic town and battlefield. When they have enough of history, they wander over to us to shop. There's no other affordable facility large enough in the area." Belinda rubbed at her face. "If I move the fair site too far, I lose the tourists as well as most of my vendors, who live locally. They won't want to drag their goods back and forth any great distance."

Lia saw the worry on Belinda's face. She'd spent years building the weekend craft fair as well as filling in the week with other activities in the barn, things like meetings and receptions, and even dance classes. To lose access to what had become her life would be devastating.

Less devastating would be the effect on the Ninth Street Knitters, but it would be a huge disappointment, just when things had barely got going for them. It had become an important part of Lia's recovery, too, and frankly, the added income had made a difference, not only to her but to others in the group.

"Don't you have a contract with Alfred?" she asked.

"Of course. But unfortunately for me there's a clause that lets him off the hook." Belinda's face hardened. "Darren won't get away with this."

"What do you mean to do?" Lia asked a little worriedly.

"He'll be sorry he went down this road." Belinda stood, ignoring Lia's question.

"Do you think you can stop him?" Lia asked.

"Don't say anything to the others," Belinda said. "Not yet." She stepped over to her window to stare through it, her thoughts obviously churning, and from the tension of her stance, Lia wasn't sure she wanted to know in what direction. Essentially dismissed, Lia left and returned to her booth, thanking Olivia for watching over it while she was gone.

"Everything okay?" Olivia asked, letting Lia know her expression was worrisome. Lia cleared it, managing a small smile, and was glad when a shopper stopped at Olivia's booth to distract her. That allowed Lia to sit down to knit and think.

During a late afternoon lull, Lia had a chat on a happier subject with Olivia. The younger woman was excited about a special order a customer had placed for a Mother's Day gift basket.

"She wants at least one of almost everything I make," Olivia said. "Two each of the herbal soaps. The basket will be enormous!" *And a terrific sale*, she didn't add, though that was obvious.

Olivia, thin, rather pale, and with limp, dull blond hair, was a worrier by nature and hadn't seen good sales for a while, for whatever reason. Lia was glad to see the shadows around her eyes be replaced with happy crinkles.

"Maybe I should pick up more baskets tonight along with the big one," Olivia said. "Fill them with an assortment of products and wrap them in cellophane and ribbons. I could have them ready for tomorrow. What do you think, Lia?"

"I think that's a great idea. Perfect for your kind of booth and for shoppers looking for a very nice but quick and easy gift. I predict you'll sell out."

Olivia smiled, a pink glow rising in her cheeks, and

Lia wished she could see that look more often. That and an occasional laugh would relax some of those worry lines that shouldn't be on a twenty-nine-year-old's face. As far as Lia knew, Olivia had a happy home life with a loving husband and young son, and all were in good health. She obviously loved making and selling her soaps and oils. A realization that her life was worth smiling about and that no meteorite was speeding in her direction to destroy it all—at least not that day—was in order. At least Lia thought so. She would never directly *say* so, though a gentle hint, now and then, might pass her lips.

They had moved on to talk of ribbon colors for the baskets when two men dressed in business suits strode into the craft barn. They ignored the craft stalls and vendors and instead wandered about, the shorter, stouter one pointing out various points, high and low, in the facility. Shoppers were few at the time, and the place was quiet enough for his voice to carry, which seemed to be his intention.

"Not nearly big enough to convert into anything like a supermarket," he boomed. "And old. Would have to be totally rewired and remodeled for any good use. Not worth the cost." His taller companion nodded agreement as they circled the area, seemingly oblivious to the stares and question marks on every vendor's face.

"Best thing," he pronounced, "is to tear it down, start from scratch."

"Oh, you'd love that, wouldn't you, Darren." Belinda suddenly appeared, striding toward the two.

"Ah, my not-so-lovely ex." Darren Peebles, whom Lia had finally recognized, stopped to face the manager, his lips curling slyly. "I didn't dare to hope we'd see you today."

"Come off it, Darren. You couldn't wait to rush over and rub this in my face. But it's not going to work. I know enough about your shady business to make Schumacher shred any contract before you get anywhere near it."

"You don't know squat, my dear. And never did, simply because there was nothing to know. And before you even think about making threats, you might keep in mind that little incident from the summer of 'oh-eight. Wouldn't like to see that spread around, would you?"

Belinda's eyes narrowed. "I knew you were low, but I didn't know how low. If you would stoop to—"

"I'll stoop as low as necessary to clear whatever gets in my way, so I'd advise you to stay out of it. Now, unless you want to air more dirty laundry in front of these lovely people . . ." He waved an arm toward the stunned vendors and shoppers. Belinda, uncharacteristically speechless and with a beet-colored face, turned on her heel.

Darren Peebles grinned as he watched her stomp off. When the office door banged, he actually chuckled and murmured something to his companion. The two turned and eventually left, though not in any kind of hurry, Peebles chatting casually the entire time.

Once they'd gone, Lia glanced around the barn. The vendors seemed frozen in place. Quilter Maggie Wood's arms were outstretched, holding a half-folded quilt. Beekeeper Zach Goodwin gripped the jar of honey he'd been stacking on a row of others. Joan Fowler still held one of her watercolor paintings for a shopper, who'd turned her back on it at the start of the argument. Both looked stunned.

Slowly, the craft fair came back to life, though the vision was eerie. Lia, standing at the side of her booth where she'd been chatting with Olivia, saw that her neighbor was okay—as wide-eyed as Lia probably was, but not overly upset. Perhaps the excitement of her big sale had been enough to insulate her? Just as well, since Lia didn't have a thing to say about what they'd witnessed, a condition that lasted until it was time to leave.

Chapter 3

Lia's daughter had texted that she'd arrived, so Lia set aside craft fair problems for the time being and drove home in a lighter mood. The professed reason for Hayley's visit was Mother's Day weekend, but she had been driving from Philadelphia often. Lia sensed a need in Hayley to regularly check on her mother—unnecessary, to Lia's mind, but she wasn't going to protest just yet, since she enjoyed the visits. When she thought they were becoming too much of a burden for her daughter, Lia would say something.

She'd given Hayley an extra key to the house and wasn't surprised to see lights on inside when she pulled up in front. Lia had bought a much smaller place than she and Tom had owned in York, but it fit her current needs. It was a well-kept-up but older home, built before the Civil War, and something about the place spoke to her when she had first toured it.

She liked the welcoming porch that fronted one of Crandalsburg's quiet side streets and the cozy parlor that was small enough for one person to feel snug in but with enough space for three or four to gather comfortably. The plumbing and wiring had been updated, a very important consideration, but the character of the house remained, making her feel, as she sat and knitted by the light of a single lamp, as though she had gone back in time. She loved imagining the lives of the previous occupants and sometimes felt pleasantly surrounded by them.

"That would creep me out," Hayley had said when her mother shared that tidbit with her, but it was fine with Lia.

As Lia climbed out of her car, Hayley stepped out onto the porch, her long blond hair, the same color Tom's had once been, catching the late-day sun and framing features that were a mix of both parents. Her temperament was totally her own, more lively than either Lia's or Tom's, but also less practical and much more impulsive, traits that had caused difficulties when she was growing up. Lia was relieved that maturity had moderated both, but Hayley was still a work in progress.

"Happy Mother's Day!" Hayley came down the short walkway to throw her arms around her mother. She wore a flower-printed tee knotted at the waist of her artfully torn jeans.

"Thank you, dear," Lia said, hugging back. "How was your drive? Any problems?"

They turned and headed back to the house, arm in arm. "None whatsoever. Unless you count the turtles on the turnpike."

"Turtles? Oh, you mean drivers going the speed limit?"

"In the left lane, Mother!" She held the door open for Lia.

"Yes, I see," Lia said, stepping inside. "Unbearable.

Are you hungry? I fixed a chicken dish to pop in the oven. But it'll take about half an hour."

"Oh! I was thinking I'd treat you to dinner tonight. We can't do it tomorrow. You'll be at the fair all day, and I have to head back before dinner. But if you have something ready . . ."

"Such a lot of driving in two days! It's very nice of you, Hayley, but you know I'm just as happy to pass on a made-up holiday like Mother's Day, especially when it means putting you to so much trouble."

"It's not a lot of trouble, Mom. I enjoy driving, really. Well, except when there's turtles in front of me. But I kinda wanted to talk to you about something."

"Oh?" Lia paused on her way through the house to look back at her daughter.

"It can wait." Hayley passed her to get to the kitchen. "If dinner's not for half an hour, got any munchies?"

"There's cheese and crackers, grapes, carrot sticks. Help yourself." Lia squeezed past her daughter, who had opened the refrigerator door to peer inside, narrowing the walking space in the already tight room. She turned the oven on to preheat and pointed out the covered dish on the middle shelf of the refrigerator. "Want to slip that in when the temp gets to three-fifty? I'm going to run upstairs."

Lia headed to the narrow, nineteenth-century, squeaky staircase to the right of her front door, wondering once again how the original occupants had negotiated it—meaning anyone with hoop skirts or standing taller than five feet four. She ducked slightly halfway up to negotiate the landing. She also wondered what Hayley wanted to talk about, something that she wasn't eager to jump into. Money problems? Lia shook her head. Not likely. Her daughter had landed a good job shortly after graduation, which allowed her to stay in Philadelphia, the city she'd come to love during her college years. Roommate trouble? Doubtful. She and Jessica had been friends since middle school. Lia was sure that any issue that came up would be worked out without her help.

Lia freshened up and changed out of her craft fair attire into more casual and comfortable clothes: elastic-waist pants and a loose blouse. Whatever Hayley had on her mind, Lia would simply have to wait to hear. She trotted downstairs and found her small dining table set for two with Lia's good china.

"Is this okay?" Hayley asked. "I thought since we weren't going out, we should still make it a special dinner."

Lia smiled. "I haven't had those dishes out since I moved here. It's nice to see them again. But where did the flowers come from?"

"My car. I forgot and left them in the back. Like them?"

"They're lovely. Thank you! You didn't have to do that." Lia gave her daughter a hug.

"I know," Hayley said. "But Dad always got you flowers, didn't he? I thought I'd keep it going."

Lia blinked away the tears that came to her eyes at that, and she caught Hayley doing the same. Eleven months wasn't long enough to mention Tom without feeling emotional, but it was getting easier, and Lia didn't mind. Shedding a few tears once in a while with her daughter was probably therapeutic for them both, and when it was just the two of them, neither was embarrassed in the least.

"Well!" Lia said. "Let's see if our dinner is ready to eat. I'm hungry!"

* * *

They lingered at the table over coffee after finishing their meal, and Lia told Hayley about the fight that had occurred between Belinda and her ex. "When it ended, everyone seemed to recover in slow motion," she said, describing the stunned vendors.

"Freaky! Do you think he'll really tear down the barn?" Hayley asked.

"It sounded like it, unless he was just trying to agitate Belinda."

"Ha! It worked. But he must be a real piece of, well, you know, a real creep to do that. Good thing she got rid of him, I mean with the divorce. But what about the craft fair?"

"It's in real jeopardy," Lia admitted.

"Oh shoot! Your knitting booth!"

"Which would go, along with all the others, and I'd hate that. The bigger problem would be Belinda's. But . . . ," Lia said, pausing to drain her cup, "it's not a done deal. Nothing's been signed or any plans put in motion. Things could still change." She didn't mention Belinda's prediction that Darren would be sorry to go down that road. Surely that came from her anger and distress and meant nothing.

"Well!" Lia said. "Enough about that. You had something you wanted to talk about?"

"Uh, yeah." Hayley stood and began picking up plates and silverware to carry into the kitchen. "How about we go out for ice cream to top off dinner? My treat. Is that little stand open yet? We can talk on the way."

Lia followed Hayley, carrying the cups and saucers and worrying a bit about what might be coming. But she helped load the dishwasher and wrapped up and put the leftovers away. Once her kitchen was set to rights, she threw on a light sweater as Hayley grabbed her purse before heading out.

"I love this little town," Hayley said after they got their cones at the stand just three blocks from Lia's house and on the edge of the town center. Licking their ice cream, they strolled on, checking out store windows. A gift shop and a clothing store sandwiched a small tea shop that was closed and dark. Those were followed by a hardware store that had interesting gadgets on display. "It's so easy to get around. Not like Philly and all the traffic."

"It is nice," Lia agreed. "But Philadelphia has a lot more to get around *to*. Restaurants, theaters, museums."

"Mm-hmm."

Lia waited. After more window-shopping, Hayley said, "Mom, I'm thinking of taking some time off from work. I'd like to come back and stay a few days, if that's all right with you."

Uh-oh. "Of course it's all right, Hayley. But this is sudden. Is something wrong?"

"That's just it. I don't know. I need to think." She turned to Lia. "It's my job. My so-called career. I don't think it's working for me."

Not working for her. Lia could almost hear Tom's reaction to that. *Last I heard, a person worked for the job, not the other way around.* But Lia took a milder tack. "What's not working about it?" she asked. "You loved your marketing courses, and you were excited when you got the job offer."

"I know." Hayley dropped her unfinished cone into a trash basket. "That was then. Now I feel differently. I'm not sure anymore that it's what I want to do for the rest of my life."

"It's only been, what, ten months?"

"Ten *long* months. Mom, I haven't made any decisions yet. I'm not jumping into, or rather out of, anything in a rush, you know, like I used to, when I was a kid. That's why I want the time off. To mull things over. Carefully."

"But time off without pay, Hayley? You probably haven't earned vacation time yet, right?"

"I have a couple of days due, and I'm willing to use them up. It's that important to me, Mom."

"Okay." Thinking things over carefully was the advice she and Tom had given Hayley for years, so how could she argue? But there was so much Hayley had left unsaid— ironic for a communications major. Lia was sure there was more to the story but decided not to press her daughter. There'd be time ahead of them, opportunities for the rest to come out.

The next morning, Lia and Hayley went to church— together, but driving separately. St. Vincent's was between Crandalsburg and the craft fair barn, and Lia had decided to continue on to the barn afterward.

In the church parking lot, Hayley said, "I'll come by around one with the picnic lunch, okay? We can eat during your break."

"That should be a good time. And you might want to pick up a cake from Carolyn Hanson's booth while you're there to take back with you. If she hasn't sold out by then."

"I might pick up more than that. I haven't had any time to bake. Remember how I used to love it? Maybe that's what I should be doing, making cakes or something, instead of marketing." Lia gave her a look, and Hayley shrugged and grinned. "Just an idea. Don't worry, I won't be making any hasty decisions."

They hugged, and Lia climbed into her white Camry, then lowered her window to wave good-bye as she drove off.

It was another lovely day. May in the Crandalsburg area wasn't any different from May in York. But Lia felt more aware of it as she drove on quiet roads lined with spring-blooming trees or acres of sprouting crops.

She thought of the alpaca farm she'd visited a few weeks ago and decided to make another trip. She loved seeing the animals, and it wasn't too soon to start knitting sweaters and scarves with those special yarns. But would she have an outlet for those items? The thought of the craft fair folding and not having any reason to knit with those yarns started to bring her down, that and her lingering concerns about Hayley. She clicked on the radio for some distracting music.

The sight of the craft barn up ahead cheered her, and she soon turned onto the approaching drive. The red-painted sides, set off by white-trimmed windows, were nicely lit by the sun, which also turned the metal rooster atop one of the white cupolas into a glowing beacon. The rooster, she'd been told, had been made by Lou Krause, the metalworker who had a booth at the craft fair. One of Lou's pieces, a wall hanging, had tempted Lia. Perhaps she'd take another look that day if there was time.

Lia slowed as she always did when she drove up the narrow drive, to soak in the sight of the three-story structure. She'd been told that the building had been used as a hospital during the Civil War, which touched her heart, especially recalling the minimal medical aid available at the time for the poor young men and the suffering they must have endured. How, she wondered, could anyone think of tearing down such a historic and beautiful structure? It boggled her mind, and Lia dearly hoped Darren Peebles's statement had been thrown out only to agitate Belinda and was not what he truly intended.

Coming directly after the nine o'clock Mass, she knew she'd be arriving earlier than the Sunday opening time of eleven and planned to knit in her car as she waited for Belinda to arrive with her keys. Lia was surprised, therefore, as she drew closer, to see the side door ajar. She pulled into the parking area behind the split-rail fence and spotted Belinda's black Acura in the lot. A second car that Lia didn't recognize, a Lexus, sat a few spaces away, though she hardly knew what everyone exhibiting at the fair drove. Maybe it was Alfred Schumacher's, and he was there to discuss the sale of his barn with Belinda, or perhaps to be persuaded against it? But the red luxury car seemed an unlikely ride for the elderly man, who claimed to need the money from the property's sale.

Lia parked and picked up the box of knitted items she'd brought to replenish her stock from the previous day. As she approached the barn, a feeling of uneasiness fell over her, though she tried to shrug it off. Surely it was only the unusual silence, when she was used to the noisy bustle of other vendors arriving. Still, it felt eerie.

Lia paused at the opened door. All was dim inside, the only light coming from the barn's high windows, and quiet, so quiet. She had to urge herself to step inside, and when she finally did, she left the door open behind her.

She needed to blink several times to adjust to the gloom but eventually was able to discern a figure in the shadows over to her left. Belinda? Lia moved toward her, calling out hello, and expected to see her friend look over.

But the woman remained tautly in the same position, slightly bent forward over something on the floor. Finally, her head turned, and the look on her face was frightening.

"Lia," Belinda said, her voice cracking. "He's dead."

Lia stopped. She couldn't have heard that, could she? But a few steps closer confirmed that she had. A man lay on the floor beneath both women's gazes, clearly lifeless.

"It's Darren," Belinda said.

"Are you sure?" What Lia saw was a man in a suit, with his face covered.

"Yes. I lifted the place mat to see."

Good heavens! It was one of Lia's knitted navy blue place mats, its white daisy incongruously cheery. Peering closer, Lia saw what looked like a circle of dried blood surrounding Darren's head, mixed with shards of broken pottery. Two tall, handcrafted candles flanked his body, and worst of all a metal sculpture of a grinning clown had been planted inches beyond Lia's blue place mat like a bizarre headstone.

Lia looked to Belinda with horror, unable to voice what sprang instantly to mind.

"I didn't do it," the craft fair manager said flatly. She stepped back and pulled a phone from her jacket pocket. Lia watched as she punched in three numbers. "Yes," she said after a moment. "My name is Belinda Peebles."

She coughed and cleared her voice before adding, "I'm at the Schumacher barn. Send the police. There's been a murder."

Chapter 4

With years of nursing behind her, Lia thought she knew how to deal with stress. But she was learning what a huge difference it made to not be the one in control. As she watched officials and technicians flood the area, she thought she understood what it was like to be the patient lying on the table, waiting anxiously for what came next.

She worried for Belinda, who'd stated to Lia that she didn't do it. Belinda had also told her that her spare key to the barn had been stolen. But she'd shut down after that, possibly as shocked as Lia and processing it in her own way. Lia knew how bad it would look for her friend, at least at first glance. Would a deeper examination find evidence to exonerate her?

Lia thought about the broken pottery, the candles, and the clown sculpture placed next to the body, all apparently taken from the craft fair's vendor stalls, including her own knitted place mat. But why? Besides the fact that Belinda was not a murderer, it would be totally unlike her to then set such a strange scene like that. But would the police see it that way?

Lia and Belinda were quickly separated for questioning. Lia told all she knew, which was minimal, but she was asked to go over it multiple times. She understood why, though the repetition was still terribly tedious. It was a relief when it ended and she was told she could leave. Lia had assured Hayley by phone that there was no need to come, but she was cheered to spot her waving behind the cordoned-off area and hurried over.

"Are you okay, Mom?" Hayley asked.

"I'm fine." Maybe not the exact truth, but she was still upright.

"C'mon, let's go," Hayley said. "My car's over there." She pointed to her burgundy Nissan parked partway down the road.

Lia blinked. Her brain had grown fuzzy with fatigue. "What about mine?"

"We can get it later, Mom. You don't want to drive right now. You need to get home."

Lia surrendered without further argument. There were times when giving up control was a good thing.

After she got home, Lia tried to reach Belinda, but her calls and messages went unanswered, leaving Lia with little choice other than to wait. She allowed Hayley to fuss over her a little and sipped at her second cup of tea, her feet propped on a hassock.

"I'm so sorry for all the vendors," she said after going through all the details of the scene at the barn with Hayley and moving on to the collateral damage of the murder. "This was going to be such a big day for sales. Everyone loaded their booths with particular things for Mother's Day. Oh, and poor Olivia! She had a special order. It would have been her best sale in a long while. She was so excited."

"At least it's not perishable," Hayley said. "Olivia's stuff, I mean. And yours and a lot of the others."

"But not Carolyn's," Lia said, shaking her head. "She and her daughters probably baked loads of coffee cakes and every other kind of pastry for today. I don't know what they'll do with it all."

Hayley clicked her tongue. "That's a shame. Maybe they can sell them out of her house? I wouldn't mind running over for one." She set her own cup on one of Lia's narrow end tables. "What do you suppose will happen to the craft fair itself?"

"Well, the barn won't be sold, at least not to Darren Peebles. But, gosh, even if it isn't, the murder itself might cause plenty of damage to the fair's reputation."

"Unless it's solved right away, over and done with, back to normal." Hayley appeared to think that cheery thought over. "But I guess a lot will depend on who did it."

"Yes," Lia agreed. "Who." If the murderer was someone connected to the Crandalsburg Craft Fair, it was doomed, and they both knew the fair's manager, Belinda, was in a tight spot. There was the very public fight she'd had with Darren, and the fact that his death would clearly benefit her. To top it off, she had been the person on the scene when Lia had arrived, gazing down at her dead ex-husband.

"But," Lia said, coming to her friend's defense, "besides the fact that Belinda would never do such a thing, if, hypothetically speaking, she had, she wouldn't kill Darren at the barn, would she? It's just common sense that she'd pick anywhere else."

"Maybe it wasn't planned, Mom. It could have been one of those heat-of-the moment things."

"But she didn't look the least bit heated when I walked in. And the candles? The clown sculpture? Why in the world would she drag those around him?"

"I don't know," Hayley said with a helpless shrug. "If you're crazy enough to commit murder, maybe you'll do lots of other crazy things."

Lia frowned. "Maybe." But maybe not, too. It didn't sit right with her.

"So what exactly did him in?" Hayley asked. She shifted position in her chair, curling her bare feet under her. "You said there was blood."

Lia nodded. "Around his head, along with broken pottery. My guess is he was hit hard with one of Annie Bradburn's beautiful pots."

"Ugh! How much strength would that take?" Hayley asked. "Could a woman do it? I mean, if not, maybe that would let Belinda off the hook."

"I have no idea, dear." But Lia pictured Belinda's solid build and remembered how effortlessly she'd lifted Lia's packed moving boxes out of the back of her car. That argument wasn't going to fly. "We'll just have to wait for an official report."

Hayley offered to stay overnight with Lia, but Lia waved the suggestion off. "No need. Go back tonight as planned and arrange for your time off. Do you think that'll be doable?"

"Sure. I'm between projects right now so nobody'll mind. Huh! They might not even notice I'm gone!"

"Is that the problem?" Lia asked gently.

"Just kidding. No, it should be fine as long as I tie up a couple of things first. Is my coming Thursday or Friday okay with you?"

"Absolutely, for as long as you need."

They heated up the leftovers from the previous night—Lia hardly able to believe it had been only twenty-four hours—and ate a quick meal, after which Hayley drove them back to the barn to collect Lia's car. They hugged one final time before Hayley took off, promising as usual to text Lia that she'd made it back to her place in Philadelphia safely.

As Lia watched her daughter drive away, she wondered about the remark that Hayley had passed off as a joke. *They might not even notice I'm gone.* Sometimes jokes could be revealing. Lia would hold on to it and wait for more to come along.

At ten the next morning, after multiple calls to Belinda continued to go to voice mail, Lia decided to go to her house. She knew how Belinda tended to hole herself up, convinced that not talking about a problem meant it would go away. That wasn't going to work so well this time.

Belinda's house was the one she and Darren had once shared and which she had retained after their divorce. It had impressed Lia and Tom when they first saw it years ago, with its vaulted-ceiling living room, roomy eat-in kitchen, and airy sunroom, along with the beautiful landscaping. But Lia saw signs of neglect in that landscaping—overgrown or dead shrubs—and siding that needed a good power wash, along with several missing or broken slates on the roof. Whether the unkempt condition was from lack of money or time, Lia didn't know, but it set a depressing tone as she drove up.

She rang the doorbell, banged the knocker, and called out until she finally saw an upstairs curtain twitch and in a minute or so heard the locks turn. Belinda stood before her, dressed in sweat pants and a long shirt. Her hair looked like she hadn't touched it since getting out of bed.

"What are you doing here?" she asked, looking puzzled and just a little annoyed.

"I came to see how you're doing. You aren't answering your phone."

"I've been too busy using it. All the events at the barn have to be rescheduled, which is a major headache. Then there's the cleanup. Did you know you can't just send in a regular crew? It has to be done by a licensed crime scene cleanup crew. I just spent half an hour explaining that to Alfred Schumacher, who'd love to push the expense onto me. In his dreams!"

"I'm sorry about all that. But I'm mostly concerned about you. May I come in?"

Belinda looked hesitant, but she stepped aside. Lia headed directly through the large foyer and down the hallway to the kitchen at the back of the house.

"Have you eaten anything today?"

"I had coffee."

Lia looked in the double-door refrigerator, glad to see staples like eggs and milk. Not exactly bare but not much. "Scrambled or fried?" she asked, pulling out the eggs.

"Neither." At Lia's raised-eyebrow glare, she gave in and pointed to the freezer. "There's bagels in the freezer. And I think there's a tub of cream cheese somewhere near the back. I'm not sure how old it is. Want coffee? I've got the hazelnut K-Cups that you like."

Glad to see her friend cooperating, Lia let Belinda make coffee as she pulled out a bag of frozen bagels and dropped two halves into the toaster. She found the cream cheese and checked it carefully. Seeing nothing suspicious, she set it next to the bagel plate.

Within a few minutes, with one toasted bagel consumed and the coffee doing its work, Lia could see positive signs of tension leaving Belinda. She sipped from her own mug, then asked, "So, how did it go with the police yesterday?"

"I don't know." Belinda licked cream cheese from her lips. "Not terrible. They asked a lot of questions. I gave them what I knew, and that was it."

"You were still there when I left."

"Yeah. Every time a new guy showed up, I had to go through the whole thing again. Like, was it too much trouble for one of them to tell the other what I'd said?"

"You told them about one of your keys to the barn missing?" When Belinda nodded, Lia asked, "Did they seem to believe it?"

"Why wouldn't they? It's true."

"They might think it was very convenient. You know you're going to be their first suspect, right? I mean, because of your relationship with Darren and how his death benefits you."

"Of course I know that. But I can't be the only one who would have wanted to kill Darren. There'd probably be a line from here to Pittsburgh of people who'd be happy to do away with him."

"But his body didn't end up in any of their workplaces, which makes you first in line. Have you thought about getting a lawyer?"

"No, because I don't need one, and I'm not going to

waste the money!" Belinda's bravado faded. "I can't afford to. Lia, if anyone thinks Darren's death is going to benefit me, they only have to look at my bank account. I've been living week to week. Losing this time at the barn will cost me. The police can suspect whoever they want, but I've got to keep my events going or I'm going to go under—lose this house, for one thing! So if you'll excuse me, I really have to get back to work. Thank you for stopping by." Belinda stood up and waited for Lia to do the same.

Lia sighed. At least she'd got some food into her friend, and she'd learned that no charges had been made. Belinda wasn't ready to discuss anything further than that, and Lia couldn't force her to. "Will you please call me if anything new comes up? Or if you just want to talk? Please?"

Belinda's expression softened. "I will." She walked Lia to the door, then gave her hand a squeeze at the last moment before closing it. Lia shook her head lightly as she stood on the narrow porch. It had struck her when they'd first visited as the kind of porch that said *don't linger*, which was exactly the message she'd just gotten. She hitched her purse onto her shoulder and stepped down to squeeze between two overgrown rhododendrons on the way to her car.

She wouldn't linger, but she would be back after she picked up a few groceries to fill in Belinda's meager fare—things like easy-to-cook frozen dinners, fresh fruit, and a few packs of cut-up veggies. Belinda might receive it with another puzzled scowl, but Lia knew that deep down she would be grateful. It just was so darned hard for her to express it.

Chapter 5

L ia spent much of the next few days knitting in front of
the television, which spouted nonstop talk about the
murder. With Crandalsburg normally such a peaceful,
crime-free town, it had become topic number one, and she
suffered through on-the-street interviews with people
who seemed happy to float wild theories in order to be
on-camera. She dropped stitches when one such resident
began with "Well, everyone knew the ex-wife had a grudge
and was capable of . . . ," and again when another recom-
mended keeping one's distance from the craft fair because
"You never know!" But she kept watching, feeling the
need to catch any nugget of information that she could,
though it required plenty of sifting.

The gold nugget that finally appeared was the news
about Darren Peebles's time of death: several hours before
Lia had come upon Belinda standing over him in the barn.

Lia was excited to hear that, though further thought tempered her joy. The time of death might not let Belinda totally off the hook. But it was still an important step.

Meeting up with the Ninth Street Knitters offered a welcome respite, as the weekly Thursday night get-together came up. Although it meant a longer drive since her move to Crandalsburg, the trip to York was doable, but she would have driven twice the distance in bad weather if she had to. She'd already spoken with each of her knitting friends by phone soon after the murder and had dealt with the immediate questions, so she looked forward to an evening focused on catching up with everyone's lives as they knitted and nibbled at the various treats brought along.

Jen Beasley's house on Ninth Street had become the regular meeting place some time ago, both because of its central location and because of Jen's insistence that she loved hosting. She also had the largest living room and an extremely lovable cat, which altogether made the decision a no-brainer.

When Lia pulled up, she saw the others had already arrived and hurried to gather her shrimp dip and knitting, keeping the two carefully apart. She didn't bother to knock—none of them ever did—and walked right in. Jen's husband, Bob, happened to be crossing the foyer, and he pointed to the kitchen.

"They're all in there," he said before turning away to sneeze.

"Caught a cold?" Lia asked.

"I'm not sure. Maybe. But I'll keep out of everyone's way just in case."

Lia wished him well and followed the voices coming from the kitchen. Hugs were exchanged amid the chatter, dishes were uncovered or unwrapped, with some carried into the living room, where the women gradually settled themselves in. Jen lifted her fluffy tan-and-white ragdoll cat, Daphne, off the sofa and onto a floor cushion from which the feline blinked her amazing blue eyes amenably at them all before curling up.

Lia chose the chair next to Daphne's cushion as she usually did so she could reach down and pet her once in a while. It had been a while since she'd had a cat of her own, and Daphne helped fill that void a little. Lia also loved the feel of Daphne's thick, silky fur and knew her yarn was safe next to that calm, contented creature. When questioned about how she came up with *Daphne*, Jen said it was the name of one of her grandmother's shrubs in North Carolina, a plant she'd always loved for its sweet aroma. To her mind that translated to the perfect name for her sweet southern belle of a pet.

"So, Lia," Jen asked as she began to work on a ribbed green hat with cabled trim, "will the craft fair go on and will the Ninth Street Knitters have a booth to knit for?" Jen was the oldest of the group by just a few years, though she didn't look it with her still-dark hair and a figure kept trim by years of yoga and wise eating.

"I hope so!" Tracy Kaufmann, blond, petite, and the youngest, was also the fastest knitter in the group. Her hands fairly blurred as she worked at a small pink-and-white cardigan. "I've made so many fun things since you took that booth, Lia, pieces I wouldn't have a reason to do otherwise. My boys have been turning up their noses at anything handmade. You'd think I was forcing ugly Christmas sweaters on them!" Tracy had twin sons in middle school, an age where wearing anything without the proper logo was out of the question. Lia had gone through that with Hayley and understood.

Maureen Evert and Diana Reynolds both started talking at once, something they often did. Lia was only surprised that they'd waited this long. The two were usually bursting with opinions and stories to share first thing at the meetings. Lia loved them both and often found their chatter soothing as she knitted, especially now that she lived alone.

"Girls!" Jen called out, clearly not finding it as soothing. "Let Lia answer the question." She turned to Lia. "Well?"

"Sorry, but I don't have an answer about the craft fair yet. All I can say is I'm hopeful it will reopen."

All four added their fervent hopes, too, which confirmed how important the Ninth Street Knits booth at the craft fair had become to them. The conversation then turned to other topics, as needles clacked and rows of stitches grew, giving Lia the breather she'd wanted and needed. She admired the beautiful raspberry yarn Diana was knitting into a sweater that looked luxuriously soft and smiled at the delicate flower-decorated baby cap Maureen was working on.

When she'd caught up with the others' lives, Lia brought up Hayley's situation. "She's just not giving me a good reason why she wants to leave her job. I could sympathize more if it was something I could understand."

"What has she said?" Maureen asked. Maureen worked in the personnel office of a small business and so had a particular interest.

"Very little. Just that it's not working for her. I don't know if it's the work itself or the workplace."

"If it's the workplace, it'll be an easy fix," Maureen

said. "Or at least easier. She can probably find a situation that's better for her. If she's found she just doesn't like the work, that'll be trickier."

"I know. She'll be coming to stay with me for a few days to think. I'm really hoping she'll open up more during that time. I can't offer advice if I don't know what the problem is."

"She might not be looking for advice," Jen said. "Just support."

Lia sighed. "True. And I realize she's old enough to make her own decisions. It's hard, though, to hold back."

"Hayley's a smart girl," Diana said. "I wouldn't worry about it too much. When I was twenty-three there were so many things I wanted to do. It was awful to have to pick just one."

"That's something she threw out," Lia said. "That she wasn't sure it was what she wanted to do for the rest of her life."

"If she wants to try something different," Maureen said, "this is the time to do it. But I wouldn't go too far afield if I were her. Or jump ship too soon. She's been at this first job less than a year, right? That might not look too good on her résumé."

Lia nodded. All things she'd thought of herself and agreed with. But would Hayley?

They moved on to other topics, Tracy happy about her twins' apparent preference for playing baseball instead of the more injury-prone football, and Diana asking for any book recommendations—and getting several. During it all, Daphne stayed contentedly by Lia's side, ignoring occasional invitations from the others to come over for a petting.

When Lia set aside her afghan squares—which were

adding up nicely—to give her fingers a rest, she lifted the large cat onto her lap. In true ragdoll mode, Daphne went almost totally limp during the move, as if to say, *I'm yours. Do with me what you will.* Jen had apparently taken notice over time of Daphne's and Lia's particular connection, because at the end of the evening, as everyone was packing up and saying good-byes, she asked Lia to stay behind for a minute. When they were alone, she sprang her surprising request.

"I have a huge favor to ask. Would you take Daphne for a while?"

"Take her? You mean take her home? Now?"

"I know, it's last-minute and a terrible imposition. But the neighbor who was going to take her got sick. We have painters coming to do our hall, stairway, and bedrooms. Daphne needs to be away from the hassle. She'd be upset to be shut away from it all, but if she wasn't, she'd only get herself into trouble. I wouldn't ask except I see how comfortable Daphne is with you. And you like her, too, right? It would just be a few days. You could bring her back next week, or I could come get her when things are back to normal. How about it?"

Lia looked at the desperation in Jen's eyes. As a former cat owner, she understood the need to keep pets safely out of the way during certain home projects. Hayley was coming the next day, but that shouldn't be a problem. And Daphne was an awfully sweet cat.

"Sure," she said, and soon found her car loaded with a litter box, litter bag, food and water bowls, cat cushion, and toys, along with a Daphne-loaded carrier that was buckled safely onto the back seat. Lia had come to her knitting group for a respite and was going home with a cat.

"Hang on, Daphne," Lia said as she took a deep breath and pulled away from Jen's house. "This will be a change for both of us. But it'll be a temporary one. No matter what you think of it, keep that in mind. You'll be back with Jen before you know it."

Chapter 6

"You got a cat?" Hayley, two bulging totes in hand, stood at Lia's front door and stared at Daphne, who blinked her electric blue eyes back from her place on the sofa.

"It's Jen Beasley's and just for a few days," Lia said. She was amazed at how easily Daphne had adjusted to the move. After fully inspecting her new quarters from top to bottom, the cat settled in to sample her food and water bowls in Lia's kitchen. She'd nibbled and lapped a bit, then claimed the left cushion of Lia's sofa as her own. The previous night she'd spent in Lia's bed.

"She's adorable!" Hayley squatted down before Daphne, who, after a brief sniff, licked at her hand. "Or is it a he?"

"She. Her name's Daphne, and she's luckily okay with being here. I don't think I'd be able to deal with a frazzled cat, what with everything else that's gone on." Lia picked up the smaller of Hayley's bags and led her up the stairs to the guest room. As Hayley unpacked, Lia updated her on the murder news.

"Since you were here I've learned that Darren Peebles's murder happened hours before I showed up at the barn."

Hayley paused midway between bag and dresser with a folded tee in hand. "And before Belinda arrived?"

"I spoke with Belinda a couple of days ago by phone. She told me that a neighbor assured police she had seen Belinda drive off from her house half an hour before I got to the barn Sunday morning, which means she probably arrived only minutes before I did. That same neighbor said she could see Belinda through sheer curtains, pacing inside her house most of the night before."

"Nosy neighbor." Hayley slid the tee into a drawer.

"A concerned neighbor. Also a woman who apparently was up most of the night herself with a colicky baby."

"Well, that's good! Not about the baby, I mean, but that clears Belinda."

"It seems to, although someone could argue that the baby's mother couldn't possibly have been aware of Belinda's movements the entire night or even be sure it was her. But it doesn't look like they have any incriminating evidence from the crime scene, against Belinda or anyone else, since no one's been charged."

"That's a good thing, right? For Belinda?" Hayley slipped a denim jacket onto a hanger and hung it in the closet.

"Short-term good. I'm not so sure about long-term," Lia said, taking socks from Hayley's bag to stack in another drawer. "What I mean is, not charging *anyone* leaves a lot of suspicion hanging out there. I've already overheard some foolish speculations voiced in the supermarket when I was there on Monday. That kind of thing has a way of spreading."

"You better believe it," Hayley agreed. "Twitter, Facebook. Gossip can make it around the world in minutes."

"Oh, you're right! The Crandalsburg Craft Fair has a Facebook page. I didn't think to check it."

Hayley grabbed her phone from the bed and started tapping. She studied her screen for several seconds. "Nothing much on that page."

"Good."

"But that's not to say nobody's talking on their own pages."

Not good.

"Are you friends with many locals on Facebook?"

Lia shook her head. "I use it mostly to keep in touch with my old friends back in York."

"Well, you might want to connect with the craft fair's followers—you know, people who liked its Facebook page—just to keep tabs. Twitter, too."

Lia nodded. She watched Hayley put away the last of her things and close up her bags. "Did you have any problem getting time off?"

"No, not really." Hayley grinned sheepishly. "They kinda think you needed looking after, you know, what with coming across a dead body and all."

"Hayley!"

"Well, I *do* worry about you. That sort of thing can be traumatic."

"Do I look traumatized?"

"People show their feelings in different ways. I learned that in my psych class. Okay, so I exaggerated a little. But you have to admit that it's frightening to have a murderer on the loose. Wouldn't you worry about me if I were living alone?"

"I would," Lia admitted. "But I doubt that our murderer is someone roaming the streets with a lethal handcrafted pot in hand, looking for a new victim. Darren Peebles was surely murdered by someone who had a major grudge against him. Unless I happen to threaten this person in the same way, which I can't imagine, I'd say I'm pretty safe."

Hayley folded up her totes and dropped them in a corner, then followed Lia out of the guest room and down the stairs. "What I'm most worried about," Lia said over her shoulder, "is what this unsolved murder means for Belinda and the craft fair." When they reached the bottom of the stairs she asked, "Coffee?"

Hayley shook her head. "Water. I'm trying to drink less caffeine." She went on to the kitchen, where she filled a glass and added ice cubes. Lia considered following her daughter's lead but instead fixed a hazelnut coffee for herself in her mini coffee maker. They carried their drinks to the living room, where Hayley carefully settled on the sofa next to Daphne. The cat lifted her head briefly before tucking it back between her paws.

"What I meant a minute ago," Lia said, taking a chair, "is that suspicion hanging over Belinda's head or over the craft fair's reputation will be a bad thing for both. If Darren's murder becomes a cold case, the Crandalsburg Craft Fair might become known for that instead of for all its fine offerings."

"The Handcrafted-Murder Fair!"

"Yes, and it wouldn't be a joking matter."

"I know. And I'd hate to see Belinda go through that. She's not the easiest person to like—" At Lia's wince, she shrugged. "I'm sorry, but she isn't! Yes, she has her nicer side—"

"She was very good to me," Lia said. "You remember when Dad died, and both of us were total wrecks. Belinda stepped right up. She helped me make all the necessary arrangements when I could barely see straight, and she got us over the worst."

"She *was* amazing," Hayley agreed. "I remember her running out for ice cream at that time, when I didn't think I could eat, and coming back with my favorite double chocolate fudge. But not everyone sees that side of her, do they? And she doesn't hold back when someone irritates her. I'm talking about even little things like, oh, someone dawdling too long ahead of her in a checkout line or something. But that just makes it easier for people—*some* people—to want to think the worst of her when they're given a chance."

Lia had to agree that Hayley was right. "I don't want to just sit by and let that happen, Hayley. Belinda would simply dig in, and that won't help. I'd hate to see her world come crashing down around her because someone decided to murder her ex-husband."

"And you plan to prevent that by . . . ?"

Lia paused, thinking. "Maybe," she said, "by looking at the situation from a different angle than the police are. From the inside out, you might say. I've noticed in just about every crime show I've seen that people freeze up a little when they're asked questions by the police. And they hold back things, thinking that the little tidbit they know couldn't possibly be important enough to mention. But they might share it with someone like me, or you."

"Me?"

"You're good at talking to people, Hayley. You always

have been. And you said you love Crandalsburg. This could give you a chance to get to know it better. As long as you're careful, of course, and don't let on about what you're going after.

Hayley smiled. "And talking to craft fair vendors might give me some ideas, too. I mean career ideas." She reached over to Daphne to stroke her soft fur.

"Oh?"

"Right. I've been thinking a little about what I might like to do instead of marketing. I used to love making baskets, remember?"

"Hayley, that was back in Girl Scouts."

"I know, but I could do more with it. Or maybe make cupcakes. That's a big thing now."

It wasn't exactly what Lia had in mind when suggesting Hayley could help out. She'd wanted to keep her active and not moping around the house. Cupcakes? Good heavens! But Lia said, "Talking to the vendors about their own work would be interesting, certainly, but my hope is that it would bring out something useful for clearing Belinda."

"Sure, Mom. But might as well aim for both, right?"

"Right." Lia drained her coffee mug and stood. "First things first. I should get a few things started for dinner."

"Let me take you out. I never did that for Mother's Day, you know." When Lia hesitated, she added, "And if we're out and about, I can start getting to know Crandalsburgers. Ha! Sounds like they come with ketchup and onions! But you know what I mean. We won't make any progress by staying at home."

Lia smiled. That was her goal, after all. How much they might learn while sitting in a restaurant was debatable, but with Hayley, one never knew. "Okay. Let's try Hoffman's," she said, naming a family-run place that wasn't too expensive. "With luck, they'll have a table available."

Lia changed from her comfortable at-home clothes to a knee-length skirt and a nice top. Hayley, though, had merely run a brush through her hair and added a touch of pink lip gloss, staying with her jeans and tee. A bit more casual than Lia thought was appropriate before quickly correcting herself. Not appropriate for *herself*, necessarily. But twentysomethings, she was aware, approached it differently. *Clean* and/or *relatively new* was dressing up for them. And she had to admit her daughter looked lovely as usual and relaxed, both very good things.

They walked the few blocks to the town center, where Hoffman's was located, the number of pedestrians gradually increasing as they closed in. The mild weather and a Friday night had drawn many, like them, from their homes. Lia saw a policeman up ahead, strolling and nodding to greeters, and she noticed Hayley staring at him. As they drew closer, Hayley cried, "I don't believe it!"

"What?" Lia asked.

Hayley darted forward. "Brady! Brady McCormick. Is that you?"

The officer turned, and Lia saw the stunned look on the officer's face gradually replaced by a huge grin. "Hayley Geiger! What are you doing here?"

"What am *I* doing? Never mind that. What are *you* doing here? And in a police uniform!" Hayley gave the young man a hug, which, Lia noticed, brought a flush to his face that nearly matched his red hair.

Lia caught up with her daughter, who turned to her. "Mom, this is Brady McCormick. We were in drama class together at Mercer," she said, naming their high school.

"And social studies," Brady added. "And English."

"That's right! So what are you doing here in Crandalsburg?"

"I'm on the police force."

"Well, obviously! But why here?"

"After high school, I joined the army. When I got out, I took classes at the community college, which helped get me into the police academy. When I graduated, Crandalsburg had an opening, so here I am."

"Wow! That's so cool!"

"Your parents must be very proud of you," Lia said. She'd never met his parents, or Brady, either. But he certainly came across as pride-worthy.

Brady acknowledged Lia's comment with a modest smile and asked Hayley, "So what are you doing here? Do you live in Crandalsburg?" Lia thought he looked hopeful.

"No, my mom does. I live in Philly, but that might change. Who knows, I might end up here! Hey, Brady, it's so neat running into you like this. We have to keep in touch." Hayley whipped out her cell phone, and they exchanged numbers, Brady taking great pains to get hers right.

Hayley and Lia left him to his police duties, which, as far as Lia could tell, consisted at the moment of strolling the very well-behaved beat of Crandalsburg's town center. If she were his mother, she would hope that would be the worst he'd be called on to do.

I don't remember you mentioning Brady before," Lia said as she scanned the menu at Hoffman's. "Did you know each other well?" The German-themed restaurant, she found, offered dishes like sauerbraten and bratwurst along with lighter fare.

"Hardly at all." Hayley flipped a page in her menu.

"Then why so eager to reconnect?"

Hayley looked up, her lip pulled to one side. "Maybe a little bit of guilt?"

"Guilt?"

"I think I was a bit of a snobby brat back in high school. Brady was a nice guy, but kind of quiet, and he didn't fit in with my group of friends, my clique." Hayley made air quotes along with an eye roll. "I'd like to make up for that."

Lia nodded. "The teen years tend to be self-centered ones. Not everyone gets an opportunity to make things right. So you're not interested in Brady other than that?"

"Mom, it's not like back in your day. Not every boy-girl thing has to be a romance. Now girls have guy friends all the time and vice versa."

"My day wasn't exactly in the Victorian age," Lia said with a laugh, "but, yes, I realize that some things have changed." Lia was pretty sure that the look she'd seen on Brady's face when Hayley hugged him was not "guy friend," but she let it drop. "So you'll come to the craft fair tomorrow?"

"Uh-huh. How about I bring lunch like I was going to last week? Then just hang around and try to talk to people."

"Perfect." Lia closed her menu. "I think I'll have the pork chop that comes with German potato salad. What about you?"

"Not sure yet," Hayley said, her eyes still scanning. "All I know is . . . whatever I get, it's gonna have a side of these fried pickles I'm seeing here!"

Chapter 7

The next morning, Lia spoke with a few of the vendors before the doors opened for the Crandalsburg Craft Fair. Most were subdued and as worried as she was about the craft fair's survival. Lia had hoped to have a few words with Annie Bradburn, whose pottery jug had been the murder weapon, but Annie arrived at the last minute and dashed to her spot without stopping to talk to anyone.

When their security guard, Bill Landry, opened the doors, only a scattering of tourists, all of whom looked like first timers, wandered in, gazing about curiously. Nothing near the eager rush of shoppers they'd seen the previous Saturday.

A handful of browsers stopped at Lia's knitting booth in the first hour, and she made one small sale—a pair of baby booties Maureen had made. When that customer left, Lia glanced over to her neighbor's booth to see Olivia looking more downcast than usual. A line of medium-sized cellophane-wrapped baskets sat on her counter, filled with Olivia's products—what she must have excitedly prepared last week for Mother's Day.

"My big order never showed," Olivia said when Lia asked about it, adding, "Of course. I mean, there was no way either of us could find each other Sunday, was there? With the barn totally blocked off by all the police and press vehicles? The whole thing must have scared her away. I wish I'd given her my cell number, but I never thought of it. Who knew there was going to be a murder that night?"

Lia sympathized. "Maybe your other baskets will sell," she offered. "Even though Mother's Day is over, they'd be perfect for somebody's birthday or as a housewarming gift." She knew the odds were not in Olivia's favor, especially with the slow turnout, but she wanted to offer a glimmer of hope. A shopper stopped to browse at Olivia's booth, and Lia moved back to let her wait on the woman.

She gazed across the way and saw Maggie Wood sitting and stitching quietly at one of her quilts in progress. Zach Goodwin caught Lia's eye as he stood behind his stacked jars of honey. He shrugged as though saying, *Things are slow, but what can you do?* Or maybe he meant, *Wish I'd stayed home today!* Lia considered strolling around, but then she got a customer. Or a would-be customer. The woman oohed and aahed over a delicate pink baby sweater and matching bonnet but ultimately decided to think it over.

Belinda had remained holed up in her office after a quick walk-through before opening time. Lia wished she would come out to encourage the vendors. She wished *someone* would cheer them all up. One of Tom's favorite quotes came to mind, and she could almost hear him say, *If wishes were fishes and cattle were kings, the world would be full of wonderful things.*

Though she smiled at that, thinking about Tom turned her wistful, which must have showed, for the next thing she knew, Hayley was asking, "Mom, you okay?"

Lia immediately brightened. "Where did you come from?"

"Um . . . the door over there?" Hayley grinned. "I waved when I came in, but you looked about a million miles away."

More like thirty, Lia thought—the distance from Crandalsburg to the home they'd all once shared. "Just thinking," she said. "It's been quiet."

"Yeah, I see. Are you ready for lunch yet?"

"Not really. It's a little early."

"I know." Hayley shoved her hands into her tunic top pockets and rocked on her heels. "After I fixed the sandwiches, I ran out of things to do, so I drove over. How about I wander around? Give me a shout when you're ready."

"I will." Lia was pleased to see that Hayley first stopped to say hello to Olivia, whom she'd met before, then bought a bar of herbal soap from her. She watched Hayley browse at a few other booths, chatting as she did so and always leaving the vendors with smiles on their faces even if they hadn't sold her anything. It was a gift she'd seen in her daughter almost from the moment Hayley learned to talk, and it usually worked very positively. Though once in a while it got her into a bit of trouble. Too much talk with too little thought sometimes worked that way.

After an actual buying customer—who took ages to make up her mind—Lia felt in need of a break. She waved Hayley back.

Checking that Olivia could watch over her booth and leaving her cashbox safely with her, Lia picked up her purse. "I'd love some fresh air," she said to Hayley. "Why don't I grab one of the picnic tables while you get the food from the car."

Outside, Lia saw that several other vendors had the same idea. When she spotted Annie Bradburn sitting alone at one table, Lia made a beeline for it.

"Hi, Annie. Mind if I join you?"

The potter, a woman in her mid-thirties with a mass of curly light brown hair, looked up from the magazine she'd been paging through and smiled. "Sure, Lia, have a seat."

"Actually, I'll take two seats. My daughter will be joining me in a minute." Lia glanced over her shoulder. "Ah, here she comes now." When Hayley came, Lia introduced them, then helped unpack the insulated bags, asking Annie, "Did you eat yet? We have plenty, including drinks."

"I had my lunch, but I wouldn't mind an iced tea if you can spare one. It was great soaking up some sun, but it's made me thirsty again." She reached gratefully for the bottle Lia held out to her.

"Not in a hurry to get back, then?" Lia asked.

Annie wrinkled her nose. "To what? I've barely sold a thing all morning." She brushed a blown leaf off of her long printed skirt. "None of us have. Turns out murder isn't good for business. Who'd a guessed?"

"We're all hoping the slump will be temporary." Lia unwrapped a flaky croissant filled with chicken salad, impressed with Hayley's lunch making.

"I sure hope so. A lot of us, you know, depend on the craft fair for a big part of our income. Yes, there's always Etsy, but I've been doing well enough here that I've neglected that part. It soaks up a lot of time to keep an online presence going, you know. I have only so many hours in a week, and I need to devote the major chunk of them to actually *making* the pottery. In other words, losing my craft fair income would mean bringing in hardly anything for probably weeks until I could get the online sites back in gear."

"Aren't there other fairs you could get into?" Hayley asked. She bit into her brown bread and veggie sandwich.

Annie shook her head. "I can't do a lot of traveling. I have young kids and, well, other responsibilities that keep me close to home."

"I imagine the police talked to you," Lia said, moving on to the murder. "That was one of your pots that was used in the murder, wasn't it?"

"Oh lordy, yes." A lock of hair blew onto her face, and Annie brushed it back. "And what a shock that was to hear! At least they saw right away it wasn't me who broke it over the guy's head. Other than the fact that I would never do such a thing, especially with one of my own creations, I was home at the time, looking after Ken and the kids. But it got into the papers that my pot was the murder weapon. Not the kind of hashtag I need attached to my business, believe me." She grimaced, then swung her legs over the picnic bench to stand and shake out her skirt. "I'd better get back," Annie said. "Carolyn Hanson will want me to keep an eye on her stuff while she takes her break. Thanks for the tea!"

Hayley looked after her while taking a swig from her water bottle. "Bummer about that bad publicity. One of your place mats was left on the body. Has that hurt Ninth Street Knits?"

Lia shook her head. "As far as I know, the place mat was never named in the media as one of ours. Gilbert Bowen's candles, either, or the metal clown sculpture. Only Annie's pottery, sadly for her."

"Probably because it was the murder weapon. Annie

made it sound like hers was the only income for her family, but she mentioned a husband. Doesn't he bring anything in?"

"Ken had a good job at one time, from what I've been told. But he was in some kind of accident about a year ago and is still recovering. I suspect they're struggling to keep their heads above water right now."

"Yes, they are!"

Hayley and Lia turned to see a plump, gray-haired woman approaching with some effort from the direction of the barn. "Didn't mean to eavesdrop," she said. She tapped at her ear. "New hearing aid. Picks up more than it should sometimes." She came over to their table and introduced herself—"Florrie Goodwin, Zach's wife"—before sinking down on Lia's side of the table with a "whoof!"

"Oh yes," Lia said, remembering having met her some time ago. "Zach is the craft fair's beekeeper," she explained to Hayley. "He sells honey, and you, Florrie, make jams and jellies, don't you?"

"I do." Florrie smiled. "In season, of course. Today I just brought lunch over for Zach. Anyway, I overheard you talking about Annie's husband, and you're new enough that I thought you might not know. Ken's been in a bad way ever since that car accident. He might not ever be the same again."

"Oh, I'm sorry to hear that!" Lia said.

Hayley asked, "What happened?"

"Well, the long story is he was driving home late on a back road, came around a sharp curve, and slammed into a bulldozer that was parked where it had no business being. The short story is it shouldn't have happened at all." Florrie shifted her position, wincing as she rubbed at a knee.

"The bulldozer operator," she continued, "was working a site. When it got to the end of the day, he called his boss, who told him to leave the dozer where it was and just put some cones around it. Said he'd send a flatbed to pick it up right away. It was still light out, so the guy did that and went on home. The dozer was sitting there hours later when Ken came around that curve." Florrie drew a deep breath. "They said it was lucky he wasn't killed, though from what he's been going through since, he might feel differently."

"That's terrible," Lia said, shaking her head.

"What happened to the bulldozer people?" Hayley asked.

"Not much. Some fines were paid after everyone pointed fingers at everyone else. The dozer operator said he did what he was told and thought the rest would be taken care of. The boss said he called for the flatbed that never showed. The flatbed people claimed they never got a call. For my money the blame goes to the top guy. Maybe he was thinking he'd save a few bucks by waiting till morning? Or maybe he got distracted and just forgot. Either way, the buck stopped with him, to my mind."

Florrie pushed herself up with a soft groan. "Funny thing, though."

"What?" Hayley leaned forward.

"That boss? It was Darren Peebles, the guy who just got killed here in the barn."

Silence fell between Lia and Hayley, and they exchanged glances.

"Well, just thought you'd want to know the whole story." She glanced at her watch. "Look at the time! I've got someone coming to check out our air conditioner. Better get going." Florrie smiled. "Have a nice day!"

"Oh wow," Hayley said after the older woman had gone. "What do you think of that?"

"I don't know what to think. It's a disturbing story."

"It's a good thing Annie has an alibi, because Florrie Goodwin just outlined a heck of a motive for her to knock off Darren Peebles. And with one of her own pots."

"I'm not so sure about that alibi, Hayley. I hate to say it because she's obviously dealing with a rough situation. But an alibi that places you at home with a husband and kids during the time of the murder isn't exactly rock-solid. How hard would it be to slip out unnoticed when everyone else was asleep, especially young children and an ailing husband who might be on painkillers? Or for them to back up a fake alibi?"

Hayley grimaced. "You're right, though I hate to admit that. I like Annie. "

"It's not to say that's what happened. It's just something we need to keep in mind."

"Sure." Hayley brightened. "I just hope we can come up with someone else, someone who we wouldn't feel bad about."

"I hope so, too," Lia said. "Because the only two suspects we know about at this point are my good friend Belinda and a young woman I think I'd hate just as much to find guilty of murder."

Chapter 8

Lia returned to her booth to find a familiar figure browsing through her knits, though she didn't get her hopes
up for a sale. The plumpish forty-something woman,
Ginny Norton, visited the craft fair regularly and seemed
to love everything in it, from Maggie Wood's quilts to Bob
Langston's suncatchers, as well as just about every item of
Ninth Street Knits that Lia laid out. But Lia had never
noticed her actually buy.

Lia put that down to limited finances and, perhaps,
loneliness, since Ginny had dropped a few hints to that
effect during their brief chats. The woman, who often
dressed in colorful outfits—items that Lia found interesting but not always flattering—apparently lived alone after
losing one family member after another, another fact
she'd once bravely shared. The craft fair, Lia thought,
might offer a way to socialize, as wandering a shopping
mall did for some people. What she did for a living, Lia

had no idea, and, she reminded herself, it was none of her business.

"Hello, Ginny," Lia said as she slipped behind her counter after retrieving her cashbox from Olivia. "How've you been?"

Ginny refolded the lacy scarf she'd been looking at and returned it to its place atop several others. "Oh, I'm fine. Lovely scarf," she said, patting it. "Just not my color."

Lia refrained from pointing out the other color choices beneath it. Ginny, of course, was not really shopping.

"Quiet in here today," Ginny said, glancing around. "I guess because of what happened last week, huh?"

"Probably." Lia might have said more, but Annie Bradburn's story still filled her head. An actual customer stepped forward and asked about sweaters for five-year-old girls, and Ginny wandered away as Lia pulled up a collection from below her counter for the woman to look through.

Lia was pleased to make that sale—a pretty yellow cardigan with a knitted white duck on the front that fellow Ninth Street Knitter Tracy Kaufmann had made—but a glance around the sparsely populated barn hinted that it might be her final one of the day. Hayley returned from a long chat with baked-goods vendor Carolyn Hanson.

"I'm thinking cupcakes might not be a good choice, I mean if I was going to strike out in a new career. Carolyn clued me in about all the time it takes, and she has daughters who pitch in. I'd just have me, unless . . ." Hayley wiggled her eyebrows at Lia.

"Don't look at me. I'm a knitter, not a baker!"

"Just kidding. But the more she described her schedule and other things, the less it sounded right for me."

Thank you, Carolyn.

"So I'm leaning toward baskets. No perishable-type

worries if the weather keeps customers away or if there's any, you know, murders."

"Not a joking matter," Lia said, though not really scolding. She knew what Hayley's feelings were. "Things are really slow today. I'd like to circulate a little myself and talk to a few people. Want to come along, or have you had enough?"

"Oh, I've barely started!"

Lia didn't bother Olivia about keeping an eye on her booth. The craft barn was empty enough for her to do that herself. She set her BACK IN A MINUTE sign on the center of her counter before coming around to join her daughter.

They passed a few unmanned booths, whose sellers had apparently grown as weary as Lia of waiting for non-existent customers. As they neared Joan Fowler's area, Lia could hear the artist complaining loudly to the vendor on one side of her.

"This craft fair has been horribly managed from the start! Frankly, I don't know why I've stayed this long."

A surprising statement, since Lia had seen crowds gathered around Joan's booth on most weekends, eager to buy her watercolors and drawings. Joan's sounding board, scenic photographer Mark Simmons, was surely just as aware of her steady success and looked just as puzzled. But the wiry artist's negativity only grew, the wide sleeves of her vibrantly patterned top flapping as she gestured and groused in a voice that carried well beyond the immediate area.

"Belinda doesn't have a clue what she's doing," she insisted. "She's a totally disorganized mess!"

Hoping to at least tone down the volume, Lia approached to say, "Actually, I think Belinda's been running the craft fair very well."

Mark's eyes widened. Perhaps one of the most mild mannered of the craft fair people, he quickly moved to the far side of his booth to busy himself with straightening and shifting his photos.

Joan drew a deep breath, but instead of letting out an expected blast, she responded in an ominously low voice, her eyes narrowed to slits. "You're entitled to your opinion, but you're sadly mistaken. Look around you. Is this pitiful turnout a sign of a well-run fair?"

"It's had negative press," Hayley said, pitching in. "That's bound to hurt business for a while. You have to give it time to calm down."

"And whose fault is that bad press?" Joan asked, turning her steely eyes on Hayley. "Belinda Peebles!"

"You can't blame the murder on her," Lia said.

"I can't?"

"No, you can't," Lia restated firmly. "If the police haven't, neither should the rest of us."

"It was *her* ex-husband, my dear. If she hadn't married the scoundrel in the first place and then divorced him, he wouldn't have had the least interest in buying this barn. He wouldn't have been anywhere *near* this barn to be murdered in it. Her stupid decisions have had far-reaching consequences. For all of us!"

Lia was stunned into silence by the woman's convoluted logic.

Joan took Lia's silence as victory and smugly turned away.

Hayley drew Lia away from the artist's booth with a head jerk. "What an awful woman," she said once they were out of earshot, "which is so weird, 'cause her artwork is really beautiful. It's like everything good in her got used up in her paintings, isn't it?"

"She has a point, though." Ginny Norton's voice coming from her left startled Lia, who hadn't noticed her there. "I mean about Belinda's marriage—or rather, her divorce—bringing on a lot of this trouble. But, you know, Joan and Belinda have always had their problems."

"They have?" This was the first Lia had heard that, though with two such bullheaded women it wasn't hard to believe. "What, exactly?"

"You'd best ask Belinda about that," Ginny said, suddenly prim. "Not really my business."

Lia, though frustrated, nodded. Better to get information from the horse's mouth. Ginny wandered off in the direction of Lou Krause's metal creations, and Lia turned to Hayley.

"Mind taking over my booth for a minute? I'll see what I can pry out of our very closemouthed manager."

Lia headed down the side hall to Belinda's office and knocked once before trying the knob. The door was locked. She knocked again.

"Go away!" Belinda barked.

"It's me, Belinda. Let me in."

"I'm busy."

"You're always busy. I'll just take a minute. Let me in."

Lia waited, then heard a chair scrape and the clomp of footsteps. The lock clicked and the footsteps retreated, leaving Lia to open the door herself.

"Nice welcome," she said, walking in. Belinda's face showed signs of fatigue, including dark circles under her eyes, which helped Lia overlook the rudeness. She got straight to the point. "What are the problems between you and Joan Fowler?"

Belinda looked up from her seat behind the desk. "Problems?"

"Yes, you know, disagreements? Bad feelings? I understand they've been ongoing."

"Who told you that?"

"It doesn't matter. I just want to understand what they are and how serious."

Belinda scowled. "Joan's a major pain, but she's been a good draw for the craft fair so I put up with her. She runs her booth; I run the fair. We keep out of each other's hair."

Lia studied Belinda's face. "No hassles, no major arguments?"

"No."

"Did she have any connection to Darren? Personal or business related?"

"How should I know?" Belinda snapped. She rubbed at her eyes and sighed. "Sorry. But I really don't know. Who or what either of them did was the last thing I cared about."

"You understand I'm only trying to help, right? The more information I have, the better I can do that."

"I know." Belinda exhaled loudly. "And I appreciate it. Really." A small smile curled her lips. "This is your kind of thing, isn't it?" When Lia cocked her head questioningly, Belinda explained. "Remember that time back in elementary school? When kids were missing cash from their book bags? You were the one who figured it out."

Lia smiled back. "It wasn't too hard. Tara . . ." Lia wrinkled her nose. "Was that her name? It's been so long I can't remember exactly." She pulled over the visitor's chair to sit. "I remember that she started wearing fairly expensive stuff to school, small things like earrings or bracelets that I suppose she could hide from her parents. So I kept an eye on her during recess until I spotted her slipping back into the classroom. I caught her going through other kids' bags that were kept in the cubbies."

"Yeah, but she was someone no one would have suspected, wasn't she? One of the so-called *good* kids." Belinda made finger quotes along with an eye roll. "And I was one of the many that little witch stole from. But wasn't there also something similar at the hospital?"

"You mean the missing equipment? Well, yes. Again, it was just a matter of keeping my eyes open."

"My point is you've always been pretty sharp about reading people and picking up on things. So I'm glad to have you in my corner, Lia." She grinned lopsidedly. "Even if I don't always show it. But I can't tell you anything more about Joan than I have. She's a miserable person, but I don't see her murdering Darren for any reason, if that's what you're thinking. Besides, how would that be a good thing? Pinning it on one of the craft fair vendors isn't going to help me keep it running, is it? It'd be just one more nail in the coffin."

Lia shrugged. "I don't know what I'm thinking about Joan or anyone yet. I'm just trying to get a clear picture."

"You could try looking outside the craft fair, though, couldn't you?"

"Any suggestions?"

Belinda stared over Lia's shoulder for several moments. "There's Martin Brewer."

"Who?"

"He's been Crandalsburg's unofficial historian for as long as I know. He's always putting together exhibits about past stuff and writing guest columns for the paper. He's a retired professor from somewhere. I can't imagine he would have been thrilled over Darren wanting to tear this barn down, what with its Civil War connection."

"Where do I find him?"

Brenda started fumbling through the papers on her desk. "He was giving a talk. I have a flyer about it here some- where. Ha! Got it." She pulled out a yellow sheet and looked it over. "It's tonight at the library." She handed it over.

Lia read the title: "'The 1863 Battle of Crandalsburg.' Sounds interesting."

"Yeah," Belinda said, sounding totally uninterested.

"Maybe I'll go to it. Want to come?" The stricken look on Belinda's face made Lia laugh.

"I would," Belinda protested. "Because I know you're going for my sake. But I'm so darned worn-out. I haven't been able to sleep." She added dryly, "Maybe I should go. His lecture might do it for me."

"No, go home tonight, try to relax. Drink some chamo- mile tea. I'll be fine on my own and try to get this professor's measure."

"Thanks." Belinda sank her head tiredly in her hands, and Lia left to relieve Hayley from guard duty at her booth.

As she picked up and began knitting on an afghan square, she hoped Belinda was being totally open with her. Lia didn't believe for a minute that Belinda had murdered Darren, but she also knew that for an outspoken woman, her friend could be very good at holding her cards close to her chest. Unfortunately, this was not the time to do that.

Chapter 9

Lia drove to the library, a charming building that had been somebody's grand home a century or so ago, with a columned entryway and a warren of interior rooms, one of which was used for public meetings. Hayley had begged off, wanting to do a little research on basket-making. She hadn't said much yet about her reasons for wanting to leave her job, but Lia hoped to gradually nudge her in that direction.

Lia parked in the side lot among a dozen or so vehicles and headed inside, picking up the pleasingly familiar scents of books and floor polish. An added aroma of coffee led her to the meeting room at the back. As she entered, she saw a scattering of people of all ages, some obviously couples, and she felt a twinge, reminded of the many times Tom had accompanied her to events of this sort and how she had taken his comfortable presence for granted. She saw an empty seat beside another lone woman and headed toward it, pleasantly surprised, as she closed in, to recognize her neighbor Sharon Kuhn.

"If I'd known, I would have given you a ride," Lia said, plopping down next to her.

"Lia!" Sharon looked up from her cell phone and shook her head, smiling. "I decided at the last minute. If I'd had my wits about me, I would have checked with you."

Sharon and her husband, Jack, had been good neighbors from the day Lia moved in, approximately her age and sharing several interests. Sharon, petite and with no-nonsense short-cropped hair, was a bundle of energy and a font of highly useful information for a newcomer, things like the best local dentist or hairdresser. Jack had willingly stepped in when Lia's electronics needed setting up, something Tom had always handled before.

"Jack didn't come?" Lia asked, glancing back in case he was wandering about.

"He's dealing with a cold. Thought it best not to spread it around."

"Tell him I appreciate that and hope he feels better soon."

"Will do. So, this must be your first Martin Brewer lecture."

"It is. But not yours?"

"Not at all. I try to make as many as I can. He's good, and I like learning about our area's history."

"Are his topics always about Crandalsburg?"

"Mostly, and it's always something new."

"He sounds passionate about his subject."

"And about historic preservation."

"Oh?

"Ah, there he is." Sharon pointed out a tall man in a sports jacket, open shirt, and slacks walking in with a woman whom Lia recognized as one of the librarians. His neatly trimmed white goatee and wire-rimmed glasses gave the sixtyish man a scholarly look. His lecture still needed to confirm that for Lia, but Sharon was obviously convinced, and her opinions had so far not steered Lia wrong.

The smiling librarian introduced Brewer, beginning with, "a man who needs no introduction in our community," and continuing with a list of his credits, which included published books on Pennsylvania history and a past professorship at Penn State. Lia was properly impressed.

Brewer rocked back and forth on his heels as the librarian went on, obviously eager to take over, and he did so with vigor once the welcoming patter of applause died down.

"Thank you, Miss Morgan; thank you, all. It's good to see many of you here again. Let's get right down to business: the 1863 Battle of Crandalsburg. I'll go through it along with several photos from the time that should help. Please hold your questions until the end. Now then . . ."

Brewer launched into his topic with the enthusiastic energy of a man who had much to say with a limited time to get it all out, clicking through the PowerPoint slides. The photos were of the town, taken before and after 1863, the later ones showing buildings and houses that had been burned by Confederate troops during the Gettysburg campaign. Then there were posed photos of the generals involved and a few of the citizens of the time. It was all very interesting to Lia, who had thought herself reasonably well informed about the Civil War but had never known about this particular event.

She was forming a highly positive opinion of Martin Brewer, but it was dampened when she saw him shoot a glare at a white-haired woman sitting up front. The woman had pulled out her knitting to work on during his talk. She'd done it discreetly and worked her circular needles quietly as she stitched, but Brewer clearly disliked it. Perhaps he thought she should be taking notes of his every golden word instead of knitting? But that was her choice, wasn't it? And it was one of which Lia totally approved. She herself often found it easier to concentrate on a discussion while knitting at the same time. But Brewer obviously wasn't a knitter.

When he wrapped up his talk, a few hands shot up for questions, which he answered fully. After the questions petered out, Miss Morgan stepped forward to thank him and invited everyone to visit the refreshments table at the back.

"Go ahead," Sharon said to Lia. "I just got a text from Jack that I'll answer first."

So Lia headed back, keeping an eye on Martin Brewer as he spoke with an attendee while packing up his equipment. She picked up a paper cup of what looked like cherry-flavored punch, along with an oatmeal cookie, then glanced around. The knitting lady stood nearby, recognizable by her cloud of white hair and the tote at her feet that had knitting needles poking out. Lia went to join her.

"What are you working on?" she asked, nodding at the tote, which brought a smile.

"A shawl for a friend of mine," the woman said in a soft enough voice that Lia needed to lean closer to hear her. "It's my third one for her. They wear out or get lost because she takes them with her everywhere, especially during warm weather. She likes to have something to slip on indoors. So many places set their air-conditioning to *freeze*."

Lia nodded knowingly, having shivered at many a restaurant under a stream of icy air. "I should do that." She sipped at her punch, which was indeed cherry. "Professor Brewer didn't seem to approve of your knitting."

The soft-spoken woman's eyes twinkled saucily. "The professor forgets that he's not teaching in his university classroom but in a public library. He doesn't get to make the rules here. After the first time he gave me the evil eye, I've made a point of bringing my knitting every time and sitting up front."

Lia grinned. This soft-spoken lady wasn't anyone's doormat.

"He does know his stuff, though," the woman added. "I'll give him that."

"Yes, there was quite a lot of—" Lia stopped when her companion suddenly put a hand on her arm.

"Excuse me, dear, I'm so sorry, but I'm afraid there's a lady I've just now spotted who I urgently need to speak to. Melanie!" she called, raising her voice slightly. "Hold up a minute." She smiled apologetically at Lia and picked up her tote.

Lia nodded genially and stepped out of the way. As she did, she saw that Brewer had finished his packing and come over to the refreshments table. Lia took a bite of her cookie and moved closer, overhearing him receive compliments on the evening's talk from several people. One man asked about particular buildings in Crandalsburg and if they had been built after the Civil War or had survived the 1863 attack.

Lia was impressed to hear Brewer rattle off a list of structures that had been constructed post 1863, those that had been partially destroyed during the attack and rebuilt, and the few that had managed to survive unscathed. As-

suming it was all correct, which Lia didn't doubt, the man
had a phenomenal memory for historical details.

"What about the Schumacher barn?" the man asked,
which perked up Lia's ears. "Was it around at that time?"

Brewer paused, and a woman who'd been listening in-
serted herself into the discussion. "Oh, that's where the
murder happened!"

"Was it?" Brewer asked. He turned to study the library's selection of cookies.

"Yes, it was." The sharp-faced woman leaned forward
to continue her point. "It definitely was. It's where they
hold those craft fairs every weekend. A murder there, of
all places! Who knows what could happen next? It's shocking that—"

Brewer turned back and found himself blocked in. He
looked annoyed and began to squeeze his way out. "I'm
afraid I haven't kept up with . . . Excuse me, I need to . . ."
He pushed past the original two and others who looked
ready to speak to him, brushing them off and only pausing for a brief word with Miss Morgan, the librarian. He
then snatched up his bag and disappeared out a side door.

Lia stared after him. For a man who'd shown a remark-
able retention of history-related details, he'd just claimed
surprising ignorance of a subject that had been all over
the news. In addition, he'd passed up a chance to expound
on the Schumacher barn and its historical use as a mili-
tary hospital.

Interesting.

Chapter 10

Sharon came up to Lia as she stood mulling over Professor Brewer's sudden departure. "Oh, he's gone!" she said, following Lia's gaze to the meeting room's side door. "Shoot! I wanted to ask him something."

"For a while there, he seemed ready to hang around. Then he suddenly skittered off. Does he often do that?"

"No, I don't think so." Sharon thought a moment. "Actually, probably never," she added with a grin. "What did you do to scare him, Lia?"

Lia smiled. "Not a thing. But the subject of the murder at the craft barn seemed to—"

"I thought I saw you here." Maggie Wood, the craft fair's quilting vendor, engulfed Lia in a hug.

Surprised but delighted to see the tall, heavyset older woman, whose mass of unnaturally bright red hair seemed a perfect fit to her ebullient personality, Lia explained to Sharon, "Maggie and I often gaze at each other across the barn at the craft fair but don't get that much of a chance to actually talk to each other."

"Oh, I know you avoid me like the plague, you sly thing, don't give me that." Maggie jabbed Lia lightly with an elbow and said to Sharon, "She knows once she gets within three feet of me I'll start talking and never let her go."

Lia laughed. "Not at all."

"Then why didn't you bring that pretty daughter of yours around to say hello today?"

"I should have," Lia acknowledged, "and I will next time, promise. We made it halfway around the barn but kind of hit a wall with Joan Fowler."

"Ah yes, Joan."

"Is she the artist?" Sharon asked.

"She is," Maggie said. "And an excellent one. But she had her back up today. You don't want to get too close to Joan when that happens. Poor Mark."

"Mark Simmons has a photography booth next to Joan," Lia told Sharon.

"What was Joan upset about?" Sharon asked.

"The low turnout today. All the publicity about the murder probably scared people away. But Joan first blamed it on Belinda's bad management of the craft fair, which was totally unjustified. Belinda has always done a great job. Then Joan claimed the murder wouldn't have happened at all if Belinda hadn't married and divorced Darren Peebles in the first place."

"Wow," Sharon said.

"Yes, wow," Maggie agreed. "But that's Joan. So," she said to Lia, "I take it this was your first time at one of the professor's talks. What did you think?"

"Very interesting," Lia said. "And it made me very grateful that my little house escaped the burning."

"You and a lot of others," Maggie said. "The worst damage was done to the more important buildings of the time, like our town hall. Not that it was the first time or the last for that one. We've gone through a few town halls over the years, but we're getting better at it. The current one has been around at least fifty years."

"Sounds like you know your Crandalsburg history," Lia said.

"Not as well as our professor. But I do volunteer a bit with the historical society."

"Do you? Is Professor Brewer the head of it?" Lia asked.

"Uh-huh. We never had one until he got it going. It's all volunteer, including his work. We run on donations, which sometimes means running on fumes," she added with a cackle. "But Brewer manages to keep it all going. He's very passionate about it."

"How is he to work with?" Lia asked. "I mean, sometimes people who are that driven can be pretty demanding." A particular surgeon came to mind. Great at his job but drove the staff crazy.

"Thinking of volunteering?" Maggie asked with another elbow jab. "We could use you. But, yeah, Brewer isn't the easiest. There was the time he nearly tore the place apart when he thought the papers he'd brought in were lost. All was well once we found them.

"Another time, though, he went ballistic when he learned an old house had been torn down. The place had no historic value other than being old; I mean, nothing of any consequence had happened there, and it was only one of several others of the kind. Plus, it was already half-crumbled, but that didn't matter to the professor. We all walked on eggshells around him for a *long* time. But that sort of thing doesn't come up often."

Really? "Did he know about the possibility of the Schumacher barn being sold?" Lia asked.

Maggie paused, suddenly serious. "That's been tickling the back of my mind, too. Did he know what Darren Peebles was up to before he was murdered? I don't have an answer. You'd think he'd always be on top of things like that. Then again, he sometimes misses stuff, like he did with that old, dilapidated house."

"The barn does have historical value," Lia pointed out.

"Yes, it does," Maggie agreed.

"You said he's gone ballistic. Has the professor ever been violent?"

"No, never." Maggie shook her head firmly. "Shouting, yes, and the occasional fist pound, but never anything more than that."

"Well, if you're wondering if he could commit murder to preserve a historic barn, I'd say he'd be more likely to go to court," Sharon put in.

"Does he have that recourse?" Lia asked Maggie. "I mean, are there statutes in Crandalsburg to protect historical buildings?"

Maggie grimaced. "Actually, no. That's something Professor Brewer has been pushing hard on." She drew a breath. "But it hasn't happened yet."

I'll bet he's our guy," Hayley said after Lia returned home and described the evening.

"I'm not so sure. Yes, he would be horrified to see the craft fair barn torn down. But he's a scholar, an intellectual, and, yes, he gets upset, but according to Maggie he's not a man who resorts to physical violence to get his way."

"She isn't around him twenty-four/seven, though, is

she?" Hayley argued. "She probably only sees the more controlled side of him. And if he can lose it in front of his volunteers, what would hold him back alone in a remote place with a man he must have been furious with?"

"But why would Brewer be meeting Darren at the barn in the first place? And so late?"

"I don't know. Maybe he tried talking to him reasonably and got nowhere? So he worked out some kind of trap. You said he was passionate."

"About historic preservation, yes," Lia conceded. "But passion doesn't necessarily lead to murder."

Hayley reached down to Daphne. The cat had left to explore the house and returned to find her preferred sofa cushion occupied. A few seconds of a mild accusatory stare was all it took to get a warm lap as replacement. "You hate to think the worst of people, Mom. You're going to have to get over that." She scratched at Daphne's ears.

"I am?" Lia smiled.

"We're looking for a murderer, you know, someone who so far has gotten away with it. Which means that person was pulling the wool over everyone's eyes for a long time. Everyone he or she knows has been convinced that they're way too nice to do anything terrible. So the person we're looking for must be hiding a dark side, right?"

Lia looked at her daughter. "When did you get so wise?" she asked.

"The psychology course you and Dad paid for back when I thought I might major in it wasn't a total waste." Hayley grinned. "That and plenty of crime shows. "

"Uncovering a dark side will be difficult if our person of interest has become very good at hiding. I'm afraid one psychology course isn't going to do it for us."

"What about all those years of working as closely as

you did with your surgery patients? You must have learned how to read people."

Lia sighed. "Remember, my patients were unconscious most of the time. This is going to be a challenge."

"Well, I'll go for a run first thing tomorrow," Hayley said. "That's always been my best time to think. Maybe I'll figure out something. Want to come?"

Lia shook her head, saying, "Not on a craft fair day. And I do my best thinking as I knit."

Hayley ruffled Daphne's fur and leaned forward to ask, "Wanna come along for a run?" Daphne stood up to stretch, but then circled into a back-to-sleep position. *Silly question* was clearly her answer.

Chapter 11

Hayley headed back home after they attended Mass at St. Vincent's, but Lia lingered, chatting with whoever was willing to chat, which turned out to be mostly about the weather. She was simply killing time. It had been only a week since she'd shown up early at the craft fair to discover Belinda standing over the dead body of Darren Peebles. Though she knew deep down she was being silly, Lia couldn't face a repeat of that solitary approach to the barn's near-empty parking lot. The memory of seeing the side door ajar, inviting her into the dim interior and what awaited within, was too strong. She preferred to arrive that Sunday morning when the other vendors did, with their comforting numbers and hustle and bustle.

Hayley had told her about running into Brady earlier that morning. "Not *literally* running into him," Hayley added, laughing. "But he was up early for a jog, too! What a surprise." They'd run together for a while, she'd said, and somehow or other Hayley had convinced Brady to help with their search for Darren Peebles's murderer.

"He's police," Hayley pointed out unnecessarily. "There's things he'll be able to find out that we can't."

"I hope he wouldn't be overstepping his position."

"Oh no." Hayley had answered breezily, but Lia couldn't help having some concern. Sometimes a young man's emotions—and she was sure she'd seen them on Brady's face when Hayley had hugged him—could lead him into trouble. Lia would be glad of any help as long as it came without too much cost to the helper.

The craft fair began as slowly as it had the day before, but Sunday mornings were often that way, she reminded herself. Lia looked over the items she'd brought back from the Ninth Street Knitters meeting, lingering over a girl's pale pink cardigan that Tracy had made with a lofty eyelash yarn. Lia loved its fluffy softness. Surely a young mother or doting grandmother would fall in love with it, too, if not that day, then another weekend. She sighed. Assuming the craft fair would survive the current slump. If sales lagged too long, vendors would start leaving for greener pastures, especially cranky Joan Fowler, who was the fair's biggest draw.

Lia glanced toward Joan's booth. Shoppers were looking over her paintings, but instead of attending to them, Joan was engaged with her neighbor, Mark, in what looked like another tirade. Lia noticed Maggie watching the same scene from her quilting booth across the way and knew she was thinking the same thing. *Poor Mark.*

Ginny Norton, the fair's biggest fan but worst customer, wandered by and confirmed Lia's impression that Joan had been complaining once again about Belinda and her management.

"Nothing new," she said, pushing up the sleeves of her flower-printed smock, whose pleats only added unflatteringly to her shape. "Joan seems stuck on that same script."

"Maybe some of us should help her find a new one."

"Good luck with that!" Ginny stepped aside as an actual customer approached. To Lia's pleasure, it was a fifty-ish woman named Paulette, who had bought from her before. She'd come, she explained, with a special request. She wanted a sweater knitted from alpaca yarn.

"Would that be possible to order from you?" Paulette asked.

Lia's face lit up with delight. "Absolutely. As a matter of fact, I was meaning to visit the alpaca farm and fiber mill to see what they had. What did you have in mind and how soon do you want it?"

The sweater would be a dreamed-of gift to herself, Paulette explained, something that she'd wanted for ages but had put off because of the cost. "I finally decided I'm worth it!" she said, laughing. "Plus, regular wool makes me itchy." She described the color and style she had in mind, and Lia checked through her books for a pattern that might fit the bill.

"That's it!" Paulette cried when Lia showed her a photo of a cream-colored cardigan with a Fair Isle–patterned border at the bottom in contrasting colors. Those various shades of brown and rust also trimmed the V-neck opening. "Exactly what I want."

"An alpaca sweater will keep you nice and warm in cooler weather and be beautiful for years. Besides being extra soft and silky, it won't be itchy at all. I'll be thrilled to make it for you."

Lia wasn't exaggerating. She loved working with alpaca yarn and didn't get the opportunity often enough.

She was definitely going to do it herself, she decided, not pass it on to another Ninth Street Knitter. Her afghan squares were nearly done, and now she would have a wonderful new project to look forward to.

They worked out the timing and the cost, and Paulette put down her deposit, excited to take the first step toward her dream sweater. She reached out and gave Lia a big hug. "I can hardly wait!" she cried, nearly dancing as she took off.

"Wow!" Olivia said, looking after the woman. Ginny, who'd been sniffing samples of Olivia's fragrant herbal soaps, glanced over but then turned back to sort through a tray of Olivia's lip balms. "I've never made a customer that happy," Olivia added. "What did you do?"

Lia told her about the special order. "I'll head to the alpaca farm tomorrow to get the yarn. I can hardly wait to get started."

"Oh, the Weber Farm? I've been there. We took Michael to see the alpacas," she said, referring to her young son. "He loved petting them. They're so friendly! I know one of the workers."

"Do you?"

"Uh-huh. Shelby Fischer. We were in school together. She always loved animals, so this is her dream job. She taught Michael a lot about alpacas."

"Michael is what, six?" Lia asked, getting a smiling nod. "Is he close in age to any of Annie Bradburn's children?" The potter had mentioned having young children, but Lia didn't know how young.

"Ryan Bradburn is Michael's school friend. They're both in first grade. I've set up playdates for the boys a few times—for Michael's sake but also to help out Annie a little. She has a lot on her hands. You know about her husband?"

"Yes, so unfortunate."

"Shelby worked in Darren Peebles's office at the time of the bulldozer accident."

"Did she? What was her job?" Lia asked.

"I'm not sure, exactly. Basic office-type stuff, probably. But she was glad to get out."

"Didn't like the job? Or the boss?"

"Well, she wasn't an indoor-work kind of person, so when the opportunity at the alpaca farm came up, she jumped at it. But she said the atmosphere at the office, especially after the accident, was pretty awful. That's all I know."

It sounded to Lia like a very good reason to look up Shelby Fischer when she visited the farm.

Olivia got a customer, and Ginny ambled back to Lia's counter. "I couldn't help overhearing Shelby Fischer's name. She worked for Belinda for a while, too, you know."

"You mean at the craft fair?"

"Not just the craft fair. She was some kind of general assistant to Belinda for the different events she runs at the barn. But it didn't last long."

"Why?"

"I don't know, exactly. I ran into Shelby once, and she just said Belinda was really tough to please."

Lia sighed.

"I'm glad she found a job she likes." Ginny fingered a set of knitted coasters. "I hear alpacas are easy to get along with."

Chapter 12

It took only one word to catch Hayley's interest when Lia mentioned her planned excursion the following morning: *alpaca*.

"I'm going with you! I've been dying to see those fuzzy, furry things ever since you first told me about them. They sound adorable."

"Fleecy," Lia corrected, "not furry, but, yes, they are really lovable. They're used to people because of being raised by them and are like friendly puppies in a way. Only bigger."

Hayley frowned. "Do they spit?"

"Not if you don't scare them, I imagine. But the handlers can tell you more."

"I'll definitely ask. Forewarned and all that."

"I'll have other things to ask Shelby Fischer, one of the workers there. I hope I'll get the chance." Lia explained what she'd learned about Shelby's previous job in Darren Peebles's office.

"Whoa! That should be interesting."

"Could be. We'll see. More coffee?" Hayley had gone for an early morning jog again and was just finishing breakfast after her shower.

"No, I'm good. Should we take a lunch?" she asked, draining the last of her mug.

"There's a small café there," Lia said. "They've offered tours for a long time to help support the farm. The tours grew so popular that they added the café and a gift shop. All very nice and convenient."

"This should be great." Hayley leaned down toward Daphne, who'd been loitering near the breakfast table. "Shall we bring something back for you? A fleecy toy alpaca?"

"Oh, I almost forgot about Daphne!" Lia said as she loaded her dishwasher. "I'm out of the habit of having a cat around. I'll make sure her bowls are filled before we leave."

"And I'll check the litter box," Hayley offered. "When do we have to return her?"

"It was left up in the air but possibly Thursday, when I go back for the next Ninth Street Knitters meeting. Unless Jen calls before then. Her room painting should be finished soon."

"I'll hate to see her go," Hayley said, picking up the genial cat for a cuddle.

"She's certainly an easy pet to look after." Lia rubbed Daphne's head lightly as she walked by and admitted to herself that she would miss her. But she was Jen's cat, after all. And Lia would get to see her on Thursdays.

When they had themselves, the house, and the cat accommodations set, Lia and Hayley stepped out onto the porch and into perfect weather for their excursion. They heard "Good morning!" and looked over to see Sharon kneeling on a gardening cushion in her yard, surrounded by seedlings and garden tools. A straw hat shielded her face from the bright sun.

"Looks like a very good morning," Lia said. "Flowers or vegetables?" she asked.

"Flowers," Sharon said, sitting back on her heels. "I'll get my fresh veggies at the farmers' market when the time comes. Much less work," she added with a grin. "I'll take you to my favorite one if you like, Lia."

"Thanks, I'd like that. Enjoy your day!"

Hayley waved good-bye and followed Lia to the car. As they buckled in, she said, "How great to live in Crandalsburg, with farmers' markets around and all."

"I thought you liked big-city living. You raved about Philadelphia all through college." Lia pulled away from the curb and headed toward the route that would take them out of town.

"Yeah, I know. But it was different then."

"How so?"

"I don't know. Just different."

Lia focused on her driving for a while, and Hayley gazed out her window, neither saying anything. Finally, as Lia drove onto the highway and settled into a lane, she said, "You've never said exactly why you're unhappy at your job."

Hayley heaved a great sigh. "It's so hard to explain, Mom. I guess I just feel like I don't fit in."

"You're new, Hayley."

"Right! I'm the new girl. Everyone else has been there, like, forever."

"So you don't feel, what, part of the team?"

"Yeah, but that's not all."

Lia waited, but Hayley was quiet. "Has there been any kind of harassment?" she asked and was relieved when Hayley shook her head.

"I'm still figuring things out, Mom. Just give me a little more time, okay?"

"Sure." Lia glanced over. Hayley didn't look distressed, so she turned her attention back to the road and let the topic be. Hopefully not for too long.

They both perked up when the first sign for the Weber Farm appeared, featuring a picture of an alpaca.

"Yay!" Hayley cried as Lia turned at it, then continued on the country road for a few more miles.

"I think I see them!" Hayley said before long. She pointed toward a field in the distance where Lia spotted what looked like long-necked sheep grazing contentedly. Soon she was turning into the farm's parking lot to pull next to a bus that must have brought a visiting group.

"If you hurry you can get in on the tour. It's just starting," a young man told them as they walked over to a gate. Lia had already taken one, but she was glad to go again with Hayley.

They hustled in the direction the young man had indicated and joined a group of a dozen or so senior citizens lined up along a fence that encircled several alpacas. Hayley's voice instantly joined in with the *oohs* and *aws* aimed at the extremely cute animals, which stood about three feet high at the shoulder, their curly heads stretching several inches higher. The animals gazed back with their large eyes at the humans, looking as though they considered them just as cuddly.

"These animals have recently been shorn," a female tour guide in jeans and a green Weber Farm–logoed tee explained, "something we do once a year as the weather warms up. We want their fleece, of course, but we also want to keep them comfortable. If you come back to see us in the winter, they'll look more like teddy bears."

The alpacas were huacayas, she explained, which accounted for their fluffy, crimped fleece. "Suris," she said, "have silkier, heavier locks that hang down. Our huacaya fleece is wonderful for knitting, whereas suri fiber is usually blended with cotton, wool, or silk to be woven into high-end fabrics."

"Do they bite?" one gray-haired woman asked.

"They don't bite. Alpacas are extremely docile."

"What about spitting?" Hayley asked.

"Alpacas spit when they are distressed or feel threatened. They will sometimes spit at one another when they are competing for food or trying to establish dominance. They won't spit at people unless they have been abused. We make sure that doesn't happen."

The guide, a woman of about Olivia's age who Lia thought might be Shelby Fischer, talked about the humming sounds contented alpacas made and the shriek they emitted when danger was near. As she spoke, a couple of the animals wandered close enough to be petted, much to the delight of their visitors. Hayley coaxed a third one over long enough to run her fingers through its fleece, which, from the look on her face, made her day.

"What do they eat?" one man in the group asked.

"Grass," the guide answered, "or a good grass hay, not alfalfa, which can be too rich for them, though we might give it occasionally to put a little weight on an animal."

A few more questions were thrown out, but all eyes were on the sweet-looking creatures that strolled before them.

When the talk ended, Lia went up to the guide to introduce herself and ask if she was Shelby Fischer.

"Yes," the woman said with a smile. She ran a hand through her light brown curly hair, which mimicked the animals she cared for.

"Olivia Byrd mentioned that you might be here," Lia said. "She runs a booth next to mine at the craft fair."

"Oh, Olivia!" Shelby said. "We go way back. How's she doing? I should get in touch with her."

"She's fine. She told me you had once worked in Darren Peebles's office. Would you mind talking to me about that?"

Shelby's cheery expression darkened. "You're not a reporter, are you? If you're looking to write something about how bad his employees feel about what happened, you won't hear that from me."

"I'm not a reporter," Lia assured her. "I'm a friend of Darren's ex-wife, so I have a pretty good idea of what he was like, at least in his personal life. I need to learn more about the other side of him, the business side. This could help my friend a lot."

Shelby thought about that a few moments. "She's the one who found the body?" When Lia nodded, Shelby said, "Okay. But can you wait until my break in about half an hour? I have a few things to do for these guys," she said, gesturing toward the alpacas.

"That'd be fine. I can look around the yarn shop." They agreed to meet in the café, and Lia and Hayley went off to the farm store, Lia to choose the yarn for her customer's sweater and to hope Shelby wouldn't have a change of heart in the meantime.

"Oh, wow!" Hayley exclaimed when she saw the colorful array of yarns. "I thought they'd all be beiges and browns."

"No, they can be dyed," Lia said. She knew which colors she would eventually pick, but she couldn't resist wandering past all the others. And touching.

Hayley either, apparently. "They're so soft!" she said.

"Softer than sheep's wool," Lia told her, "and stronger, too. Oh, and hypoallergenic," Lia said, explaining about the lack of itch-producing lanolin in alpaca wool. "That means it isn't water resistant, but it is very warm."

Hayley checked the price. "And expensive."

"Right! And exactly why I only buy it for special orders. It's definitely an investment." Lia watched Hayley linger over a beautiful periwinkle blue yarn, a shade Lia knew would look lovely on her. A future Christmas or birthday surprise, perhaps? She'd have to think about that.

Lia chose her yarns, a luscious cream for the body of the sweater and rust, tan, and dark blue for the trim. As she brought the skeins to the cashier, Hayley browsed through the jewelry, finally picking out two bracelets made of felted alpaca fiber with ceramic beads woven in. After paying for them, she presented one to Lia.

Lia took it with pleased surprise. "How pretty!"

"I love them. But," Hayley added solemnly, "we can't wear them at the same time."

"Heavens no!" Lia agreed, playing along with a smile. She dropped hers into her purse as Hayley slipped her bracelet on. "Thank you, dear." She glanced at the clock. "Time to meet up with Shelby. Fingers crossed that she hasn't changed her mind."

Chapter 13

Several members of the senior citizens group were finishing up their stop at the Weber Farm's café, which worked perfectly for Lia and Hayley, as they had their choice of empty tables. Shelby Fischer hadn't arrived, but Lia and Hayley went ahead and ordered their sandwiches and drinks from a waitress, who seemed in a hurry to serve them. Lia hoped Shelby would join them soon. By the time their food arrived there was no sign of the tour guide, but as Lia lifted her sandwich for her first bite, the woman dashed in. She seemed back to her cheerful self, her concerns about speaking with Lia appearing to have vanished during her time with the alpacas.

"Sorry! A cria got separated from its mom. I needed to take care of it."

"Cria?" Hayley asked. "Oh, that's right. That's what you call the babies, right?"

"Uh-huh. The moms and babies get upset when they're separated for too long. I hate to see that."

"You really love your job, don't you?" Lia asked, setting her egg salad sandwich down.

"I do," Shelby agreed with a smile. She ordered tea and a veggie burger from the waitress who'd hurried up to their table. "I've been crazy about animals all my life and love being outdoors instead of stuck in a stuffy office."

That was a good cue for Lia to begin questioning the woman about her time in Darren Peebles's office, but she decided to give Shelby a chance to eat first. She listened quietly as Hayley and Shelby chatted about alpacas, during which time Shelby's food arrived. When the farmworker finished her burger and leaned back to sip her tea, Lia brought up Peebles.

"Olivia said you were working for him around the time of the bulldozer accident."

"Gosh, yes. That was awful. The whole office was walking on eggshells for days."

"I guess Peebles was pretty upset, huh?" Hayley asked.

Shelby huffed. "More like mad. And Mr. Mathis was furious, too."

"Mathis?" Lia asked.

"Adam Mathis. He's partners with Mr. Peebles. Was, I guess I should say."

"Tall guy? More fit than Darren?" Lia asked, remembering the man who'd accompanied Peebles to the craft fair barn hours before the murder.

"No, Mr. Mathis isn't tall, and he's on the pudgy side." She rolled her eyes. "You should have heard some of the fights between them. They'd close the inner office door, but their voices still carried all the way down the hall."

"Fights about the accident?" Hayley asked.

"That, and about nearly everything else that came up. How they ever became business partners I can't imagine. They couldn't agree on a thing. I heard Mr. Mathis accuse Mr. Peebles of leading them toward bankruptcy."

"Wow!" Hayley said.

"Yeah, wow," Shelby agreed. "It wasn't a great atmosphere to work in. I was glad to get away."

"Did you ever hear them discuss buying the craft fair barn?" Lia asked.

"No, but that might have come up after I left. When I heard that Mr. Peebles had been negotiating a deal on it, I figured Mr. Mathis wouldn't have been happy about it," she said, adding with emphasis, "At *all*."

"Why was that?" Lia asked.

Shelby took a sip of her tea. "I think the firm's finances were stretched pretty thin. Too many properties sitting undeveloped for one reason or another." She grimaced. "Poor Charlotte."

"Who's that?" Hayley asked.

"She was Mathis's assistant. He blamed every glitch that happened on her. Like, once a project got stalled when some old bones were dug up. They have to be examined, you know, by the county coroner and archeologists, and that takes time. Mathis made Charlotte feel she should have somehow known about them and it was her incompetence that was losing him money. He could be really nasty."

"Sounds like he might have made Darren Peebles look good by comparison," Lia said.

"Well," Shelby said with a tight smile, "maybe less bad. Mr. Peebles had his moments, too. I'm sure there must be businessmen who are great people and honest, and all that. But those two turned me off in a big way. Especially when I finally decided to quit."

"Oh?" Lia asked, remembering Shelby's reaction when they'd first approached her. That dark look had returned.

"Yeah, when I'd had enough, I gave them my two weeks' notice. Normal procedure, right? Oh no, not with those two. They yelled and told me to get out on the spot. Practically threw me out and made me feel like crap."

"No!" Hayley gasped.

Shelby nodded. "When I applied for a job here, I wasn't about to ask them for references. I told the Webers I'd had disagreements with my former bosses but without going into details. Maybe they knew enough about Peebles and Mathis to understand, I don't know. But they hired me, for which I'm very grateful." She paused, jerking her chin up. "And I don't think Mathis is going to cause me any more trouble. He has other things to worry about now."

"Such as?" Lia asked.

"Well." Shelby leaned forward on the table. "With his partner dead, Mathis gets full control of the business, doesn't he? I mean, there's no wife or anyone else to inherit, at least as far as I know. So I'm guessing the police will be asking him a lot of questions. And frankly?" Shelby looked from Lia to Hayley. "I hope he did it."

She's right, you know," Hayley said after Shelby left to get back to work. "About Darren's partner having a good motive. But wouldn't there be easier ways to grab control of a business?"

"Better ways, certainly," Lia said. "But knocking off your partner would be quicker. And cheaper. As long as you don't get caught, of course." Lia reached for her iced tea and took a long swallow. "What still bothers me is *where* Darren was murdered. None of the three people with motives that we've come up with so far have any reason that I can see to do it at the craft fair barn."

"But the timing—middle of the night—works for everyone. Easy to show up with no one the wiser."

"Though not so easy to get Darren to show up. How was that managed?"

"Skillfully," Hayley said. "We won't know exactly how until we discover who."

"You're probably right. And maybe not even then," Lia added, not liking the idea of such unfinished business. "But," she said, "on a more positive note, I have a fantastic knitting project I can't wait to get started on." She gathered up her bag of yarn, her fingers itching to dig into it. "With a little luck, something useful will come to me while I knit."

When they got home, Lia realized she'd missed a call on her cell phone from Jen Beasley. The voice mail message Jen left simply asked Lia to call.

"Does she want Daphne back?" Hayley asked, swooping up and hugging the cat as though she intended to stop that from happening.

"I'll see." Lia called Jen and after a short chat reported to Hayley. "She asked me to keep Daphne a little longer. Some complications came up. Looks like we have a cat until the next Ninth Street Knitters meeting on Thursday."

"Woo-hoo! You get to stay," Hayley said to Daphne, who purred either at the news or at Hayley's happy squeezes. Hayley's own phone pinged, and she reached for it, juggling to keep hold of Daphne with one arm before finally sitting down to read the text. "It's from Brady," she reported. "He has news and wants to meet up."

"News about the murder?"

"That must be it. He's on duty but has a break soon and will be at the tea shop. I'll tell him I'll run over. Want to come?"

"You go," Lia said, sure that Brady hoped Hayley would show up alone. She also doubted that the tea shop, with its more delicate fare, was Brady's usual break choice and might have been picked for Hayley's sake. No use spoiling the young man's plan by pulling a third chair up to the table. Lia trusted Hayley to get the full story of whatever Brady had to share.

"I'd better clean up a little first," Hayley said heading for the stairs. "I grabbed a lot of alpaca snuggles on our way out of the farm. But I loved them all!" She paused. "It'd actually be a fun job to be around them all day like Shelby is, wouldn't it?" she asked, then trotted on up.

Lia refrained from pointing out all the financial considerations that instantly popped into her head and instead reached into her bag of supersoft yarn for a major dose of her own kind of sensory comfort.

Chapter 14

Lia had hoped to catch up with Belinda at her home the following morning but learned that her friend was at her office in the craft fair barn, where the weekly dance class was going on. When she proposed a trip to the barn, Hayley readily agreed and insisted it was her turn to drive. Lia didn't argue.

As they paused at one of Crandalsburg's few stoplights, Hayley continued a discussion that had been ongoing since her report of her meeting with Brady. "I still think it's significant," she said, referring to a years-ago incident concerning Martin Brewer that Brady had dug up.

"But it was decades ago," Lia said, sticking with her original argument. "The fact that Brewer once physically attacked a fellow historian during a debate doesn't automatically mean he's capable of murder."

"It was bad enough that the other guy pressed charges," Hayley pointed out.

"Yes, but Brewer was in his late twenties then. He's in his sixties now. People change."

"He's not decrepit." Hayley stepped on the gas as the light changed to green. "You said he looked in good shape and full of energy. He's just as passionate about history now, maybe even more so." Hayley paused to navigate a left turn. "And he obviously really hates to be disagreed with or when things don't go his way."

Lia had a momentary worry for the quiet-mannered woman who consistently defied Brewer by knitting during his lectures.

"Yes, all good points," she said. "I would be more convinced if our professor had shown anything more than a bad temper lately. As it is, I struggle to imagine a man of his position and intelligence resorting to such violence."

"Don't rule him out because of his degrees, Mom. A lot of people can be book smart but really life stupid."

Lia glanced at her daughter. "That I can totally agree with. There were one or two doctors I worked with who were brilliant surgeons but made spectacular blunders in their personal lives. They always came through for their patients, though."

Hayley was quiet for a while. "Do you miss your work at the hospital?"

"In a way," Lia said. "Dad's death was a shock." She paused for a deep breath. "But remember, we'd had plans to retire early. Dad's dream was to buy a small farm, and we were both more than ready to leave our jobs. The farm idea got scrapped, of course, but our finances were in good enough shape to allow me to come here and start a new life. That, I think, was the best thing in the world for me to do. Belinda was a big help with that, and it's partly why I want to help her now."

"You will," Hayley said firmly. "We both will."

They fell silent for a while, each absorbed with her own thoughts, until Hayley turned onto the drive that led up to the barn.

"That really is a beautiful building," she said as she took in its red sides and the metal rooster up top. "It would have been a crime for Darren Peebles to tear it down just to spite Belinda."

Instead, the crime had been turned on him, Lia thought. But was the barn the catalyst? Or was it something else?

Hayley parked near the open side door. As they climbed out of the car, they could hear dance music. Lia knew it was a class of mostly senior citizens and had expected sedate waltzes or fox-trots. Instead she was intrigued to hear the sultry rhythms of the tango.

They stood in the doorway, watching as couples moved in elegant synchrony, backs arched, heads held high, and clasped hands gracefully outstretched. The instructor—a woman whose own salt-and-pepper hair matched that of most of her students—clapped her hands to the beat and called out, "Slow, slow, quick-quick, slow, quick-quick, slow."

Lia found herself swaying to the music. Hayley noticed and nudged her. She tilted her head toward the group along with an encouraging eyebrow wiggle.

"Uh-uh," Lia murmured. "They're much too good."

"You could learn."

"Maybe someday." Lia did enjoy dancing, but she wasn't ready to think of partnering with anyone other than Tom. She cocked her head toward Belinda's office, and the two slipped quietly down the hall. Lia tapped lightly on the door and opened it to find Belinda at her usual spot behind the desk. "How can you concentrate with that music coming through?" Lia asked smilingly as they stepped in.

"Music?" Belinda looked genuinely puzzled for a moment. "Oh. Doesn't bother me. Hi, Hayley! I didn't realize you were still in town. Vacation?"

Hayley went to give Belinda a hug. "Just a short break," she said.

"While she's here, she's been helping me look into what happened to Darren," Lia said as they both sat down. "I wanted to run a few things by you." Lia told Belinda about going to Martin Brewer's lecture and shared what Maggie Wood had told her about him.

Belinda blinked. "Maggie volunteers at the historical society?"

"Maybe you should get to know your crafters better," Lia suggested with a smile. "Maggie confirmed my impression that the professor would likely have been highly upset over Darren's plans for this barn."

"And I learned from a police friend of mine that Brewer has a record of attacking people who crossed him," Hayley said.

"One incident," Lia clarified. "Years ago, but it at least tells us he bears looking into. Can you add anything more about him? Something Darren might have mentioned?"

Belinda shook her head. "Darren and I weren't exactly on speaking terms for some time. I'd love to be able to tell you he was getting threats from Brewer, but I can't. And I barely knew the man."

"Okay, then what about Adam Mathis?" Lia asked.

"Darren's partner? He's a snake. I never liked him. Did you find something on him? That would make me very happy."

"Only that the two fought a lot," Hayley said.

"And Mathis probably gains from Darren's death, acquiring the entire business. Is that right?" Lia asked.

"I suppose so. I sure don't get anything, which should clear me right there."

"How did they happen to partner up?" Hayley asked. "It sounds like they disagreed on everything."

"Not at the beginning," Belinda said. "They were like two peas in a pod when they first set up their firm, probably because they both were fine with bending the rules as much as they could get away with, something I didn't catch on to for a while. As long as the money was coming in, they were great buddies. When problems cropped up that slowed the flow, they probably went for each other's throats, like most snakes and bullies do."

"Would you say Mathis was capable of murder?" Lia asked.

Belinda thought for a moment, then nodded. "Yes, but probably not in the way Darren was murdered. If he chose to do it, he'd probably set it up carefully to look like an accident or frame someone else for it."

"You were kind of framed for it," Hayley said.

"*Kind of* wouldn't be enough for Adam Mathis," Belinda said. "If he'd planned it, there would have been enough faked evidence pointing to me that I'd be locked in a cell right now."

"I can't imagine faking evidence is that easy," Lia said. "Whoever did it has so far gotten away with it, which might be the best he could do. If it was him," she added.

Belinda shook her head, disagreeing, so Lia let it be. She asked about the man who'd accompanied Darren the day he'd walked into the craft fair. "I understand that wasn't Mathis. Was it someone else who worked with Darren?"

Belinda waved a hand dismissively. "That was Todd

Mullins. He and Darren knew each other for a long time. He's one of the few who continued to put up with him." She glanced in the direction of the ongoing dance class. "He's probably out there right now. I know he joined the class."

"He is?" Lia perked up. "Would you point him out?"

"Sure." Belinda rose, and they all trooped out of the office. She studied the twirling couples for several moments, then pointed. "There," she said. "The tall guy in the red polo shirt."

Lia stared, recognizing the man she'd seen circling the barn's interior that day with Darren Peebles. He was now circling the same area in graceful, rhythmic steps, he and his partner appearing to be two of the younger ones of the group. As they turned, Lia was able to see his partner's face. It was Paulette, the woman whose alpaca sweater Lia had just started knitting.

Chapter 15

Belinda returned to her office as Lia and Hayley waited for the class to end, watching the couples step and turn. Lia was impressed with Paulette's dancing ability. Until then, she'd only known her as an enthusiastic customer of Ninth Street Knits, since all their conversations had been about sweaters, scarves, or afghans. Lia saw that she'd only scratched the surface of the fifty-something woman, who clearly had much more to be discovered. But the part of greatest interest to Lia right then was Paulette's connection to Todd Mullins. Was he just a dance class partner or something more, and if so, what would that mean?

The class wound down, and as the music stopped, chatter began. Many of the dancers wandered over to a table against a far wall, where cool drinks awaited them, but Paulette broke away and headed straight to Lia and Hayley.

"I thought I saw you!" she cried. "Are you joining our

group?" She pulled a handkerchief from a skirt pocket and dabbed at perspiration on her face and neck. Tangoing was apparently a vigorous activity.

"No, I just stopped by to speak to our craft fair manager for a minute." Lia introduced Hayley, then said, "I had no idea you were such a good dancer."

"Oh!" Paulette laughed and shook her head. "I have a long way to go! But it's such fun! You should try it. Both of you!"

"It does look like fun," Hayley said, looking pointedly at Lia.

"Maybe someday," Lia said. "I picked up your yarn yesterday," she said, changing the subject. "The colors are going to be beautiful together."

"I can hardly wait!" Paulette turned as Todd Mullins approached carrying two tall paper cups of water. "Todd," she said, "this is Lia Geiger, the wonderful knitter who'll be making my new sweater, and her daughter, Hayley."

"Nice to meet you," Todd said pleasantly. He handed Paulette her cup, then offered to bring them something. "Paulette and I stick with water, but there's other choices."

Lia and Hayley declined, and the four began chatting about sweaters and the tango. Lia was wondering how she might bring up Darren Peebles when Paulette said, "You know what? Todd and I usually go to lunch after class. The dancing makes us ravenous! Why don't you come with us—both of you—and we can talk as much as we want there?"

Todd nodded agreeably, and Lia thought if she was going to turn the conversation to Darren, that would be her better chance. She looked at Hayley questioningly.

"I have things to do, but go ahead, Mom. I can pick you up later."

"Well, if you're sure," Lia said, to which all three nodded vigorously, and soon Lia was climbing into Todd Mullins's white SUV as Hayley drove off in her Nissan waving breezily.

They ended up at the tea shop where Hayley had met up with Brady the day before—Antonia's Tea Trolley—a place Lia hadn't been to yet and which she quickly realized she'd mischaracterized as far as not carrying food that would appeal to a young policeman. It did offer teas—an amazing variety, including many she'd never heard of—but it also had coffee on the menu and plenty of heartier fare besides dainty tea sandwiches.

"Antonia's has changed with the times," Paulette explained after the waitress took their orders. "Happily, they've kept their wonderful pastries. I love to pop in on midafternoons just for a lovely cup of chai and a blueberry scone. But others like Todd want their coffee and maybe a soup and sandwich. They cater to us all now, and they're thriving because of it."

"That's partly because Antonia's daughter and son-in-law stepped in to help, at her request, after she'd run it herself for many years," Todd said. "Fresh ideas."

"And apparently Antonia's openness to them," Lia said. "Change isn't always easy." Something she knew well from her own recent struggles.

"No, it isn't," Paulette agreed. "I made the switch a few years ago from a salaried position to self-employed. It was scary, but it worked out. I'm so happy I took the risk."

"What do you do?" Lia asked.

"Physical therapy. Now, instead of a set schedule, I can be flexible, and it's so much easier for my patients. I mean, these are people who might have trouble getting around, for whatever reason. Instead of making them travel to a clinic, I go to them at a convenient time for both of us."

"That makes a lot of sense. I'm glad it worked out for you," Lia said. She paused as the waitress served their food, then asked Todd, "And what about you?"

"I'm a dog walker." He dug into his steak-and-cheese sandwich, giving Lia a moment to think about that.

"Well, I imagine that offers flexibility to your schedule, too," she finally said, which brought out a ripple of laughter from Paulette.

"That's not all he does," she said, her eyes crinkling. "Todd works at home on his computer."

"Graphic designing," Todd admitted. "The dog walking gets me out of the house and gives me exercise. Plus, I enjoy the animals. I don't know which job I like better."

"Sounds like a great combination," Lia said, smiling.

"It was because we can make our own schedules that we were both able to sign up for the tango class. And it's how we met!" Paulette and Todd exchanged smiles.

"From the looks of it, this wasn't your first class," Lia said.

"Oh no. We started with the beginners' group last fall. The tango is quite intricate and takes practice."

"Paulette's a natural," Todd said.

Lia watched the interaction between them and understood the two had become more than just dance partners. That would normally be fine, but according to Belinda, Todd was one of Darren's few friends. What did that say about him? It was time to find out.

"Todd, I remember seeing you before," Lia said. "You came to the barn with Darren Peebles that day, when the craft fair was going on."

A shadow passed over his face. "Yes. That was the last time I saw him."

"Oh my gosh, Todd. Was that the day he was killed?" Paulette asked.

He nodded, wincing.

"I hope you don't mind my asking," Lia said, "but did he give you an idea why he would return to the barn later that night?"

"It's okay. The police asked me that, too. No, Darren never mentioned any intention of doing such a thing."

"I thought that was awfully odd, too," Paulette said. "I mean, who shows up to meet someone so late at night? Todd, I had no idea you two were friends."

Todd shrugged. "I'd say we were more friendly than friends. We knew each other for a long time, and we'd connect now and then." He reached for his water glass and moved it around as he shifted in his chair. "I realize he had his shortcomings. But he was also a pretty interesting guy and always full of energy. Just fun to be around."

Lia raised a single eyebrow. "He planned to tear down the craft fair barn," she said. "The barn where you take your tango classes."

"Tear down that beautiful barn!" Paulette cried. "That would have been disastrous!"

"I know that's what he was saying," Todd said, squirming uneasily. "But I thought he was just trying to get his ex-wife's goat."

"He had made an offer, which Alfred Schumacher was on the verge of accepting," Lia said. "I think Darren had every intention of following through."

"Then I'm sorry I didn't understand that," Todd said. He reached apologetically for Paulette's hand. "If I had, I would have tried to talk him out of it. Not that I would have gotten anywhere, knowing Darren. But I would have tried."

Paulette nodded and smiled, apparently ready to forgive Todd for associating with a dreadful man.

"Darren did get a call shortly after we left the barn that day," Todd said.

Lia leaned forward. "Oh?"

"I don't know whether or not it had anything to do with his showing up at the barn that night. But it didn't sound like a business call."

"What *did* it sound like?"

"Personal, I'd say. I didn't hear much. Darren dropped his voice and turned away. But he seemed pleased afterward. With business calls he'd usually have a determined or even a combative air about him."

"You didn't hear a name? Or plans to meet up?" Lia asked.

"Nope. Nothing like that. So it might have nothing to do with what happened later that night."

"You told the police?" Lia asked.

"Sure. But nothing seems to have come of it."

"Right." But Lia thought it might be worth checking with Brady to see what he could find out. "Thanks, Todd. And I'm sorry if Darren's death was upsetting for you."

Todd nodded, and Paulette put her hand over his. Todd had described his friendship with Darren as casual, but Lia knew how some people—men in particular—tended to keep most of their connections with friends very loose, feeling more comfortable that way. Todd might or might not have felt a loss from Darren Peebles's death, and it was actually startling to Lia to come across someone who had a positive relationship with the man, but either way it seemed clear Paulette was there for him.

Chapter 16

Lia had intended to walk the short distance home from Antonia's, despite Hayley's plan to pick her up, but Todd insisted on dropping her off, saving them both the effort. When she went inside, she found Hayley unpacking groceries.

"I just picked up a few things," Hayley said. "I'm going to make tonight's dinner."

"Great! What are we having?"

"It's a surprise. You just sit and knit or whatever. I'll take care of everything in the kitchen."

"Sounds lovely." Lia eyed the various items spread out on her kitchen counter, which included an eggplant, onion, garlic, peppers, and mushrooms, and wondered what lay ahead. Hayley had never been a particularly interested cook growing up, despite Lia's attempts to draw her in, but time living on her own might have changed that.

"So, what did you find out from the dancing duo?" Hayley asked, following Lia to the living room.

Lia picked up Daphne, who'd been circling her feet, and shared the more intriguing information concerning the mysterious call Darren had received the afternoon before his death. She sank carefully into her knitting chair as she held on to the large but pliable cat and asked, "Do you think Brady could find out about that? I mean, the police must have checked Darren's phone records, something we can't do."

"I can ask," Hayley said. "But would it really help? If the call came from the murderer, luring Peebles to the barn, the police would have arrested somebody by now, wouldn't they?"

"No, they wouldn't know what was said, and the caller could make up any story about the call if he or she wanted to. But I'd still love to know who made it. If it was from somebody who hasn't shown up on our radar yet, we'd at least be aware of them. Then we could decide if we want to look into them ourselves."

"Oooh, maybe Darren was seeing someone secretly. A married someone." Hayley immediately shook her head. "No, scratch that. Crazy thought. Who'd have an affair with *him*? Okay, I'll try to reach Brady." Hayley glanced around. "Bummer. I must have left my phone upstairs."

As Hayley trotted up to her room, Lia set Daphne down on the floor and reached into her yarn bag. She'd finished studying the directions for Paulette's sweater and was ready to cast on when Hayley returned.

"Brady's going to see what he can learn, and," she tossed off casually, "he'll be joining us for dinner tonight."

"Oh! That'll be nice. How did it come about?"

"Well, he said he'd stop by to let us know what he came up with, and I thought, hey, we have lots of food! So I told him to plan on staying. Besides, he sounded hungry."

Lia wasn't sure how someone sounded hungry over the phone, but having Brady join them was fine with her. She began casting on her stitches, and Hayley disappeared into the kitchen, soon making chopping noises while instructing Alexa to play various tunes from the Echo device Tom had given Lia on his last Christmas. When the music changed to a tango, Lia's eyebrows went up, trying to picture what might be going on in her tiny kitchen. But she stuck with her promise to remain where she was, knitting assiduously and trying not to disrupt her gauge with her rhythmically tilting shoulders and tapping feet.

When her fingers grew tired and her legs needed stretching, Lia set her knitting aside, gave Daphne, who'd been dozing on the rug by her side, a light head scratch, and stepped outdoors for some fresh air. She was strolling along the row of blooming red azaleas that had been planted by the previous owner when a blue Impala pulled up in front of her neighbors' house, and Sharon climbed out.

"Planning some gardening?" Sharon asked as she spotted Lia and veered in her direction.

"There's nothing needed," Lia said, "other than to pull a weed or two now and then. The Potters left me a perfectly landscaped yard."

"They did plan it very nicely," Sharon said. "And the low maintenance is great for most people. I, on the other hand, am someone who can't simply let things be. I love to change, try new plants, and putter around a lot."

"Yes, I've noticed," Lia said with a smile. "When something of mine dies, I'll come to you for advice on a new one."

"And if I ever take up knitting, I'll know who to turn

to. Not that I ever will. I don't have the patience. By the way, are you on Twitter?"

"I am, but I don't go there much. Why?"

"You might want to take a look at what that artist Joan Fowler has been posting."

"Uh-oh. What kind of stuff?"

Sharon's cell phone dinged, and she held up a hand as she checked her text. "Sorry, gotta deal with this. An appointment needs changing. Just go online," she said as she tapped at her screen. "You'll see." Sharon walked away, and Lia headed back inside, dreading to find out what Joan had been up to.

Indoors, tantalizing aromas drifted from the kitchen while the music had changed to slow and soothing. Lia grabbed her phone and clicked her way into Twitter, then searched for Joan Fowler's tweets.

#CrandalsburgCraftFair—terrible management! Craftspeople can't create under such mess and stress. Many are looking for new outlets, including this artist. Stay tuned for updates.

Lia scrolled to the woman's previous tweets. Several were highly critical of Belinda in one way or another, though thankfully they never accused her of a crime. The worst hinted darkly at a messed-up private life that had badly affected the Crandalsburg crafters. Lia was shocked. How could the woman post such off-base negativity, which would surely hurt herself as much as Belinda, along with the craft fair in general?

"Mom?" Hayley stepped out of the kitchen. "Brady will be here soon. Got a minute to set the table for me?"

"Of course, dear. Anything else?"

Hayley pulled her blond ponytail off her neck and fanned it. "Maybe check on the rolls in the oven. But they have a few minutes to go. Everything else is ready. You really should have a rice cooker, Mom. So much easier! I'm going to run upstairs and clean up."

"Go ahead. I'll take it from here."

Lia briefly considered the table setting—her too-seldom-used china or the everyday dishes? But she already knew informality was the answer and would likely be more comfortable for Brady. She took a quick peek at the rolls before pulling out her plates, saw that they in fact needed more time, then peeked into the large pot on the stove to see chunks of various-colored vegetables mingling with pieces of chicken and an aromatic blend of seasonings. For a reluctant chef, her daughter had put together quite a meal!

She got to work on the table and within seconds of finishing heard her doorbell ring, then footsteps as Hayley clomped down the stairs, calling out, "I'll get it."

Lia went to the kitchen and, seeing perfectly browned rolls in her oven, slid them out. She transferred them to a napkin-lined basket, then went out to greet Brady, who looked different out of uniform and dressed in civvies: clean jeans and a tee. Hayley had changed to fresh shorts and a tee, both outfits fitting perfectly with Lia's casual table, as she'd expected.

"So nice to see you, Brady," she said as she joined them. "You're just in time. Hayley's dinner is ready to be served."

"Thanks, Mrs. Geiger," Brady said, running a hand over his red hair and trying unsuccessfully to smooth down a stubborn cowlick.

"Brady brought us wine," Hayley said, holding up the bottle.

"I hope it's the right kind," he said.

"There's no such thing as a wrong wine in my book," Lia said. "Thank you, Brady. That's very nice."

The three got busy, Lia adding wineglasses to the table, Brady working on the cork, and Hayley dishing out her dinner, which she announced was chicken ratatouille, into serving bowls.

"Jessica's mom gave us the recipe," she said, referring to her roommate and looking quite proud of her achievement. She instructed that it should be spooned over the rice she'd made, once again bringing up Lia's need of a rice cooker. That, plus the freshly baked rolls and Brady's wine, made for what they all eventually agreed was an amazing dinner, Brady even asking—much to Hayley's delight—for a second helping.

"Though I feel guilty," Brady said. "I didn't find out much about that phone call you asked about."

"Well, in that case . . ." Hayley laughingly pulled back the dish she'd been about to hand him.

"We're glad to have you just for yourself, Brady," Lia said, offering him the rice bowl.

Hayley seconded that, then handed him the ratatouille after he'd spooned out the rice. "So, you didn't find out much. What *did* you find out?"

"Only that the call Darren Peebles got that afternoon couldn't be traced. It came from a disposable phone."

Hayley wrinkled her nose. "Bummer!"

"Does that strike the investigators as suspicious?" Lia asked.

Brady nodded, his mouth full. After he'd dealt with it, he said, "But it could also mean nothing. It could have been just a spam call."

"Except that Darren did speak with the caller, according to the man who was with him at the time, Todd Mullins. And he seemed pleased afterward."

"Nobody answers a spammer," Hayley said. "It must have been the murderer, who didn't want to be traced."

"Unfortunately, if that was the case," Lia said, "it worked."

The three contemplated that glumly for several moments; then Lia shared her distressing discovery of Joan Fowler's recent tweets, explaining to Brady who both Joan and Belinda were.

"What a pain in the you know what that woman is, artist or not!" Hayley said.

"I have to agree," Lia said.

"Why doesn't Belinda just kick her out of the craft fair?" Hayley asked.

Lia shrugged helplessly.

"Has Belinda seen these tweets?" Brady asked.

"I don't know. I just found out about them myself. I don't even know if Belinda's on Twitter."

"Even if she isn't, she's bound to find out eventually, one way or another," Hayley said. "And knowing her, it's not going to end well."

A second silence fell over the three until Lia clapped her hands briskly.

"Well, enough of that for now," she said, looking from one to the other. "Dessert, anyone?"

Chapter 17

As Lia made coffee, Hayley brought out the sheet cake she'd also made, admitting it had come from a box mix. "It was all I had time for."

"Box cake is my favorite kind," Lia said. "I'm amazed at all you accomplished while I sat in my chair and knitted."

Tom had once laughingly claimed that he realized their daughter had reached adulthood when she picked up the check for the first time at a family dinner out, which had happened when Hayley worked a summer job before her last year of college. But to Lia's mind, being presented with an entire meal cooked by Hayley topped that. And if her daughter ever showed an interest in knitting, well, that would put Lia over the moon. But one thing at a time.

As Hayley cut the cake, Daphne, who'd made herself scarce on Brady's arrival, reappeared at his side, apparently having decided he was safe. More than safe, in fact, since after sniffing at his shoes for a few moments, she suddenly leaped onto his lap.

"Whoa!" Brady cried, startled.

"Daphne!" Lia scolded. "Just set her down, Brady," she advised as Daphne rubbed her face against his and purred loudly.

"You've made a friend," Hayley said, grinning. "Let me take her." She pushed back her chair.

"No," Brady said, "it's okay." He leaned back to evade more Daphne kisses. "I like cats."

"Well, this one definitely likes you," Lia said. Daphne settled down onto Brady's lap, and Lia decided to let her be.

Hayley served the cake and, over Daphne's continued purrs, described their trip to the alpaca farm, where they'd spoken with a former employee of Darren Peebles.

"You should have seen those alpacas," Hayley told Brady. "So cute and so friendly! I just loved them. Anyway, Shelby said the atmosphere in Peebles's office was really tense and that Peebles and his partner, Adam Mathis, argued a lot about money. Are you looking into Mathis? Does he have an alibi?"

"Um, it's not me looking into anybody," Brady reminded her. "But I'm a hundred percent certain everyone connected to Peebles is being checked out by the detectives on the case. The problem with having alibis is that the murder happened late at night, when most people are sleeping."

"Or can claim to have been," Hayley said.

"Is Mathis married?" Lia asked, wondering if a wife could verify where he'd been. "Or does he live alone?"

Brady shrugged.

"We should have asked Shelby that," Hayley said. "Maybe we should go back."

"She mentioned a woman named Charlotte, who is Mathis's assistant," Lia said. "According to Shelby, she got the brunt of Mathis's temper when things went wrong. Maybe we could track her down and see what she can tell us."

"How do we do that?" Hayley asked. "Shelby didn't give us a last name."

"Pratt."

The two women turned to Brady.

"Her name is Charlotte Pratt," Brady said.

"You know her?" Hayley asked.

"Sort of. I almost gave her a ticket once. For parking too close to a fire hydrant."

"Almost?" Hayley prodded.

Brady flushed. "I felt bad for her. She was all flustered. Said their office copy machine was down, and she had been in a big rush to get to the office supplies place when she parked and never noticed the hydrant. Her boss, Adam Mathis, was apparently having a fit over some papers that needed to be copied. I've run into her a few times since." He grinned. "She thanks me every time."

"Where do you run into her?" Hayley asked. "I mean, where would we find her to talk to?"

Brady thought about that. "Mostly at the coffee shop. But she's usually in and out pretty quick."

"Probably picking up her awful boss's special coffee," Hayley guessed.

"That he wants *stat*," Lia added. "I doubt she'd stop and talk to strangers, in a hurry or not."

"I've also seen her after work at the park," Brady said.

"There's a guy who runs a walk-on clinic at the tennis courts. I did one once myself. They're cheap—ten bucks a pop—and you do drills for different shots. Maybe you could catch her there? It might be easier to strike up a conversation."

Hayley brightened. "I'd love to do a tennis clinic! Wouldn't you, Mom? Do you have a racquet I can use?"

"I hung on to my old one after I got a new one, not that I've used either for a while. I'm pretty rusty. Are these clinics for better players?" she asked Brady.

"All levels," he assured her. "Terrell divides the group up if he thinks it's necessary."

"Okay, then," Lia said, smiling. "That sounds like it'll work. There's nothing like doing a group activity that makes for easy conversation. Thanks, Brady."

"I'd say you earned your dinner tonight," Hayley said.

"And an extra piece of cake?" Brady asked.

"You got it!"

When it was time to leave, Brady peeled Daphne off his lap with some difficulty. After he set her down, she stuck to his heels as he headed to the door.

"Daphne, you can't go home with Brady!" Hayley mock scolded.

Brady grinned. "I swear I didn't load my pockets with tuna."

"Maybe you remind her of Bob Beasley," Lia said. "He and his wife, Jen, are her owners—I'm just a temporary. She probably misses him."

"You'll just have to come by a lot to visit," Hayley teased, which brought a slight flush to Brady's cheeks.

Lia picked up the flirty ragdoll cat to allow Brady to open the door and, holding tightly, bid Brady a pleasant good night as he made his exit.

* * *

The next day, Hayley got a call while Lia was in the kitchen. Lia could tell from Hayley's tone that it wasn't one of her friends and guessed it was work related. She was right. In a couple of minutes, Hayley walked into the kitchen, not looking particularly happy.

"I'll need to go back."

"To Philadelphia?" Lia folded the rooster-printed towel and set it down next to the sink.

"Uh-huh. Seems my grace period at work has ended."

"Right away?"

"I can drive back tonight. I want to take that tennis clinic first and see what Charlotte has to say."

"You won't be too tired for a long drive?" Lia asked, then realized the silliness of her question. She—Lia— would be tired after an intense session of tennis drills. Hayley, who rose early to start her day with a jog, never seemed to run out of energy. A two- to three-hour drive was a drop in the bucket to her. "Have you made any decisions?" Lia asked, moving on to the more important question.

"Still thinking," Hayley said, then grinned ruefully. "But I'm getting close."

Lia gave her daughter a hug. "I'm sure you'll make the best one for you. I'll support whatever you decide."

"Thanks, Mom. And don't worry. I won't do anything too foolish."

Too foolish? Was that leaving the door open for *kind of* foolish? Lia didn't want to go there.

Lia's phone rang, and she saw it was Jen Beasley calling. She quickly swiped right and answered cheerily as Hayley wandered off.

Jen greeted her hesitantly. "Lia, I have a proposal for you, but I don't want you to feel in the least obligated." She paused. "How would you feel about keeping Daphne?"

"You mean for a few more days?"

"No, I mean for good."

"Oh!"

"I know," Jen rushed to say, "it's asking a lot, so I'll absolutely understand if you say no. We've discovered that Bob is allergic to her. Since she's been gone, he's felt so much better. No more headaches, sniffles, or sneezes. The doctor said the allergy must have snuck up on him gradually."

"Goodness!"

"And it breaks our heart to have to part with her, but Bob's well-being has to come first. I know how you and Daphne have always had a special connection, and that's why I'm asking."

"Daphne's an absolutely wonderful cat, and I've enjoyed having her here. But . . ." A thousand conflicting thoughts rushed through Lia's head, each clamoring for attention. "Can I think about this?" she asked.

"Of course. Take as long as you need."

They shared a few more words about the next day's meeting of the Ninth Street Knitters, then ended the call. Lia stared numbly at Daphne, who was grooming herself contentedly, unaware of the pending change to her life.

"What's up?" Hayley asked, walking into the room and seeing Lia's expression.

"Jen needs to give up Daphne. I get first dibs."

"Wow! How come?" Hayley took in Lia's explanation with a small frown, then asked, "You'll take her, right?"

Lia looked at her daughter. "It's a big commitment."

"But we've had cats. You know all about taking care of them."

"I also know about losing them," Lia said. "When first Coco, then Misty died after being with us for seventeen years, it was awfully hard. I don't know if I want to go through that again."

Hayley gave her mom an understanding squeeze. "That must feel like the last thing in the world you want to face right now. But you could also think about all the good years that Daphne and you could enjoy together. She's a young cat, isn't she?"

"Around five, I think."

"And she's in good health." Hayley stepped back. "But it's your decision."

Lia appreciated Hayley not pointing out that Daphne was obviously happy in Lia's home and would have to go through a major adjustment should Jen have to settle on a perfect stranger to take her. Or be put in a shelter? Heavens! Surely Jen wouldn't resort to that, but the thought was terrible.

Lia was definitely fond of the cat and had truly enjoyed having her around. But that had been when Daphne's presence was considered temporary. Taking ownership meant taking on full responsibilities, things like vet visits and finding cat sitters for when Lia would be gone. But was that so hard?

As if on cue, Daphne finished her grooming and wandered over to Lia. She looked up with bright blue eyes, begging to be picked up, which Lia did, knowing it probably meant her downfall. She hugged the sweet cat and received a soft-tongued face lick in return.

That did it.

"Okay, you little temptress. You're going to stay here."

"Yay!" Hayley cried as Daphne purred.

Lia smiled. Now that she'd made the decision, it felt good.

Yes, a little bit worrisome, but mostly good. In fact, it felt darned good!

Chapter 18

Lia and Hayley walked into Gunther Park shortly be-fore five o'clock, dressed in shorts and tees and each carrying a tennis racquet. They spotted two others dressed similarly and followed them down a twisty path they assumed led to the tennis courts.

It was a perfect evening for batting a ball around, comfortably cool, with only a slight breeze—nothing strong enough to carry off high-flying balls or disrupt a straight-line track. Lia breathed in the lightly scented air and felt energized, while at the same time uneasily hoping she wouldn't look too foolish on the court with her rusty swings. But she reminded herself that their real purpose was to pump Charlotte for information on Adam Mathis. If Lia had to go through a bit of embarrassment in the process, she could deal with it.

"There they are." As they rounded a curve, Hayley pointed to two fenced-in, side-by-side tennis courts. Several players, a mix of young and old, male and female, had formed a line in front of a fit, dark-skinned man of about thirty in white shorts and tee. Since he was collecting fees, she assumed he must be Terrell, the pro.

Hayley and Lia got in line, both checking out the others for someone who fit Brady's description of Charlotte Pratt. "I think that's her," Hayley murmured into Lia's ear, nodding toward a thin woman in her mid-thirties with close-cut dark hair. She chatted with the tennis pro as she handed over her payment, then headed off to one of the courts where a couple of players were warming up.

When it became Lia's turn, she was greeted smilingly by the man. "Hi, you're new! Welcome." He introduced himself as Terrell Smith and took Lia's and Hayley's names and estimated levels of play. He seemed satisfied that they would both fit in and benefit from the clinic. After accepting their fees, he waved them over to the court and, since they had been the last, picked up his gear and followed.

"Okay, folks," Terrell addressed the eight players from across the net, where he stood next to a waist-high orange wire basket filled with tennis balls, "line up, and let's start with forehands." He demonstrated the proper swing a few times, then hit a ball to the first person in line, a man with thinning hair and a noticeable paunch, who hit it back easily, then hurried to the back of the line as a teen girl stepped forward to take the next ball.

They went through that exercise three times, some hitting into the net—which Lia did on her first try—and some placing the ball nicely onto the far court, each shot drawing comments from Terrell, either complimentary—"Nice!"—or suggesting a way to do better.

They repeated the drill with backhands, Lia finding to her surprise that she did better with that shot and drawing

"Good one!" from Terrell. Hayley struggled, never having played much, but she simply laughed at her wild shots and continued to try. Charlotte, Lia noticed, hit nearly every shot perfectly. So well, in fact, that she didn't look in need of the lessons, though according to Brady she showed up often.

After helping to pick up the balls and reload Terrell's basket, they learned the next drill would be overheads. That turned out to be a comedy of errors as one player after another flubbed their attempts, hitting wildly or into the net, or totally missing the ball. Charlotte, however, did great. Lia and the others watched in awe as she lined herself up perfectly, pointed upward with her left hand as Terrell had demonstrated, then swung, placing the ball inside the line with such power that it bounced at least ten feet. On one try, Terrell had to jump out of the way as it flew too close to him. Charlotte immediately apologized but drew praise from her near victim.

"That's exactly how it should be done, people," Terrell said. "Watch how she does it. Simple motions, guys. You can do it."

Right. Lia and Hayley exchanged amused, in-our-dreams looks. Lia wondered where delicate-looking Charlotte got her strength. Was more than a little anger powering those shots?

They went through that drill two more times, then returned to forehands, which both Lia and Hayley were pleased to find had improved. Instant results! When that drill ended, so did the clinic, and water bottles came out as the players rested and chatted with Terrell or one another. Charlotte was packing up her bag, which she'd left against the fence, and Lia headed over with Hayley, anxious to speak with her before she took off.

"Hi," Lia said. "Are these yours?" she asked, holding out a pair of sunglasses. "They were hooked over the net."

"No," Charlotte said, holding up the pair she'd taken off.

"I'll check with the others," Hayley said, taking the glasses from Lia and trotting off as Lia lingered.

"I was very impressed with your shots," Lia said.

"Really? Thanks." Charlotte pulled off her visor and ran her fingers through her short hair. "I've been coming a lot. It's great exercise, and Terrell's an excellent instructor." She gave a short laugh. "It's also pretty good therapy, after certain days at work."

"Tough job?"

"Not the job so much as the boss."

"I know what you mean," Lia said. "I used to love my work at the hospital when I was a nurse. But some of the doctors . . ." She rolled her eyes. "But it helped to remind myself of the pressure they were under."

"Hah. My boss creates the pressure." Charlotte paused. "Though I have to admit learning that your partner's been murdered must be stressful."

"You mean Darren Peebles? You work in his office? That must have been a shock."

"It was. Getting through that next day at work was . . . well, we were all zombies. Most of us, anyway."

"The office stayed open?"

"Oh yes. When I heard it on the news that night, I called Mr. Mathis, expecting he'd say to spread the word that we'd be closed. Nope. Business as usual."

"Well," Lia said, adding a note of uncertainty to her voice, "some people deal with grief by staying busy."

Charlotte's lip curled. "I wouldn't say he was exactly overcome by grief." She zipped her tennis bag closed.

"Oh?"

"They fought like cats and dogs most of the time. And I'd get caught in the middle, more often than not."

"Ugh. Sounds awful. I happen to be friends, by the way, with Darren's ex-wife, Belinda. Do you know her?"

"No, they split up before I started working there. She must be one tough lady. I can't imagine being married to that man."

"She is, and she acknowledges her mistake freely. What about Mr. Mathis? Is he married?"

"Amazingly, yes," Charlotte said with a lopsided grin. "And she must be a glutton for punishment."

Lia cocked her head questioningly.

Charlotte leaned in closely. "There were rumors that something was going on between her and Mr. Peebles."

"Wow. Do you think Mathis knew about the rumors?"

Charlotte shrugged. "I couldn't say. But that tells you something about the kind of people they were. I mean, true or not, nobody took that rumor as too unbelievable." She lifted her bag and slung it over one shoulder. "I've got to find a new job." She started walking toward the gate. "Are you coming next time?"

"I might," Lia said, following along. "It was fun to get back into the game. I think I learned a lot tonight."

They left the court, and Hayley joined them outside the gate, having pocketed the sunglasses Lia had offered Charlotte, which were, in fact, her own. The three continued on toward the entrance to the park, making small talk about tennis until Lia spotted two men standing up ahead near a historical plaque. They looked like they were having an animated conversation. As she drew closer, she recognized Professor Brewer, who dominated the exchange—loudly, and with much gesturing.

"We can't risk that barn falling into the wrong hands like it almost did," Lia heard him say as he shook a finger in the face of his companion, a shorter man who, unfortunately for him, had backed up as far as possible against the plaque, with nowhere left to go. "You have to talk to Schumacher, convince him that it should be donated to the town. If he won't do it immediately, he should put it in his will."

"But, Martin—," the other man began.

"No buts," Brewer cut him off. "If you won't do it, I will."

The shorter man stammered something Lia didn't catch, as they'd passed the two by then.

"Was he talking about the craft barn?" Hayley asked softly.

"Yes," Lia said. "That's Professor Brewer, whose lecture I went to at the library."

Hayley rolled her eyes. "Was he that worked up then?"

Lia shook her head, but Charlotte said, "I've never seen him *not* worked up. He came into our office many times. Same subject: the Schumacher barn." She stopped as they reached a split in the path. "Well, I go this way," she said, pointing right. "You?"

Her mind still on Brewer, Lia automatically gestured to the left.

"Okay, see you next time. Nice talking to you."

Lia bid her a good night, wishing she'd thought fast enough to stay with Charlotte. After the woman had gone far enough, Lia turned to Hayley. "Lots to tell you."

Chapter 19

After they returned from the park, Hayley showered, packed her things, and drove off to Philadelphia and her job. Lia waved good-bye from the curb, then noticed how strangely quiet the house was when she returned to it. She sat down next to Daphne on the sofa.

"Now I'm twice as glad to have you," she said, running her hand gently over the cat, who blinked up at her. "The place won't feel quite as empty. And," she added, "I can talk out loud and not feel like a crazy woman!"

Daphne gave a soft meow, which Lia interpreted as *You're the least crazy person I've ever known,* though it could possibly have been *Can I have a treat?*

Lia remembered that the kitchen needed tidying up from the snack she'd put together for Hayley's drive and got up to take care of that. As she cleaned, she thought about the discussion they'd had on the way back from the park about Adam Mathis. If the rumors about his wife and Darren having an affair were true, Mathis had acquired a second motive for killing Darren Peebles. Hayley was excited about that, but Belinda's argument that Mathis would have made the death look like an accident or have planted strong evidence pointing to someone else stuck in Lia's head.

Lia didn't know Mathis, but he was smart enough to have built a successful business. If he wanted to get rid of Darren, Lia leaned toward him doing so in a way that would shield himself from suspicion. What would be the benefit of murdering his partner in the craft barn and dragging those craft items around him?

She looked down at Daphne, who'd jumped down from the sofa and followed her hopefully into the kitchen. "Maybe the man's just gone bonkers and nobody noticed yet?" At Daphne's bright, blue-eyed stare, Lia gave in and reached for the pouch of cat treats. "Just one," she said, holding it out to the cat. "And don't think I'm going to fall for that look every time."

Daphne gobbled her nugget in an instant and gazed back at Lia, who shook her head firmly. But she put Kittie Krunchies on her mental shopping list. The single pouch Jen had passed on to her clearly wasn't going to last much longer.

Thank you so much for taking Daphne," Jen said when Lia arrived for the Ninth Street Knitters meeting at her house, backing up her words with a heartfelt hug.

"I'm really glad to," Lia said. "But I hope you won't miss her too much."

"I'll miss her, but it makes a huge difference to know

she'll be happy with you. And Bob is feeling so much better. No stuffiness, no headaches."

"That's wonderful."

The others commiserated with Jen on hearing the news and cheered Lia for stepping up. "I never wanted to say anything before," Tracy said. "But I think Daphne's cat dander bothered me a little, too. But I still miss seeing her. She's such a sweetie."

"She is," Lia agreed. "And anyone who wants to is welcome to come visit her—and me, too. Now, let me show you what I'm knitting," she said, pulling out the beginnings of Paulette's alpaca sweater from her bag along with the picture of what it would eventually become.

They all oohed over it, reaching out to touch the silky-soft yarn as Lia explained about the special order she'd received from her craft fair customer Paulette. "Funny thing," she said. "I ran into her a couple of days later, and it turned out she has a connection to the craft fair murder victim, Darren Peebles. It's through the man she's been seeing, Todd Mullins, who had a long-running friendship with Darren, though he took pains to describe it as a very loose one." Lia also shared what she'd been doing on Belinda's behalf.

"I admire your loyalty to a friend," Maureen said. "Particularly someone who I, for one, didn't find very easy to like." Maureen had met Belinda once on a visit to the craft fair and apparently hadn't been charmed.

"You unfortunately met her on a bad day," Lia said. "The barn's owner had promised to have some needed repairs taken care of but hadn't followed through, which caused her—and the fair—several problems. I realize Belinda has her rough edges. But I've known her a long time.

I know the good person she is. She doesn't deserve the suspicion that's been thrown on her just because she made an unfortunate marriage choice. Plus," she reminded the group, "anything that hurts Belinda also hurts the craft fair, and if the craft fair goes down . . ." Lia raised her knitting with one hand and did a thumbs-down with the other.

"That's right!" Maureen said. "Our amazing knitting outlet dissolves. We should *all* pitch in to help Belinda."

"But what can we do?" Diana asked. She paused her work on the raspberry-colored sweater that was on her lap.

"Lia's doing all the legwork," Jen said. "We can try to fill in what she's digging up with anything we know about those people. I can start since I happen to know a little about Annie Bradburn."

"Who is that?" Tracy asked.

"One of our craft fair vendors," Lia said. "Her pot was used to kill Darren Peebles."

"Well," Tracy said. "That says a lot, doesn't it?"

"It might," Lia agreed, "except it was a Saturday night, when everyone's craft fair items were sitting there. The murderer could just as easily have used one of Zach Goodwin's honey jars. On the other hand, I don't know that Zach has any reason to want Darren Peebles dead, whereas Annie does." She explained about the accident that had disabled Annie's husband.

After the group's mixed reactions of distress and suspicion, Diana asked, "Alibi?"

"Home with her family," Lia said. "The time of death was between midnight and two a.m."

"Yes, and that's what my information concerns," Jen said. All eyes turned to her, and she went on. "Most people would be asleep in bed at that time, right? And you'd naturally assume that of a woman with small children, wouldn't you?"

"Uh-huh," Tracy said as the others nodded.

"Well, my next-door neighbor Maddie has a sister-in-law who works the night shift at a 7-Eleven in your area, Lia. Long story why she took the job, but it turns out one regular customer at the place is Annie Bradburn, who shows up often in the wee hours."

"Why would she do that?" Tracy asked.

"Exactly what I asked," Jen said. "It turns out they've chatted some, since the place is usually pretty empty when she comes in, and the sister-in-law learned that Annie often works on her pots late at night, when her family is asleep and she's able to focus. She'll show up at the 7-Eleven when she needs a break and pick up things like milk or bread for the next day."

"Wow!" Tracy said.

"Did Annie stop in the night of the murder?" Lia asked.

Jen shrugged. "The sister-in-law didn't work that night."

"But she might have," Diana said. "I mean Annie might have. Or she might just as easily have gone to the craft fair barn. The woman doesn't really have an ironclad alibi anymore, does she?"

"She doesn't," Lia had to agree. "And I'm sorry about that. It puts her under the same suspicion as Belinda, with their good motives for wanting to do away with Darren."

"I'd say Annie has the stronger motive," Maureen said. She had started a new baby cap, having apparently finished last week's flowered one, and the oddity of discussing murder while knitting dainty stitches on that sweet item didn't escape Lia. "She must be reminded of the accident every time she looks at her poor husband, an accident that wouldn't have happened if Darren Peebles had done his job. Can you imagine the simmering anger she must have?"

"But why link his murder to yourself by using one of your own pots?" Tracy asked.

"Because it just felt so good to use it?" Maureen offered. "And who thinks rationally at times like that?" She looked around. "At least, that's how I'd imagine one would feel," she added with a small smile.

"That's a good point," Diana said. "But just a starting point. Lia needs evidence. We should all think about what we can do about that."

"Think about the other suspects I came up with, too," Lia said. "Adam Mathis and Martin Brewer. Anyone know anything about them?"

"The name Mathis rings a bell," Tracy said. "Is his wife's name Eve?"

"Adam and Eve?" Diana crowed. "I hope not!"

Lia shrugged. "I don't know."

"Let's see what I can find." Tracy grabbed her cell phone, her fingers flying over it as swiftly as they worked her knitting needles, as the others watched in silence. After several moments she cried, "Ah! Here's something. He attended a charity dinner with his wife, Eva." She looked up. "Not so bad as Eve, at least."

"Do you know her?" Lia asked.

"I don't recognize her," Tracy said. "But that name is familiar. Maybe it'll come to me. If it does, I'll get back to you."

Lia smiled gratefully.

No further thoughts came from the women, and they took a break to refresh their drinks and help themselves to the nibbles. Jen's husband, Bob, popped in to thank Lia for taking Daphne. His eyes looked less reddened and his voice sounded clearer, but Lia detected regret at being the cause of giving up their pet. She did her best to assure him he needed to consider his health first and that Jen felt exactly the same.

When they'd settled back down, Maureen asked about Hayley. "Has she made up her mind about her job?"

"She said she's getting close. She went back to work today. Maybe that will help her decide."

"I hope she'll be thinking long-term," Maureen said. "As well as benefits, and all that."

"Tom had a good talk with her on those points, back when she was first sending out applications."

"I'm sure she'll be fine," Jen said. "She learned from the best, after all. You and Tom."

Lia smiled, appreciating the sentiment but aware that Hayley was her own person. All Lia and Tom had been able to do was to show their daughter what they believed were the best ways. It was up to her to agree or not. Many times she went along with their advice, but there were occasions when she'd decided, a bit impulsively, to do things her own way—and not always with great results. Although some claimed mistakes were the best teacher, Lia would much rather her daughter learn from *others'* mistakes. That, unfortunately, was out of her hands.

Chapter 20

Friday morning, Lia got a call from Belinda. "How'd you like to snoop around Darren's place with me?"

"Isn't it sealed off?"

"It wasn't the crime scene," Belinda pointed out. "So, no. And I have a key."

"You have a key?"

"Well, I can get my hands on one."

"What do you hope to find?" Lia asked.

"I don't know. Probably nothing. I'm sure it's been searched already, so there won't be anything sitting around that will point to his murderer. I just want to look. Who knows? Maybe it'll be of some use."

Lia thought about it. Yes, the police would have carried off anything needed for their investigation. But Belinda knew Darren better than the cops did. There might be something that wouldn't have caught their attention but would catch hers.

"Okay."

"Good. I'll come pick you up."

By the time Lia buckled herself into Belinda's car, she was having second thoughts. "Is there a chance this is illegal?"

"We won't be *breaking* in. And," Belinda added with a sideways smile, "it's possible there was something of mine I wanted to retrieve. I mean, if anyone happened to ask."

"Something such as . . . ?"

"It'll come to me any minute, now."

Despite Belinda's assurances, Lia remained uneasy. She hoped none of Darren's neighbors would be around to take notice of them, coming or going. Maybe they should have waited until dark? Or would that have looked more suspicious?

Belinda drove to a newer development on the outskirts of Crandalsburg and through opened, unmanned wrought iron gates that defined the entrance of a group of upscale homes, all beautifully landscaped. When she pulled up in front of a large colonial-style brick house fronted with a manicured lawn and tidy shrubs, it was clear that Darren had come through the divorce in better shape than Belinda.

The street and surrounding houses were quiet, but who knew how many eyes might be watching? Lia did her best to project an air of confidence as she followed Belinda up the walk, though it began to slip as Belinda paused near the door, her gaze scouring a small flower bed uncertainly.

"It should be . . . ," Belinda said. "Aha!" She stooped to pick up a small gray rock lying beside a clump of marigolds. She flipped it over and worked at it until it came apart. Inside the hollow interior lay a house key. "Fake rock," she said, showing it to Lia. "Darren was always losing his keys. He took this with him after the divorce. Couldn't just buy a new one. I knew he'd still be using it."

She unlocked the front door and stepped inside, holding the door open for Lia. The hall and living room were dim, and Belinda moved toward the closed draperies.

"No," Lia cried. "Don't open them. Use the lamps."

Belinda shrugged, but she clicked on one lamp next to the sofa, glanced around, then added the light from its twin at the other end.

The room fit the style and affluence of the house and neighborhood, everything in it shiny and new but also impersonal. It could have been the showroom of a furniture store. Lia pictured Darren writing a check to a decorator with directions to "make it look good" and nothing more. There were no photos anywhere, nor memorabilia. But this was an area where Darren might hold business-related gatherings. His personal items might be in more private areas like the bedroom or home office.

"Hmph," Belinda said as she gazed at the large water-color painting of sailboats on a windswept lake hanging above the sofa. "Like he ever set foot on a boat. Darren got seasick watching a waiter fill his glass."

"It doesn't look like a room he spent much time in," Lia said.

"The kitchen was always his favorite place. Not to cook. To eat." Belinda led the way through a formal, chilly-feeling dining room and into a large, stainless steel–equipped kitchen.

"Did he have a housekeeper?" Lia asked.

"Nobody regular would be my guess. He didn't like anyone poking around his things without him there. But he probably had someone come in once in a while and before a big bash. When we were together, if I didn't cook, we'd eat out, or he'd get stuff delivered." A peek into the refrigerator confirmed this was still the case, with shelves full of take-out cartons. Belinda sniffed. "Somebody should probably dump all that. It won't be me."

"What happens to his property?"

Belinda shrugged. "Beats me. We don't have kids, his parents passed several years ago, and he didn't have siblings. Maybe some relative will crawl out of the woodwork and claim it, unless he left a will." She turned toward the hall. "Nothing to see down here. Let's look upstairs."

As they walked toward the wide, curving staircase, Lia asked, "Did you know Adam Mathis's wife?"

"Eva? Sure."

"What is she like?"

Belinda paused at the staircase. "Odd. She and I never clicked."

"Odd in what way?"

"A little spacey. Big on New Age stuff. Lots of weird kinds of wellness ideas."

"Attractive?"

"Yeah, I suppose so. Always dressed in the latest, and she drove to Philadelphia to shop and get her hair done. Probably spent ninety percent of her time on herself."

"And that was fine with Adam?"

"Oh, he doted on her. Whatever Eva wanted, she got." Belinda started up the stairs. "Why do you ask?"

"Darren was being cagey about something. There was a phone call he got after he left the barn that afternoon from a caller who didn't want to be traced. I wondered if he might have been having a secretive affair with a married woman."

"And you think it was Eva Mathis?"

"I don't know. There were rumors it might have been. What do you think?" Lia asked.

They'd come to the upstairs landing, and Belinda paused to consider that. "I'd be surprised for a lot of reasons. First, that she'd put what she had with Adam at risk. I mean, she had everything she wanted that he could afford. Then again, maybe she wanted more? And the excitement of the game? But I'd also be surprised on Darren's part. I mean, the one thing he had going for him was brains. Eva might be attractive in her own way, but an affair generally means long-term, right? She'd bore him to death in half an hour." Belinda started down the hall. "Let's check out his office," she said and turned into a doorway on the right.

The room had obviously been thoroughly searched, with bookshelves in disarray and desk drawers left open. "Looks like they took his computer," Lia said, noting an empty space on the desk surrounded by papers. She glanced at the walls, which held framed awards and photos of Darren shaking hands with local politicians on flag-flanked stages. There was also a framed headshot of himself, one that she recognized having seen on the firm's website. Hanging it on his own wall said a lot.

Belinda noticed Lia looking at it. "Yeah." She snorted. "I'm surprised he didn't put it over his living room sofa. Bet it crossed his mind." She rifled through the papers scattered over the desk, picking up a few to scan, then held out one stapled sheaf to Lia. "This is interesting."

Lia flipped through the papers. It was a contract for demolition of a property. "What's interesting about it?"

"It's to do with the Graham mansion," Belinda said. "That place is in the heart of Crandalsburg and has been crumbling away since the last occupant died about fifty years ago. From what I've heard, Martin Brewer has been badgering the mayor for ages to buy the place and restore it."

"It's historic?"

"It was built during the robber baron age in the nineteenth century. The first Graham made a bundle of money and put it up as his showplace. I think the history comes from the guests they entertained—people like Vanderbilts and such. It must have been gorgeous at one time."

"And Darren bought it and planned to tear it down," Lia said.

"Probably made better sense financially than trying to restore it."

"Martin Brewer wouldn't have seen it that way."

"You're right about that. But if you're thinking it gives him a reason to kill Darren, wouldn't that be after the fact?" Belinda asked. "I mean, the property was bought. His partner, Adam, could go on with demolition plans."

"True." Lia's thoughts went further. Maybe losing the Graham mansion tipped Martin over the edge? Or maybe Adam Mathis saw it as a way to throw suspicion on the historian while getting rid of Darren for his own reasons? All conjecture and too wild to share with anyone until she had more to go on.

Belinda pawed through the desk drawers, then straightened, shaking her head. "Nothing more to see here." She whisked out of the room and strode down the hall and into the master bedroom, with Lia following.

The room was a jumble, which also might have come about from the police search. Belinda went straight to the closet and threw open double doors to reveal an area about the size of Lia's small living room. Darren Peebles owned more clothes than Lia thought she'd ever possessed, including before downsizing: suits, shirts, pants, and—good heavens—rows and rows of shoes! The man could have put Imelda Marcos to shame.

Belinda wasn't interested in the clothes but started checking various-sized boxes stacked on the shelves.

"What are you looking for?" Lia asked.

"I don't know. Sometimes Darren would put things in odd places and forget about them. Things you'd never think he'd want to keep. I'm curious if he still did that." She flipped covers off a couple more boxes. "Ha! This is what I mean." She held the box out for Lia.

"Notepads?"

"Right. Sticky notes. And piles of pens with logos on them. He probably picked it all up at some convention. They're that giveaway kind of stuff that people might not ever use but makes them feel like they're getting something for free. *One* something. But he's got dozens. And where does he put it all? In a box in his closet where he'll never find it again."

Lia didn't know what to think about that, so she turned toward an end table beside the bed. The drawer was partly open and had obviously been shuffled through. The top held a lamp, a box of tissues, and a book. She picked it up to read the title: *Finding Health and Peace Through Astrology.*

"Was Darren interested in astrology?"

"What?" Belinda had opened a second box and was peering into it. "Astrology? God no. Why?"

"He had this book on his end table." Lia held it out.

Belinda moved over and took the book, then turned it over as if it were some mysterious object. "Why in the world . . . ?" Her jaw dropped. "Good Lord! Eva! It must be hers, or it came from her."

"You think so?"

"Of course! Why else would he have something like this? Wow." Belinda sank onto the bed. "So it must be true, the rumors, I mean. He and Eva Mathis. Who'd'a thunk?"

"It's not proof," Lia pointed out. But it was a strong indication.

"C'mon," Belinda said, jumping up and tossing the book away. "I've had enough. Let's get out of here." She started heading for the hall, then froze at the sound of a sharp ring from the doorbell. "Someone's at the door!"

"I'd assume that's the case." Lia said it lightly, but it jarred her, too. Was someone checking on them? Wondering why they were there? How would they explain it?

Belinda rushed to the window to look out. "It's a woman. Casual at-home clothes. Probably a neighbor who saw us go in. What do I say?"

The bell rang again, this time more insistently.

"Go on, answer it," Belinda said. "I'll be down in a second."

"Me? But what do I say?"

"Anything. Stall. Hurry!"

Lia hurried out of the room, picking up her pace as the bell sounded again. She sprinted down the stairs, then paused at the bottom to calm herself and catch her breath. With a fake smile she hoped would pass, she opened the door to a woman of about her own age, heavyset, and with a stern face that shouted *neighborhood watch* to Lia. "Yes?" Lia asked sweetly.

"I noticed you and another woman come in. I live across the street. The man who lived here is dead. Do you have a reason to be here?"

Lia spotted the cell phone clutched in the woman's hand. She was ready to call the police if she didn't get a good answer.

"I, um, that is, we—," Lia stammered.

"Hi there!" Belinda's voice sailed from above. She trotted down the stairs. "So you're one of Darren's neighbors! So good to know someone's watching over his place. I'm Belinda Peebles." She held out her hand. "And you are?"

"Kathy Linden." She took Belinda's hand automatically but didn't look pleased about it. "You're Darren's ex-wife?" The woman had obviously been following the news accounts.

"Yes, I am!" Belinda said cheerfully, then turned solemn. "So sad what happened to Darren, wasn't it?"

"Why are you here?"

Lia had stepped back. She noticed Belinda had brought down one of the boxes from Darren's closet.

"Oh." Belinda flapped a hand. "Darren's lawyer asked me to find some papers he needed. He figured I'd know where Darren might have kept them. I said I'd try, but Darren was such a pack rat. Look at this!" She pulled off the box's top to show Kathy the jumble of sticky notes and pens. "And there's piles more of stuff like this. Can you imagine? I mean, who keeps things like this?"

Much to Lia's relief, Kathy grinned and nodded. "Men! You should see what my husband hangs on to. And heaven forbid I suggest he throw out any of it."

"I know!" Belinda agreed. "You'd think you were asking them to toss out family heirlooms."

The two chuckled together as Lia smiled along, awed at how smoothly Belinda handled the situation. It ended with Belinda inviting Kathy in for coffee, which she smilingly waved off.

"No, no, I'll let you get on with your work. Just wanted to check that everything was on the up-and-up."

"That was so good of you!" Belinda said, thanking her

as she also inched the door forward. When it finally closed, she waited a few beats, then peeked out the window. "She's going home. We're clear."

"Hallelujah," Lia said quietly and drew a relieved breath. "Let's us leave, too."

"Uh-uh. Kathy thinks we've got more work to do. We'll have to wait awhile. Let's see if Darren kept any decent coffee around." She turned and marched toward the kitchen, her box of Darren's pens and sticky notes tucked blithely under her arm.

Chapter 21

Lia followed Belinda to the kitchen, and together they searched through the cupboards for coffee grounds and filter papers. Belinda set up the drip coffee maker on the counter, and Lia was glad to find powdered creamer, not trusting anything in the refrigerator. Within minutes they were sipping from two nonmatching logoed mugs, more conference giveaways, at the small kitchen table.

Lia stared through the window at the flagstone patio. "You handled the self-appointed security guard really well."

Belinda added a little more sugar to her mug and stirred. "If I'd been smarter I would have found out if she'd seen Eva Mathis coming to the house alone." She tasted her coffee, then took a longer swallow. "I'll bet she could have told me."

"Probably better to keep it short and send her on her way. You had me worried when you invited her in."

Belinda smirked. "Yeah, I took a chance there. But I

think it convinced her we were legit. Not taking me up on it and thereby holding me up from my work made her feel virtuous. A win-win."

"You know," Lia said, "if you put that kind of effort into dealing with all the craftspeople, you'd have fewer complaints and a happier atmosphere at the barn."

Belinda leaned her head on one hand. "I know. But I'm not you. Being diplomatic doesn't come naturally."

"You think I don't struggle to bite my tongue sometimes? Everyone does. Eventually it gets to be a habit. You handle the business side of the craft fair brilliantly, Belinda. You could manage to crack a few smiles and throw out more words of encouragement. You'd be surprised at what you'd get back."

"You're right, I know. It's just . . . Well, never mind. I can work on it, and I will. I should have done so a long time ago. Maybe my marriage wouldn't have been such a miserable failure if I'd learned to be a little nicer." She smirked. "Better yet, maybe I would have found someone a thousand times better than the guy I settled on."

"That would have been the preferable result," Lia agreed.

They grinned at each other, then fell silent, each sipping their coffee and mulling their own thoughts over what might have been, along with what might have been avoided, if only.

Saturday morning, the Crandalsburg craft fair doors opened, with a sparse crowd showing up for the second week in a row. Instead of the surge of shoppers Lia had grown used to during her weeks at the knitting booth, those who straggled into the barn in ones and twos looked like tourists who'd run out of things to do and were filling an empty block of time with a little browsing.

At least Lia had her work on the alpaca sweater to keep

herself occupied. Others, like Olivia with her soaps and Zach with his honey, could only wait and hope for customers. Maggie, she saw, was busily stitching a quilt. Lia intended to talk to her about the Graham mansion. With luck, she could tell Lia something useful about Martin Brewer's reaction to its planned demolition.

Lia glanced around at the other crafters. Annie Bradburn was speaking with a shopper about one of her more ornate serving platters and possibly making a sale. Good for her. But Jen's story of Annie often being out and about in the late hours of the night was worrisome. She watched the potter cheerfully reach down for a second platter to show, and then a third, looking as though she simply enjoyed chatting about them and that actually making the sale was her last concern, though Lia knew otherwise.

The shopper eventually moved on without buying but clutching one of Annie's brochures. Who knew if it would lead to her return or end up in the trash? Not Annie, at least for now, though her persistent smile belied the fact of her private heavy burdens.

During their lunchtime chat of the previous week, Annie had casually tossed out her alibi that she'd been home with her family during the time of Darren's murder, as though it was airtight. And apparently the police had accepted it. Lia now knew there could be leaks in that alibi but not ones definite enough to report. If there'd been CCTV cameras that caught her on the street around the time of the murder, she would have already been questioned about that. But Crandalsburg was a small town with minimal need to justify the cost of such surveillance technology.

Had Annie sneaked out that night and met Darren at the barn? Was her anger over his action, or rather inaction, that led to her husband's disabling accident great enough to seek revenge? Could the smiling woman who stood there surrounded by her beautifully crafted pottery be capable of murder?

"Penny for your thoughts."

Lia blinked to see Ginny Norton standing in front of her booth.

"You looked miles away." Ginny shifted the small tote bag she always carried to her other hand. Some shoppers brought totes to fill with purchases. Ginny's was a thermal bag for drinks and snacks to enjoy during her hours there.

"Not nearly that far," Lia responded.

"Planning your next knitting project?"

"Always doing that," Lia said with a smile. "Even when I already have something wonderful to work on." She held up the alpaca sweater, whose pattern was beginning to appear.

"Nice! So you went to the Weber Farm? Did you see Shelby? How's she doing?"

"Very well. She clearly loves working with those sweet animals." Lia remembered Ginny mentioning that Shelby worked briefly for Belinda in addition to having worked in Darren Peebles's office. She suddenly wondered how Ginny happened to know the much younger woman, and she asked.

"Shelby worked at the sub shop with me one summer," Ginny said.

"Sub shop?"

"Sammi's Subs. It's on Main Street?"

"Oh yes. I've seen it but haven't been in. So you work there?"

Ginny nodded with a twist of her lips. "It's all I could get after my mother died. I looked after her for years while she was sick. I was glad to do it, of course. Who else was going to? But it doesn't make for much of a job résumé. The salary at Sammi's isn't much, but Mom left enough that I can keep the house. It's nothing to brag about, old," she said, adding with a wry grin, "and with a lovely view of an auto repair shop. But it's mine, and I'm grateful for that."

"I'm sorry about your mom. Was she your only family?"

"Yup. I was a lonely only."

Lia had heard that term before and never quite understood it. Hayley was their only child, but Lia and Tom weren't the only people in her life. She always had friends, some of whom became almost part of the family. But if Ginny's mother had been ill a large part of her life, she supposed that could have made the difference. Lia thought she understood Ginny's constant presence at the craft fair a little better. It was someplace to go where people knew her and were friendly.

It was kind of sad but hopefully a way of easing back into a social life. Maybe other opportunities would come up. She was wondering if Ginny would be open to suggestions when a shopper approached her counter.

"Could I see that white shawl?" the woman asked, pointing to a delicately knitted summer shawl Jen had made that hung near the back. Lia reached for it, and Ginny moved off.

Lia's chance to speak with Maggie came during her lunch break. She spotted the quilter spreading out her things at one of the picnic tables and headed over.

"Mind if I join you?"

Midbite into her thick sandwich, Maggie could only nod and wave welcomingly toward the seat across from her. She had pinned her mass of hair back that day, and the gray strands near her face highlighted its vivid red. She wore a brightly printed peasant-style top over royal blue capris trimmed with yellow ties at the hems. Nothing about Maggie was ever muted, and Lia was amazed that she had taken to quilting, an activity that called for hours of quiet focus. She pictured the crafter taking frequent breaks of frantic mariachi dancing at her home, an image that brought up a smile.

"You look pleased with yourself," Maggie said, having swallowed. She reached for a swig of Coke. "But I didn't see you wrap up that pretty shawl that woman was looking at. Didn't she care for it?"

"She's thinking about it. It costs a little more than she wanted to spend. But for the yarn and the work my friend Jen put into it, it's really a fair price."

"She's probably hoping you'll come down. Especially since she sees the small crowd we're having. I've had a few approaches of that sort." Maggie took another bite of her sandwich.

"You've been part of the fair longer than me," Lia said. "Has it had slumps like this?"

"A few, but never this bad. And never at this time of year when the weather's gorgeous and everyone's out."

"So it's the murder and the fact that no one's been charged for it yet."

"Most likely. And not much we can do about that." Maggie reached for her Coke.

"Well . . ." Lia shifted on her bench.

"What, you're sleuthing?"

"Just keeping my eyes open and asking questions. It's not so easy when you're a newcomer. So I could use help from people who've been around longer."

Maggie grinned. "Like me?"

"Do you mind?"

"Heck no. Ask away. I'll do whatever will get this fair back on its feet again."

"Thanks, Maggie. I'm wondering about Martin Brewer."

"Ah, the professor. What about him?"

Lia told Maggie about seeing him at the park after the tennis clinic. "He was badgering a smaller man about the barn, insisting that he not let it slip through their hands again."

Maggie nodded. "That sounds like Martin."

"And I learned that Darren Peebles had bought the Graham mansion and had made plans for its demolition."

"Did he? I heard rumors about that. Wasn't sure they were true."

"So you don't know if Brewer was aware of it?"

"Hah! I'd be surprised if he wasn't. He's had his eye on that place for ages. Wanted the town to turn it into a museum. A great idea, but I don't know where he thought the money was going to come from."

"So it would have been important to him," Lia mused. "As was the Schumacher barn. And Darren Peebles was a major obstruction to both."

"You think our professor conked Peebles in the barn with the pottery?"

"Do you?"

Maggie thought about that. "I don't know. He might have liked to, but to actually do it? That's a big leap. You asked me after his library talk if he was ever physically violent, and he wasn't, at least not that I ever saw."

"Yes, and my neighbor Sharon thought he'd be more likely to go to court with any dispute. Except that wouldn't get him anywhere, would it, since apparently there's no legal basis for a lawsuit? So I'm seeing a man with extremely strong desires being thwarted, possibly to a breaking point."

"Maybe," Maggie conceded, "but maybe not."

"I know. There's no proof. That's the sticking point. Whoever did murder Darren Peebles managed it in a place where there'd be no witnesses and apparently, ghostlike, left no incriminating evidence. So what do I do?"

Maggie shrugged. "I guess you do exactly what the police must be doing. Wait and hope something more comes up. Hope whoever did it tips their hand."

Lia nodded, though she didn't much like the thought. It occurred to her that a person who had murdered to get what they wanted—a cold-blooded kind of murder that had clearly been planned—might be inclined to murder again if, to their twisted reasoning, the need arose.

Was that the "something" that they had to wait for?

Chapter 22

Lia noticed Olivia sitting behind her soaps and essential oils looking glum, and she set her knitting down. After sitting and working on the sweater a good long while, her fingers and knees could use rest and a stretch. She and her booth neighbor could both use a distraction from the slow business.

"How's Michael doing?" she asked, knowing that would bring a smile to Olivia's face. "Looking forward to the end of the school year?"

"Oh, he loves school," Olivia said. "He has a wonderful teacher. She has a way of making every day something for the kids to look forward to." She chatted on about Michael's favorite subjects and the latest group project he was involved in.

"Is Annie's boy doing as well?" Lia asked. "He's in Michael's class, right?"

Olivia's expression clouded. "I think Ryan might be

having some problems. Michael said he's being pulled out of class lately for something special. He didn't know what that was, but I think it might be some sort of counseling."

"Behavior problems?"

"I doubt that. Ryan isn't at all the kind of child to act out and disturb the class. He seemed down on himself the last couple of times we've had him over. And that was a while ago. Annie's turned down the playdates I tried to set up lately."

"Hmm. Did she say why?" Lia asked.

"Not to me." Olivia looked troubled. "Michael told me that Ryan said his mom didn't like people poking into their business. I'm afraid Annie thought I was questioning Ryan. But I would never do that."

"I know you wouldn't. Are you sure he was referring to you?"

"Michael thought he was."

"Six-year-olds don't get everything right. Did you talk to Annie about it?"

Olivia winced and seemed to pull into herself. "I didn't feel comfortable doing that."

Lia understood. Olivia's anxiety-prone nature was not up to a discussion that might become upsetting, innocent though she believed herself to be. "Would you like me to talk to her? Maybe Michael was totally out in left field with what he reported to you."

Olivia thought about it, then nodded. "I know you'd be so much better at it. Maybe if you find out what the problem is, I can take over from there."

"I'll see what I can do."

Lia looked over to the pottery booth but saw that the woman who'd been interested in Annie's serving platters had returned. That was good for Annie, and it could also be good for Lia if making the sale put the potter in a more receptive mood. She waited, but the shopper took her time. Lia picked up her knitting and sat down, glancing over every so often until an older couple stopped at her own counter. She popped back up.

"Our son and daughter-in-law are expecting our first grandchild," the woman told her, her eyes shining. "I wondered if you had any baby items?"

Only about a dozen or so, Lia thought with a smile, delighted to bring them all out. She ended up selling a matching set of baby blanket, sweater, bonnet, and booties, which was wonderful, but the transaction took an extremely long time. Lia understood. A gift for one's first grandchild, something that might be treasured for years, was important. But even the grandfather-to-be grew impatient and urged his wife to "pick one, Dorothy—any one—just pick!"

By the time they left, Lia saw that Annie's customer had been replaced by Joan Fowler. That was a surprise, since Joan rarely left her booth to make the rounds. But as she watched, it became clear that Joan's wasn't a pleasant, how're-you-doing visit. Instead, she appeared to be berating Annie. Annie wasn't simply taking it. Red-faced, she was giving as good as she got—but quietly. Both women kept their voices down—a good thing as far as the craft fair was concerned but unusual for Joan, who never seemed the least bit concerned about anyone overhearing. But angry hisses, while not audible to Lia, were clearly being exchanged.

What in the world had brought that on? Lia caught Olivia's eye. She shrugged, obviously as baffled as Lia. This clearly wasn't going to be a good time to approach Annie. Maybe not even a good day, or week!

Joan stomped back to her own booth, knocking over

one of her watercolors that had been propped on a stand and slapping it back into place. Annie left her booth and marched out the front door, possibly to walk off steam. Several crafters watched with concern but also relief that whatever had gone on was ended. A few shoppers had also glanced over. But their interest quickly returned to their browsing, and the craft fair business resumed.

Lia tidied up her counter, refolding the baby items she'd spread out and tucking several away, but couldn't stop thinking about the scene she'd witnessed. Ginny strolled nearby and, apparently reading her mind, stopped and said, "What a scene, huh?"

Lia grimaced and nodded.

"I was too far away to hear," Ginny added with some regret, "but they were both steamed, weren't they?"

"I know how easily Joan can be riled up," Lia said. "But this seemed much worse than usual."

"Joan's been working up to it, griping all day about the low sales and about Belinda."

"And what is that all about?" Lia asked. "You said there's been bad blood between Joan and Belinda, but Belinda seemed clueless when I asked her about it."

"Really?" Ginny shrugged. "I guess she doesn't like to talk about it."

"About what, exactly?" Lia prodded.

"Oh, it goes way back. Before the craft fair was even here."

"So it doesn't have anything to do with the fair?"

"Well, now it does," Ginny said. "But that's probably because Joan just can't let anything go. Maybe not Belinda, either."

"But what is it? I want to understand, Ginny. I need details."

"Details? Gosh, it was some time ago. Who can re-member details? It had to do with Joan's paintings; that I know. And I think Belinda was still married to Darren."

"Yes?"

Ginny shook her head. "I'm sure Belinda has a much clearer memory of the whole thing." She wrinkled her brow. "I'd really hate to get it wrong and maybe stir up more trouble. Talk to her. She'll get it all straight."

"But—"

A woman stopped at the edge of Lia's counter and looked hesitatingly from Lia to Ginny, as though not wishing to interrupt.

Ginny quickly stepped back, as was her habit when customers approached anyone's booth. "Belinda can tell you," she assured Lia before moving off.

"I wondered if you had any . . . ," the shopper quickly began, and Lia turned to her, trying to focus on her ques-tion while also thinking about Ginny's advice. Lia had already asked Belinda and gotten nowhere. Joan should be able to tell her, but the chances of that happening were probably zero to none. She pondered the problem as she listened to her customer with one ear but gradually was able to offer her full attention. Picking up signs of a defi-nite sale ahead helped.

On her drive home that evening, Lia set aside craft fair concerns to consider what to do about her dinner. She usually fixed something ahead for craft days, meals that needed only a quick warm-up when she came home, tired and hungry, as she was right then. But the last couple of days had been too full to manage that. Takeout was the obvious solution, and she headed to the section of Crandalsburg that offered a few choices. She lucked out on finding a parking spot central to several restaurants and climbed out of her car, still undecided but thinking the place with the shortest line would be it. As she started to walk, she heard, "Hi, Mrs. Geiger."

Startled, Lia turned. "Brady! I must have walked right past you."

He grinned and gestured to his uniform. "I'm not exactly undercover."

She laughed. "No, certainly not."

"Looking for a place to eat?" he asked.

Lia nodded. "It's been a long day at the craft barn, and I don't feel the least like cooking. I thought I'd pick up something to take home. I'm just not sure where to go for it. The restaurants on this block look pretty busy."

"If you're okay with diner food," Brady said, "Marie's is around the corner about one block down. I was going to head there myself in a little while. They probably do takeout, but I'd be glad of the company if you wanted to eat in."

"That sounds very nice," Lia said, smiling.

"Only thing, my break doesn't start for ten minutes. Would you mind going ahead and ordering for me?"

"No problem. What would you like?"

Brady asked for the hot turkey sandwich with a side of coleslaw, which Lia duly noted before heading on to Marie's, pleased with the new plans.

The waitress was in the process of serving their dinners when Brady slipped into the booth across the table from Lia.

"Perfect timing!" she said.

He grinned, his cheeks flushed. "Ran all the way after getting waylaid by a little kid who wanted to ask about being a policeman. Said he wants to be one when he grows up. I didn't want to blow him off." He took a swallow from his water glass and unrolled his knife and fork from their paper napkin wrap.

"You might have inspired a future crime fighter," Lia said.

"He could do worse," Brady said with a look of pride.

"What inspired *you*?" Lia asked as she poked a fork into her eggplant parmigiana.

Brady thought that over. "I don't know, exactly. A lot of things, I suppose."

"Were you in Boy Scouts?"

"I was." He paused before adding, "Made Eagle Scout."

"Good for you. Maybe that was a factor. What was your project?"

Brady smiled at the memory. "My team and I built a handicap ramp for a church. Took us a long time, but it was good and solid. It's still there and being used, from what I hear."

"Excellent." Lia added a smidge of sugar to her iced tea and stirred it with her straw.

"But I think it was probably my time in the army that led me to law enforcement. I liked the discipline, for one thing, even though a lot of guys didn't. But I saw the reason for it and the need. It worked for me, helped me grow up and get my head together about my future."

He dabbed at his coleslaw. "I don't plan to walk the beat for too long."

"No?"

"It's good experience, and we all have to start there. But I know I can do more. The police force offers opportunities. But it'll be up to me to work up to them."

"I have a feeling you'll succeed," Lia said.

"How about you, Mrs. Geiger? Hayley said you were a nurse?"

"Surgical," Lia said. "Challenging and sometimes grueling but very rewarding."

"Rewarding 'cause you know you're helping people, right?"

"Right."

"That's what I like about police work. It's not all about handing out tickets or putting people in jail. You're helping to keep order and protecting people. It's a positive thing."

Lia smiled. If he could hold on to that attitude, he would be a happy—and successful—man. "I really appreciate the help you've given us," she said.

Brady shrugged. "It was hardly anything."

"Not at all. It was because of you that Hayley and I managed to learn a few things about Adam Mathis from his office manager, Charlotte. We also improved our tennis game in the process," she added, smiling, "but that's a whole other thing." Lia sighed. "It's such a complicated process, trying to sift through all the people who might have wanted to murder Darren in order to figure out who actually did."

"Um, Hayley explained why you're doing this," Brady said, his brow wrinkling as much as his young face could manage. "I mean, that you're worried about your friend Belinda Peebles and all. But—"

Lia held up a hand, understanding where he was going. "I am worried about Belinda. I know her well and know she couldn't have done anything as terrible as murder, so I'm fairly confident she won't be arrested. But until the real murderer is identified, people will talk and rumors will fly. It's hurting her badly, Brady. She might lose her livelihood because of it.

"I'm sure the police are doing their job," she said. "But my thinking is that I could possibly pick up tidbits that the police would miss, simply because a person might be more comfortable talking to me about a particular topic rather than the police. Or someone might be careless about what they say around me and drop an important clue. If that happens, I intend to pass what I learn on to the police."

Brady appeared satisfied with that, and Lia turned to her dinner, having noticed that Brady's plate had been polished.

By the time they left together—Brady taking along a wrapped Danish for later—Lia felt she and Brady knew each other a little better. As far as she could tell, Hayley's interest in him was as a friend, and that was fine, her decision, and—who knew?—possibly subject to change. But Lia was pretty sure that Crandalsburg had lucked out when he'd joined their police force. All in all, it had been a very productive dinner.

L ia had just returned home when she got a call from Tracy.

"Remember I said something about the wife of Adam Mathis rang a bell? It came to me."

Lia set the leftovers box she'd been holding onto the dining room table and pulled out a chair to sit, disturbing Daphne, who'd been dozing on the opposite chair. "What was it?" she asked.

"I remembered who she was. *Is*," Tracy corrected.

"And that is . . . ?"

"She's a Bearden."

"A what?"

Tracy laughed. "Not a what. A who. The Beardens own those Under a Buck stores you see all over the place."

"They do? Well, I guess someone has to own them. So they're fairly well-off, I take it?"

Tracy chuckled. "You could say so. Their stores might be all about saving pennies, but I doubt any of them even know what a penny *is*. Or even a buck. They deal in millions. Maybe billions."

"Okay, so what does that make Eva?"

"Most likely an heiress. That's why she and her husband keep showing up at all those charity functions, like the one I found online with their photo. The family does a fair amount of philanthropy. It's probably good for business."

"So how did an heiress end up with Adam Mathis?"

"Good question. I gather she's not the brightest bulb in the Bearden tulip patch; otherwise she might be more active in the family business. But who knows? Adam's not exactly a pauper, right? Is he also a charmer?"

"I don't know. Belinda called him a snake, but that had more to do with his business practices."

"People show different sides of themselves when they want to, don't they? And I don't know anything about the Bearden family or their business ethics. None of them are in prison, so I guess that says something. Well, I just wanted to share that info about Eva. Interesting, huh?"

"It definitely is," Lia said. And what it meant as far as Adam Mathis, Darren Peebles, their partnered real estate–developing firm, and Darren's murder could be even more interesting.

Chapter 23

Lia mulled over Tracy's information as she slipped her take-home box from Marie's into the refrigerator. Belinda hadn't said anything about Eva's moneyed connections. Instead, she'd implied that Eva depended on her husband, Adam, for her various luxuries. Surely Belinda must have known. Or would she? The two women hadn't exactly been friends. *Polite acquaintances* sounded more like it, and perhaps Adam wanted his wife's personal wealth kept private. It could have been a matter of ego for him to give the impression it was his own business success that supported their lifestyle.

Another thought came to her. If Darren was actually having an affair with Eva, it would have given Adam a greater motive for murder if he feared Eva—and her money—would be leaving him for Darren.

Lia wanted to meet Adam. How should she do that? She couldn't just show up at his office and say, "I have a few questions." There had to be a better way. She grabbed her phone and called Belinda. It rang several times, then went to voice mail.

"Call me," Lia said. She disconnected and almost immediately got a text. *That was fast*, she thought, until she saw the text was from Hayley. Her daughter didn't waste any words.

Check out fair FB page. Now!

What in the world? Puzzled, Lia launched her browser and tapped her way to the Crandalsburg Craft Fair Facebook page. On previous visits, she'd found the page filled with announcements of upcoming sales or new items added to a vendor's offerings. In other words, innocuous, informative, and friendly. The first post at the top was none of those, and the poster was Joan Fowler.

Why do I keep running a booth at the Crandalsburg Craft Fair? I've stayed out of consideration for the loyal followers of my artwork, but it's getting to be too much! The heavy cloud of suspicion that hangs over the entire fair, the constant worry that I might be next if I speak up about the disastrous mismanagement! I don't know how much longer I can do this.

Good heavens! Lia had barely absorbed the horror of the post before another text from Hayley appeared.

She's on Twitter now!

Lia switched over to Twitter and navigated her way to Joan Fowler's tweet.

Faithful fans, tell me where I can take my artwork. The Crandalsburg Craft Fair is no longer
a good place for me to be. An artist needs to
feel welcomed and SAFE to create beauty. I'm
feeling neither.

Had Joan lost her mind? Lia tried to reach Belinda
again, but that call also went to voice mail. She didn't have
a phone number for Joan, but she messaged her privately
on Facebook to please give her a call. She didn't have high
hopes it would happen, but she had to try.

Lia then texted Hayley to call. When she didn't get a
quick response, Lia went back to her kitchen to scrub at
her countertops, deciding that she might as well put her
agitation to good use. By the time her counters shone, she
felt calmer and headed back to the living room, picking
up Daphne for a cuddle. She'd just settled in her knitting
chair when Hayley replied to her text.

Can't talk now. Tomorrow—promise!

Okay. So that was that. Lia set Daphne down and picked
up the alpaca sweater to work on, the best thing in the
world for her to settle the last of the agitation that Joan's
horrid social media posts had stirred. The next day they'd
all be back at the craft fair, and the problem would have to
be worked out between Belinda and Joan.

When Lia showed up at the Schumacher barn on Sunday morning, the place was buzzing. Word had
spread among the vendors who'd seen Joan's posts and those

who hadn't. Joan's booth was unmanned, but her paintings remained. For how much longer remained to be seen.

Lia went straight to Belinda's office and tried the door after a quick knock. It was locked. She stared at the door in disbelief.

"She's not in yet," a male voice behind her said. Lia turned to see the fair's security guard, Bill Landry, walking over. "She called and asked me to unlock the barn for the vendors. Said she was running late."

"Did she say why?"

"Nope, just that she'd be in soon."

"Okay, thanks, Bill." Lia left, feeling uneasy, but got busy readying her booth.

Maggie left her quilts to come over. "You saw the tweets?"

"I saw one last night." Lia set down the sweater she'd been folding. "Were there more?"

"Oh yes." Maggie rolled her eyes. "Joan went on quite a rampage."

Lia groaned. "I thought she might. I couldn't bear to look. This is so awful—for the entire craft fair! Why did she do it?"

"Who knows what goes through that woman's mind? It's a shame. Joan's been an important draw for the fair. But she's not worth the trouble she causes. Let her go and good riddance, I say. We'll survive. Who knows how many of our fair regulars actually see those posts."

"Joan continued the rants on her own Facebook page," Olivia said, leaning over the scented soaps on her counter.

"Did she? Then plenty of people must have seen them, along with her Twitter followers," Lia said.

"She's not in yet," Maggie said. "Wonder if she'll show up."

"I wouldn't if I were her," Olivia said. "But I wouldn't have said those hateful things, either."

"Belinda's going to be late," Lia said. "If Joan's smart, she'll pack up her stuff and clear out before Belinda arrives."

"That would be best for everyone," Maggie said. "We don't need a big dustup in front of whatever meager crowd might still show up. But knowing those two . . ." She raised her eyebrows and shook her head before returning to her quilts booth.

Lia saw the worry on Olivia's face. "Nothing like that'll happen," she assured her. "I'll catch Belinda as soon as she comes in and talk to her." Olivia seemed to relax, but Lia wasn't at all sure she'd be able to calm her friend. Belinda hadn't responded to her calls and might have been too steamed. Her coming in late wasn't a good sign.

Bill Landry opened the main doors of the craft barn and a few shoppers straggled in. Joan still hadn't shown up. Belinda, either, though Lia kept a sharp eye out for her as she knitted. Finally the craft fair manager appeared, looking predictably unhappy. Lia popped up from her chair, signaled Olivia to watch over her booth, and followed Belinda to her office.

"This isn't the best time," Belinda growled as she unlocked her door.

"I know you're upset."

"Darned right I am. And she's going to get an earful from me." Belinda stomped into her office but left the door open behind her. Lia stepped in and closed it.

"You can't do that," Lia said. "At least not while the fair's going on. Joan's done enough damage as it is."

Belinda stared at Lia. "How does dragging me out for nothing last night damage the fair?"

"What are you talking about?" Lia asked.

"What are *you* talking about?"

"I'm talking about Joan's horrible tweets and Facebook posts."

"Huh?" Belinda looked genuinely confused.

"You didn't see them?" Lia stared back at her. "Then what are you upset about?

"I'm steamed because Joan asked me to meet her last night, then never showed."

"What?"

"I know. Her call surprised me, too. I mean, coming out of the blue like that. And it was getting late. But she said she wanted me to meet someone who had some great ideas for pumping up the craft fair attendance to what it had been. So of course I said yes. I mean, why not? But she and this someone never showed! And never called to let me know what was up. She just left me at that stupid coffee shop to twiddle my thumbs and feel like an idiot."

Lia was flabbergasted and at a loss for something to say. Finally she asked, "So you didn't see the tweets?"

"What tweets?"

Lia quoted what she could remember and braced for the reaction.

Belinda's face reddened as the veins in her neck pulsed rapidly. "What the hell!" she shouted. "Where is she? I'll kill her!"

"Keep your voice down," Lia urged. "I know, it's terrible. Joan hasn't come in. Obviously she's leaving the fair, and those were her parting shots."

Belinda grabbed her phone and jabbed at the screen. "She can hide," she said as she put the phone to her ear, "but she's still gonna get a piece of my mind." Apparently her call went to voice mail. Belinda slammed the phone down hard enough to make Lia flinch and fear for its survival.

"For what it's worth," Lia said, "I think this storm will pass. You'll be well rid of a vendor who turns on you like this."

"Oh, I'll be rid of her; that's for sure." Belinda slumped back in her chair, looking deflated. "But the damage is done. I don't know, Lia. This might mean the end for me."

"Surely not."

Belinda shook her head. "The craft fair can't keep going like this. People are staying away. And it won't be long before my vendors take off, too. My reputation is shot, and because of that the craft fair's is, too."

"I don't believe that," Lia said. "A few negative tweets and Facebook posts by an obviously disgruntled person can't destroy an event thousands of people have loved for years."

"But there's Darren's murder." Tears had sprung to Belinda's eyes, stabbing at Lia's heart. Her friend habitually hid her feelings so fiercely that any sign of them spoke volumes.

"We'll take care of that, I promise you," Lia said. "We're getting closer. My friend Tracy gave me information just last night about Eva Mathis, which might lead somewhere. Did you know she's from an extremely wealthy family?"

"Eva?" Belinda swiped at a stray tear. "Really?"

Lia explained about Eva's connection to the Under a Buck stores. Seeing that was news to Belinda, Lia continued. "For me, that gives Adam Mathis another motive for doing away with Darren. If Eva was in fact having an affair with Darren, and if she left Adam, she'd be taking her money with her."

"Huh," Belinda huffed. "You could be right. And the

more I thought about it, the more I believe there really was an affair, freaky though it seems."

"I'd love to talk to Eva," Lia said. "Is there some way you could arrange it?"

Belinda thought about that. "Let me think about it. I'll see what I can do."

Lia left to get back to her booth, satisfied that Belinda would be fine—at least for the day.

Chapter 24

Joan still hadn't shown up, but Lia saw that Annie was at her pottery booth. She was mulling over the best way to approach her when her phone rang. It was Hayley.

"Hi, Mom. Got a minute?"

"Yes, and I'm glad to hear from you."

"Yeah, sorry I couldn't talk last night. But you saw the Facebook and Twitter posts, right?"

Lia sighed. "Along with the rest of the world."

"How did Belinda take it?"

"She didn't know about them until I told her this morning." Lia told Hayley about Belinda's strange invitation to meet up with Joan, only to be left stranded.

"That's weird. But so is Joan," Hayley said. "Mom, you need to drown those posts out."

"Drown them out?"

"Yes! Hardly anybody responded, contradicted, or just plain changed the subject. You and all the craft fair vendors need to flood the craft fair page with positive comments. Twitter, too, and Instagram, and everywhere you can. You all have let Joan have the last word. Get busy and turn that around."

Lia slapped her head. "Of course! Why didn't we think of that? Maybe we were too stunned. And we're not clever marketers like you, Hayley. I'll spread the word."

"It'll make a difference, I guarantee. I've already started, and I'll respond to and retweet anything positive I see."

Lia rang off and immediately got busy putting up her own posts. Then she urged Olivia to do the same. Leaving her booth under her dependable neighbor's watch once more, Lia went over to Bob Langston's suncatcher booth and told him about Hayley's suggestion. He lit up like one of his craft pieces and pulled out his phone. She then moved on to speak to Carolyn Hanson, whose cakes and pies had been selling steadily, she'd noticed, but definitely not as well as on other Sundays. Lia waited until Carolyn was between customers, then explained what she was getting started.

"Great idea!" Carolyn waved toward her daughter, who was helping her that day. "We'll both pitch in." Her round face darkened. "Joan shouldn't get away with that kind of meanness. We should all be pulling together, not jumping ship."

Encouraged, Lia thanked her. The next booth was Annie's. Lia had wanted to talk to her, and this gave her a great opening. But Annie was dealing with a shopper at the moment, so Lia passed by to spread the word to Mark Simmons and other vendors until she saw that Annie was free and doubled back.

"Hi, Annie," she greeted the potter and launched into the plan to muffle Joan's negative posts.

"Worth a try," Annie conceded, realigning the handmade mugs that her last shopper had been examining. "But that won't stop Joan, you know. She's on a tear."

"Why, though?" Lia asked. "If she decided to pull out of the craft fair, why not just go?"

"Probably because she's the kind of person who has to destroy whatever she leaves behind so it can't succeed without her. And because she's a miserable human being altogether. I, for one, will be glad—make that delirious—not to hear her voice all day long, every weekend, ever again." Annie emphasized her last words with an emphatic pound of a mug against the countertop. Fortunately it was sturdy enough to handle the stress.

"I can imagine that being an ordeal," Lia said. "You seemed to have reached your breaking point yesterday. I wondered at the time what had tipped it."

Annie flushed and shook her head. "Nothing I care to talk about. I just want to put it, and that woman, out of my head forever."

"Excuse me," an older woman who'd stopped at Joan's booth called out. "Do you know how I can buy one of these watercolors?"

"No!" Annie barked, causing the woman to flinch.

Lia quickly took over. "The artist isn't in today," she explained in a more soothing tone. "Perhaps I could take your contact information for Joan to get in touch with you?"

Apparently happy with that idea, the woman scrounged through her purse for pen and paper. She scribbled several lines down and handed the note to Lia, who anchored it at a noticeable spot inside Joan's booth. By that time, Annie had gone to the back of her booth, where she stood fiddling with her stock, her back firmly turned. Receiving the message, Lia moved on.

* * *

Later that afternoon, Lia checked her phone for any new social media posts by Joan and was delighted to find none. Those from the previous night had been pushed out of sight by the flood of crafters' more positive posts. *Thank goodness,* Lia thought with a sigh of relief, and she settled fairly contentedly in her chair to knit.

She'd barely finished a row when she heard, "Is that my alpaca sweater?" Paulette headed over, her expression eager.

Lia stood and held her work up by the needles. "I've finished the pattern at the lower edge of the body, as you see, and am working my way up with the solid color."

"It's beautiful!" Paulette's eyes shone. "The colors are gorgeous, just like in the picture. Can I touch it?"

"Absolutely. It's yours, after all." Lia laid the work carefully on her counter and watched as Paulette fingered the silky-soft stitches.

"It's so light!"

"You'll be surprised how warm it will keep you without the bulk. I'm really enjoying working on this," she said.

Paulette was still murmuring over her burgeoning sweater-to-be when Belinda appeared at the side of the booth and waved Lia over.

"I'm stumped. I can't think of a way for you to talk to Eva Mathis without including Adam. We were never really friends. In fact, I'm sure she dislikes me, so inviting her to lunch or something isn't going to work."

"Eva Mathis?" Paulette asked, overhearing.

"Do you know her?" Lia asked.

"I do." Paulette looked like she could say more but stopped there.

"I'd love to speak with her. Any idea how I could manage that?"

"Actually, I do," Paulette said. "I happen to know she walks her dog in the park every morning at nine like clockwork. I go that way often on my morning jog. If you want, we could, ah, *run* into her." Paulette grinned at her little joke. "Then I could introduce you."

"Would you? That'd be great. Are you free tomorrow?"

Paulette smiled. "I am now. After our lunch the other day, Todd and I talked more about Darren's murder, and I've thought about it a lot." She looked toward Belinda. "I'm really sorry about all the problems it must be causing you. I think too many people have jumped to wrong conclusions, and I'd like to help change that. In fact," she said, holding up a bag, "I made a special effort to do some shopping here at the fair, and I've been urging my patients to do the same."

"Oh! Th . . . thank you," Belinda stammered, clearly stunned and touched.

"And," Paulette said to Lia, "I'm happy to do what I can to help find who really murdered Darren."

"That's wonderful, Paulette," Lia said.

"Shall we meet tomorrow at the park entrance?" Paulette asked Lia. "A little before nine?"

"I'll be there," Lia assured her and patted Belinda's hand encouragingly as her friend stared, apparently, and uncharacteristically, still at a loss for words.

Chapter 25

L ia waited at the entrance of Gunther Park, not far from the historical marker where Martin Brewer had harangued another man about the Schumacher barn. She'd arrived early. A cool breeze played with her hair, and she was glad she'd worn a light jacket on that overcast morning. A few dog walkers came and went, but none fit the description of Eva Mathis that Belinda had given her. She hoped this wouldn't be the day Eva decided to explore another route.

"Not going to happen," Paulette had assured her when Lia brought up the possibility the previous day. "Eva's a woman who sticks to her routines fanatically. Plus, she's told me how her little dog loves the park. She fusses over the creature endlessly and wouldn't dream of upsetting it."

That had reassured Lia at the time, but as she brushed hair from her face and saw no sign of a blond woman with a small dog, she began to wonder. She brightened as she spotted Paulette crossing the street toward her, dressed in jogging shorts, a short-sleeved tee, and running shoes. The sight of those bare arms and legs made Lia shiver, but Paulette's flushed cheeks showed she'd worked up enough heat on her run to be comfortable.

"Morning!" Paulette greeted her and nodded at the thermos in Lia's hand. "Got any to spare?"

"Absolutely." She held up her small tote. "And cinnamon buns."

"You're an angel." Paulette waved toward an empty bench just inside the park.

As she doled out her treats, Lia asked, "So what do you suggest as the best approach to use with Eva?"

"Through her dog, definitely. Eva has limited interests, and the dog is a consuming one. Make friends with it, and you make friends with her."

"No problem." Lia sipped at her coffee. "I genuinely love animals."

"Well, this one is . . . Oh! Here she comes."

Lia looked toward the entrance. A slim woman with amazing long blond hair had turned into the park, holding a small dog on a pink leash. Lia went from admiring Eva's designer hoodie and leggings to puzzlement over the dog. It seemed to be wearing a baby's onesie, and as it drew closer, pulling hard on the leash, she saw it apparently was bald!

Paulette pulled Lia up from the bench and called out, "Eva! What a nice surprise."

The blond woman looked over, a tentative smile on her face before recognition kicked in. "Paulette. Hi!" She stopped, then bent down to pat the dog as though apologizing for the pause in its routine.

Paulette hurried over with Lia. "It's good to see you again."

"And you, too," Eva said. "My shoulder's so much better," she added, rolling it.

Lia realized Eva must have been a patient of Paulette's, who she recalled was a physical therapist.

"Glad to hear it," Paulette said. "Eva, this is Lia Geiger. She's fairly new to Crandalsburg. I'm showing her the park."

As Eva smiled politely, Lia said, "Your dog looks so sweet. What kind is it?"

Eva picked up the little creature, who made Lia's ragdoll cat seem like a huge, puffy marshmallow in comparison, and hugged it. "This is Eloise. She's a hairless terrier. I'm terribly allergic to dog hair, so she's the only kind I can have."

The dog stretched its nose toward Lia in a friendly manner. "May I pet her?"

"Of course. She loves people. Don't you, Eloise?" When speaking to the dog, Eva's voice took on the kind of high-pitched baby talk that tended to grate on Lia, but she smiled and stroked the dog's head, startled at how soft the skin was, and how pleasantly warm. Eloise licked at her hand. She really was a sweet dog.

"Does she need to be kept covered?" Paulette asked, indicating the flannel onesie.

"She gets chilled so easily," Eva said. "I always put something on her on cooler days. This one is kind of loose. It's not easy to find a perfect fit."

"Lia, I'll bet you could knit something that would work," Paulette said. "Lia's an expert knitter," she explained.

Taking her cue, Lia agreed she absolutely could knit

something to size. "I take special orders for my Ninth Street Knitters group all the time."

"You do? That might be perfect!"

"Why don't we walk along with you," Paulette suggested, "and you two can discuss it."

"Yes, Eloise needs to get her walk." Eva set the dog down, and they strolled behind it, talking about knitted dog sweaters and pausing when Eloise paused, which was often.

After the subject of all possible knitted dog items, including booties and hats, was thoroughly explored, Paulette introduced the one Lia was there for. "That was terrible what happened to your husband's partner, Darren Peebles."

Lia watched Eva's reaction, but she seemed more upset over Eloise chewing on a dirty stick than Darren's murder. "Eloise, no!" Eva cried, quickly pulling it from the dog's mouth. When she straightened up, there was no discernable flush to her cheeks or noticeable tear in her eye. "Adam was very upset about it," she said, nodding.

"Was he the first to be called by police?" Lia asked. "I understood Darren had no next of kin."

"They did call the house pretty soon," Eva said. "I took the call." The first sign of emotion, a faint pinkness in her cheeks, appeared. "Adam was out of town. He sometimes turns his phone off, so it took a little while to reach him."

"That must have been—" Lia jumped as Eloise let out a high-pitched yelp. Lia had inadvertently stepped on its hairless tail. Eloise then nipped at Lia's ankle, causing *her* to yelp.

"Eloise!" Eva scooped up her pet. "Are you all right?" She scowled at Lia as she cuddled the dog.

"I'm so sorry," Lia said, rubbing at her ankle. "I didn't see that she'd stopped."

"You have to be careful! She's very delicate!"

Eloise's teeth hadn't felt that delicate, but at least they hadn't broken through the skin. Lia apologized once again, fearing she'd antagonized Eva and willing to suffer a little unacknowledged pain for the greater good. She tried to make amends with a friendly scratch of Eloise's head. Fortunately, the dog licked her hand, and Eva seemed to relax. They continued their walk, Eva carrying her dog.

"Do you know what your husband intends to do about the Schumacher barn?" Lia asked after they'd gone a short ways. "I ask because I'm part of the Crandalsburg Craft Fair, which is in it. Darren intended to tear it down."

Eva shook her head. "That was a very bad idea, and I told him so."

"You told Darren?"

"His planets were not in alignment. That plan wouldn't have worked well."

"Ah, he must have been a Gemini."

Eva looked at Lia in surprise. "He was! Because of that, of course, he tended to rush his decisions."

Lia nodded, happy to have remembered Darren's birth date from a celebration Belinda had once arranged years ago that happened to coincide with Tom's birthday. "Geminis just can't help it, can they?" That she had no real knowledge of, but it seemed to be the point Eva had been making.

Eva set Eloise down, apparently no longer worried Lia would crush her. "I tried to explain it all to Darren, and I even gave him a book to study. He seemed to want to learn, but his impulsiveness reigned. It drove Adam crazy sometimes. Adam's a Leo."

"Ah." Lia assumed a look of understanding and avoided looking at Paulette, who happily had dropped back a bit. "So Adam might not go through with the sale?"

"I have no idea. What with all that's happened—about Darren, I mean—Adam's been awfully busy. He hasn't had time to discuss his own chart with me."

"I can understand that, though he really should take the time, shouldn't he?"

Eva sighed. "Not all of us understand the importance."

Lia wanted to bring the conversation back to Adam's out-of-town trip at the time of Darren's murder, but Eva preferred to get back to dog sweaters. They ended up with Lia giving Eva her address and phone number to arrange a time to look over catalogues of patterns and yarn colors for Eloise's sweater.

As they parted ways, Lia wondered how quickly she could learn enough astrology in case she was called on for future discussion of the subject. She also wondered, as she reached for her sore ankle, what Eva would think about a knitted muzzle for Eloise. *Worth a try*, she thought as she rubbed.

Paulette jogged off toward her home, and Lia pulled out an address Belinda had written down for her. It was Joan's. She had her phone number, too, but Lia wanted to speak to the artist face-to-face to try to convince her to undo the damage her posts had done. Or at the very least, learn what was going through the woman's head. Joan's street wasn't far from the park, so it seemed like a good time to go.

Still learning her way around Crandalsburg, Lia used the map on her phone to guide her. A reappearance of the sun and calming of the breeze had warmed the morning enough that she unzipped her jacket and pushed the sleeves up as she walked.

"Good morning!" a woman whom Lia recognized as living on her own street called as they neared each other, and Lia responded in kind, glad that the neighbor continued on instead of stopping to say more. Though not pressed for time, Lia was still forming her thoughts on exactly what to say to Joan. She checked her map and turned right at the next corner to continue straight ahead. After two blocks, she read the house numbers and walked until she found Joan's pretty redbrick home, glad to spot a light shining in a downstairs window.

Lia climbed the three steps up to the porch and rang the doorbell. There was no sound of footsteps from within. She rang again, then knocked several times. Still no response. Lia might have given up at that point except for the fact that Joan's red Honda was parked at the curb, the SUV Lia had seen Joan climb out of several times in the craft fair parking lot. That, plus the light inside the house, persuaded her Joan must be home. Lia pulled out her phone.

She could hear the rings from her call faintly through the door—not a landline number, but a cell phone's, which convinced her Joan was inside. Was she simply avoiding Lia? Possibly, but that would have been very unlike the artist. Joan wasn't a person who avoided confrontation. She courted it. The back of Lia's neck began to tingle. Something was wrong.

The light inside the house came through a window to the right of the small porch. Lia couldn't stretch far enough to peer through it. She glanced around and spotted a rolled-up hose at the corner of the house, and next to that an upturned bucket. Tall enough? Perhaps.

Lia trotted down the steps and over to the bucket, grabbing and placing it below the lighted window. She planted her foot on it and stepped up, reaching for the windowsill for balance, her head just making it high enough to see inside. At first she saw nothing but a sofa, a couple of small tables, and chairs. But as her eyes scoured the room, she spotted the shoes. Two brown shoes at the end of a pair of legs—legs that were splayed on the floor. Lia had no doubt they belonged to Joan. Just as she had little doubt, from the reddish-brown stain she saw next to the legs, that Joan was dead.

Chapter 26

Lia waited in the yard, clutching her jacket closely and shivering, not from the weather but from what she was sure lay inside the house. When the police car arrived, she was glad to see Brady among the responding officers and hurried up to him to describe what she'd seen through the window. He quickly confirmed it.

"We'll check all the doors and windows," he told her, asking her to stay near the patrol car. "If there's no other way, we'll have to break in. There's a chance she'll be alive."

Lia nodded but highly doubted that.

An ambulance had apparently been called by the 911 dispatcher, but by the time it arrived it had been confirmed that Joan was indeed dead. An apparent homicide, Brady told Lia, though he declined to offer details.

Lia waited for the investigating team, just as she had after coming upon Darren's body at the craft fair barn, and she went through an eerie repeat of answering questions multiple times as she'd done then. The difference was that Lia hadn't found Belinda staring down at Joan's body. That was a plus, but Lia worried it might not let her friend off the hook.

Belinda had told her that strange tale of being invited to meet Joan on Saturday night and the artist not showing up. If Joan had been killed that night, it would look bad for Belinda unless strong evidence pointed elsewhere. Joan's venomous social media posts could be taken as a motive, especially since Belinda's temper was widely known. Lia had to talk to her, though her first attempts to reach her friend were fruitless.

Lia wished Hayley was as close by as she'd been the day of Darren's murder. As it was, with her daughter at her job in Philadelphia, calling her would only be an indulgence, and an unnecessary disturbance for Hayley. When Brady realized Lia had come to Joan's place on foot, he received permission to drive her home, though he remained closemouthed about what he'd seen in the house.

"Let's just say I'm glad you weren't able to get in."

Lia nodded. She'd been pushing away uncomfortable imaginings all morning and didn't need any more to deal with. She did want to know one thing, though. "I'm puzzled how the person who did it got out of the house while managing to leave everything locked up," Lia said.

"That's easy," Brady said. "The front door has a push-button lock. The killer could have simply locked the door on the way out. There was a bolt lock in addition to the push button, but it hadn't been turned."

"Which probably means that person had been let in by Joan at some time and was somebody known to her."

He glanced at her. "That would be my guess. Although we can't know for sure."

"Of course." Who would it have been? Lia didn't think Joan was the type to welcome anyone in who showed up unannounced at her door, even if she knew them. Whoever it was must have arrived with a tale that convinced her to let down her guard.

"I don't suppose they'll find a handy fingerprint on that push-button lock," Lia said.

"If this was a sudden, unplanned confrontation, maybe yes," Brady said.

Meaning probably no, Lia concluded. She was sure that Joan's murder was somehow connected to Darren's, though exactly how she had no idea. It had to have been planned.

"Is there someone you can call to stay with you?" Brady asked as he turned onto her street. "Maybe Hayley?"

"I'll talk to Hayley a little later, but I won't ask her to come here. I'll be fine," she tried to assure him, though he probably could see how exhausted she was, both mentally and physically.

That clearly concerned him until he saw Lia's neighbor, Sharon, hurry out of her house as soon as he pulled up to the curb.

"I heard about it on the news," Sharon said as Lia climbed out of the patrol car. "I thought you could use some company. And lunch," she added as she held up a thermal bag. "If you'd rather just have the lunch and be left alone, that's fine, too."

"You're a gem, Sharon. I'd love it if you'd join me." Lia turned to wave a grateful good-bye to Brady, then led the way to her front door. She asked worriedly, "Did they mention me on the news?"

"Only as a concerned friend. But they said the victim had been part of the craft fair. Since I knew you weren't home, I made an educated guess. Jack sends his best," Sharon added. "And his offer to help any way he can."

"I lucked out when I bought a house next to you two," Lia said, picking up Daphne, who'd scurried up as they walked in, and burying her face in the cat's soft fur. "Iced tea or coffee?" she asked Sharon. She set Daphne down and made a move toward the kitchen.

"You sit down," Sharon ordered, turning her firmly toward a chair. "I'll take care of everything. You want hazelnut coffee, right?"

Lia smiled at that, but she also protested. "I'm not in such bad shape that I need to be waited on, you know."

"Anyone who just went through what you did deserves a little TLC. Now, put your feet up and relax. I'll just be a minute."

Lia did as she was told, and Daphne added herself to the mix by jumping onto Lia's lap. The cat's warmth and purrs worked wonders, and by the time Sharon set out plates and two steaming coffee mugs on Lia's table, she actually felt relaxed enough to eat.

Sharon's chicken salad on pumpernickel was delicious. That and her salad of sliced strawberries and baby spinach did their work, bringing Lia's energy level close to normal. She leaned back in her chair to sip her coffee, ready to talk about her morning's experience. When she'd gone through it all, including her reason for going to Joan's in the first place—Joan's social media blasts—Sharon's immediate question matched her own.

"Did you talk to Belinda?"

"I haven't been able to reach her."

"Hmm. What do you think about that?"

"Only that she's not the easiest person to get hold of. I don't for a minute think she could have done this to Joan. But others might think so."

"The police?"

"I'm sure they'll question her." Lia grimaced as *assuming they can find her* came to mind, but she shook that off. Of course they'd find Belinda. Her often frustrating friend was probably just ignoring her phone for some reason. Aloud, Lia said, "I'm as sure as I can be that there won't be any evidence to implicate her. But that won't stop gossip from spreading, especially so soon after Darren Peebles's murder."

"Unless they charge someone else right away. There might be news updates online. Let me check." Sharon picked up her phone to search, shaking her head as she scrolled. "Nothing I haven't seen already. We'll just have to wait."

"I can't do that. I have to find Belinda. She has to be somewhere in the area." Lia stood and started picking up plates.

"Are you sure? If you want me to come with you, I'd be happy to," Sharon offered, grabbing the mugs, and Lia wondered if Sharon worried she might stumble on another body. The way things were going, she might not be too far off. But Lia shook her head.

"No need. I'll be fine." She thanked Sharon profusely for the lunch and the much-needed comfort, then sent her home with a promise to keep her updated on both her own well-being and any future developments.

Lia had just picked up her car keys to leave when her phone rang.

"I just heard!" Maureen Evert cried. "Was that you who found the poor woman? Are you okay?"

Lia reassured her knitting friend, who tended to hyperdramatize—though in this case Lia couldn't blame her. Murder was not an especially calming event. Lia gave her a short version of what she'd been through and what she knew at that point. "Would you pass that along to the other Ninth Streeters?" she asked. "I know they'll all be upset and wanting to talk to me, but I can't take a lot of calls right now. Just tell everyone I'm okay, and I'll get in touch when I can."

"Promise?"

"Absolutely."

Lia checked her phone for any missed calls or texts from Belinda. Finding none, she slipped it into her pocket. Wherever her friend was, Lia intended to track her down. And then give her a good scolding for making things so difficult.

Lia drove up to Belinda's house, its blank windows signaling emptiness. But she went up to the door to press the doorbell, then knocked and called Belinda's landline, not liking the feeling of déjà vu that crept over her. Wasn't this exactly what she'd done that morning at Joan's? She continued the repetition by peering into the living room window, which was much more easily accessible than Joan's and required only a few steps over from the door to reach. Since the draperies were open, she was able to scan the room, holding her breath as she did so and only releasing it after seeing nothing beyond her friend's familiar furniture.

Belinda's car could have been in her garage, and with

its covered windows, Lia had no way of knowing. But with no response whatsoever to her knocks and calls, her only recourse was to assume Belinda was elsewhere.

Lia returned to her car to head next to the craft fair barn. As she drove through Crandalsburg, she checked pedestrians for a familiar figure until the streets changed to country roads and pedestrians vanished. Once she reached the barn and pulled into its parking area, she wove through the scattering of vehicles, looking for Belinda's gray Honda. It wasn't there, but she still parked and climbed out. Others were inside. It was worth finding out if they'd seen the craft barn manager recently.

As she stepped into the barn, she saw she'd have to wait a bit, as a tai chi class was in progress. Lia walked back to Belinda's office, but it was—not surprisingly—locked. She returned to watch as the group moved gracefully in unison, following their instructor. The ponytailed woman, barefoot and in loose clothing, spoke softly as waterfall-like music played. It was all extremely calming, and as it proceeded Lia began to feel some of her built-up tension slip away. For that reason, the class ended all too soon, but she was there for a purpose other than stress relief. So as the participants began to disperse, Lia called out, "Excuse me, I'm trying to reach Belinda Peebles. Has she been here today?"

Students turned toward her but as a group offered only blank expressions and shrugs. The instructor, who'd started packing up her gear, apparently was the only one who knew whom Lia was asking about. "I haven't seen Belinda at all today," she said. "Which is very unusual." Her brow puckered. "Is anything wrong?"

At that, several faces turned to Lia with greater interest. "No, it's fine," Lia quickly said. The last thing she needed to do was stir rumors. "I guess she just changed her schedule. I'll catch up with her later. Thanks."

Lia hurried off to avoid any further questions and got back in her car. *Where could she be?* Still no responses to Lia's calls and texts. Where else should she look?

Lia drove back to Crandalsburg, trying her best not to worry. It was while she was stopped at a light, glancing around with her thoughts elsewhere, that she finally spotted her friend. Lia might have missed her altogether, with Belinda's dark green shirt matching the paint color of the bench she sat on. But the top of the white plastic bag beside her had been caught by a breeze and waved, catching Lia's eye. As soon as the light changed, Lia pulled up in front, able to see, as she did, the expression on Belinda's face. It was a look of horror.

Chapter 27

She's dead!" Belinda's first words came out in a croak as Lia slipped in beside her on the bench.

"Joan? That's what I've been trying to tell you all day. Is this the first you've looked at your phone?"

"I turned it off. I couldn't stand to see any more of those tweets or people texting me about them. I didn't want to talk to anyone, either."

"So you went shopping?" Lia patted the bulky white bag.

Belinda nodded. "What happened to her?"

"I don't know, exactly. I don't even know when. All I know is whatever happened, happened in her house. That's where I found her."

Belinda's eyes bugged. "*You* found her?"

"I just saw her legs," Lia said, wincing at the memory. "And feet. Through the window."

"Maybe it was a stroke? Or a heart attack?""

Lia shook her head. "The police were pretty definite that it was a homicide."

"But who?" Belinda asked, staring blankly as she struggled with the information. "And why?"

Lia could offer thoughts on why, knowing how Joan relished antagonizing people. But before she could speak Belinda said, "They want to talk to me."

"The police?"

"They want me to come in." She held up her phone, indicating how she'd been reached.

Lia thought that was a positive sign. They had asked, not shown up with handcuffs.

"I'd better go." Belinda gathered up her bag and stood.

Lia grabbed Belinda's arm. "Take a lawyer with you."

Belinda turned to her, at first surprised. "A lawyer?" But after a moment she apparently saw the wisdom of it. "Yeah, you're right. I should." She groaned. "Great. Another expense I can't really afford."

"You can't really afford not to."

Belinda sighed. "I know."

Lia watched Belinda drive off after having elicited a promise to call when she could. A feeling of extreme weariness descended on her, the positive effects from the tai chi class not having lasted long. She wanted to go right home but paused to think about that. Sharon had fed her lunch, but dinnertime loomed ahead, and Lia had no desire or means to deal with it. Doubting that Sharon would be delighted to find her at her door begging for more food, Lia glanced around. She spotted a sub shop down the block that offered an easy out, and she headed there.

When Lia walked in, two customers were already at

the counter. She got in line behind them, listening to the discussion of choices and taking in aromas of freshly warmed bread and spicy meatball sauces. As she moved up, she got her first look at the woman behind the counter, efficiently slapping cold cuts and lettuce onto a sub roll. It took her a moment, but once the woman turned fully toward her, Lia realized it was Ginny, a familiar presence at the craft fair, but less recognizable in a different setting and wearing a cap and uniform. When it was Lia's turn, she greeted Ginny by name as the woman tidied her work area.

Ginny looked up, startled, and Lia said, "I'd forgotten that you said you worked here."

Ginny rolled her eyes and made a twisted grin. "Right. My exciting career. Nice to see you! What would you like?"

Lia recited her favorite, something she had always ordered when she and Tom occasionally stopped for subs: turkey and bacon on wheat, topped with tomato and lettuce. Just saying it out loud stirred a stomach rumble. Ginny nodded, and Lia watched as she moved swiftly from one area to another to cook, toast, and expertly assemble. When she wrapped the sub and took Lia's payment, the shop was empty except for the two of them.

"I heard about Joan," Ginny said as she handed Lia her change.

"Yes, quite a shock."

"Awful, but maybe not so surprising? I mean, she could be pretty nasty. Maybe she pushed someone too far?"

Lia thought of the social media posts against Belinda but said, "Who knows what happened. We don't even know when."

"Oh? I thought it was Saturday night. You know, because she didn't show up at the craft fair on Sunday."

Saturday night, when Belinda had gone out to supposedly meet with Joan. "I haven't heard anything official about that. I suppose it will come out soon."

"Yeah, I suppose. Well, enjoy your sub."

"Thanks. I'm sure I will!"

Lia turned to leave and paused to drop her change into her purse. The shop's door opened, and she stepped aside to make way for the man who burst in, recognizing Professor Brewer as she did so.

"Ham and cheese," he ordered, "and make it fast. No mayo."

Lia looked back and saw Ginny's mouth set tightly as she got to work. *Charming*, Lia thought grimly and wondered if there was any connection between the historian and Joan that she could dig up. It was definitely worth a try.

With Daphne lingering nearby with interest, Lia polished off the last of her sub dinner at home, grateful for a meal that made little for her to do besides a quick cleanup. She fixed a mug of coffee and carried it into the living room to turn on the local news. As expected, Joan's murder was the top story. Lia waited hopefully for any new information.

With a photo of Joan filling the screen—barely recognizable to Lia because of the unaccustomed smile on the woman's face—the news anchor led with "Local artist found murdered in her home," thankfully not adding found by whom. "Police believe the murder occurred sometime Saturday night." Lia winced, thinking of Belinda's weak alibi for that time.

But Belinda had texted that she'd followed Lia's advice

and taken a lawyer with her to speak to the police. Thank goodness for that! And apparently there'd been nothing to hold her on, since she said she was home. That didn't necessarily mean she was cleared. It was early days for that—if ever. She'd claimed to be exhausted, which Lia could understand, and promised to call with more details sometime later.

The newsman talked about Joan's popularity as an artist and her long participation in the Crandalsburg Craft Fair. A video of a police spokesman eventually came up, asking the public for any information that would help their investigation. Lia could picture the police being flooded with reports of Joan's social media diatribe against Belinda and the aforementioned craft fair, which she couldn't imagine them being unaware of. Obviously they needed more evidence, or Belinda wouldn't be at home now. But the court of public opinion wasn't always so scrupulous. Belinda and the craft fair could be in major difficulties because of that.

Lia was mulling this over when her phone rang. Lia sighed, wondering if one of the Ninth Street Knitters hadn't gotten word from Maureen about letting her be for a while. Instead, she saw it was her daughter.

"Why didn't you call me?" Hayley demanded the instant Lia said hello.

"You heard?"

"I *saw*! Jessica had the news on, and she suddenly screeches, 'That's your mom!' I come running in, thinking it was something about the craft fair and your knitting. But it's another crime scene! Mom, what's going on?"

Lia first explained how she hadn't wanted to bother Hayley at work. "But I didn't realize there were cameras around while I was there."

"They don't need TV crews anymore. Just someone showing up with a cell phone and sending their video to the station. So what happened to that crazy woman? The Philly station didn't say much."

"There isn't much to say, so far." Lia told Hayley what she knew, including her role in it and emphasizing more than once that she was fine.

Nevertheless, Hayley said, "I'm coming home."

"Hayley, no, there's no need. Really."

"You'd say that even if there was. But I want to be there. And . . . I was going to come anyway, just maybe not so soon. I was planning to tell you. I quit my job."

"Oh." Lia felt her stomach clench. "So you made your decision."

"I did. And I think it's the right one for me, Mom. Can we wait to talk about it until I get there?"

"Of course, dear. And in that case you should definitely come. How soon?"

"Sometime tomorrow. I'm not sure, exactly. I'll let you know."

Daphne jumped onto the sofa cushion next to her, and Lia urged her over to her lap. The comfort of the soft, cuddly, problem-free cat was something she could definitely use right then.

L ia had been tossing and turning in bed after having turned off the light at least an hour before, when her phone rang. She scrabbled for the device to learn it was Belinda.

"Did I wake you?"

"No," Lia assured her, sitting up and switching on her bedside lamp. "I guess you can't sleep either?"

"The way I feel right now, I may never sleep again."

"I'm glad you called. Tell me about your meeting with the police. Was it rough?"

"Not rough, exactly. Having Seth, my lawyer, there made a difference, and thank you for that. It's just that it's pretty horrible to feel like every word you say is being taken as a lie because there's no way to back it up."

"You said you'd gone to a coffee shop on Saturday evening to meet Joan. Someone there must remember you."

"Yeah, probably, and Seth's looking into that. But I was pretty steamed when I walked out of that place, and they'll also remember that. Plus I went straight home and stayed there all night. Nobody can confirm that."

Lia heard a huge sigh through the phone and was at a loss to come up with anything comforting.

"I found out how she was killed," Belinda said. "Blunt object to the head."

"Oh." The same method used for Darren. Lia realized she'd been hoping for a gunshot. Belinda, she was sure, owned no gun.

"And something else." Lia waited, knowing it must be bad. "One of her paintings."

"Yes?"

"A farm scene. Lots of barnyard animals? It had been slit."

"Oh?"

"It was pushed over her head."

Lia gasped. The memory of Darren Peebles's murder scene rushed in, his body bizarrely surrounded by craft fair items. Now Joan, left just as strangely.

"Yeah, I know," Belinda said, guessing her thoughts. "Kinda like Darren."

"Did the police point that out?"

"It was mentioned." Another long sigh.

Who was doing this? And why? Lia caught herself. Why might not matter that much. And, yes, it was bad for Belinda and for the craft fair. But it was so much worse for the two victims. Maybe the important question should be, Who might be next?

Chapter 28

The next morning, after managing a short few hours of sleep, Lia had barely thrown on some clothes and downed half a cup of coffee when she heard a knock at her door. *Much too early for Hayley,* she thought as she left her kitchen to answer it. And Sharon certainly wouldn't be bringing more food—though that wouldn't be entirely unwelcome, she thought with a smile.

"Oh! Good morning," Lia said, surprised as she opened the door. Eva Mathis stood on her doorstep, with Eloise at the end of her pink leash, sniffing at Lia's shrubs. Had they made an appointment? Lia didn't think so, but the last twenty-four hours had been such a blur. Their chat in the park now seemed like weeks ago.

"I decided to come right after today's walk," Eva said without apology. "We were both so excited about the new sweater!" *We* apparently meaning Eva and Eloise, who, at the moment, appeared much more interested in Lia's azaleas. "You don't mind, do you?"

"Um, no, of course not." Lia stepped back politely to invite the pair inside, wishing she'd put on something besides the stretched-out tee and jeans she'd grabbed. She suddenly remembered Daphne and caught a blur of tan-and-white fur flying up the stairs. "Coffee?" she asked, leading Eva to her table and clearing away the newspaper she'd spread out.

"No, water will be fine," Eva said. "Mineral water, if you have it." She took a chair and lifted her little dog onto her lap, where Lia hoped she'd remain. "I have Eloise's measurements," Eva said and held out a slip of paper. "You said you have patterns?"

"I do. They're upstairs. Just give me a second."

Lia left Eva, having to make do with a tumbler of iced tap water and stroking her little pet contentedly. At least there wouldn't be any dog hairs left behind to agitate Daphne. As Lia slipped into her bedroom, she spotted the cat's dark eyes at the edge of her bed's dust ruffle.

"Just me," Lia assured her and pulled out her box of knitting patterns to search through. While there, she considered exchanging her old tee for something better but decided to let it be. Not that Eva wasn't worth the trouble. It seemed more likely that she wouldn't have cared or even noticed. Lia's clothing, after all, had nothing to do with her beloved dog. When Lia left, she closed the door behind her for Daphne's sake, then dearly hoped a need for the litter box wasn't looming.

"Here we are," Lia said as she rejoined her self-invited guest. She laid two pattern books on the table and tapped at one. "This one's my favorite, but you might find something you like from the other."

Eva opened the first book eagerly and began paging, quickly exclaiming, "Look, Eloise. A pink sweater! Would you like that?" followed by, "Oh, this one has a little hood. Wouldn't that be cute!" After many minutes of the same, she asked Lia questions about particular sweaters, wondering if they were buttoned on and if they were washable, which Lia hoped meant a decision was coming soon. But Eva continued to flip pages until Lia, her patience growing thin, threw out a suggestion.

"How about we start with just one sweater, then choose more later on? That way you wouldn't feel like you're eliminating any, and Eloise would eventually have a whole wardrobe of sweaters."

Eva's face lit up. "I like that! Would you like that, Eloise?" she asked the dog, her voice switching to the baby-talk pitch that made Lia's teeth hurt. But Eloise seemed agreeable, so a pattern was settled on and then a yarn color, without too much trouble.

"How soon will it be ready?" Eva asked.

"I'm going to give this to one of our Ninth Street Knitters, Tracy, to handle. She's made loads of wonderful baby sweaters and is a very fast knitter with the small needles that this pattern calls for. I'll check with her on a time frame, but it shouldn't be long."

That seemed to satisfy Eva. They discussed a deposit, and as she wrote out a check, Lia mused about how Eva hadn't brought up Joan Fowler's murder, which had been all over the news. Did she even watch the news? Adam Mathis's wife seemed too absorbed in her own world to be interested in things that didn't directly touch it. The death of a local artist wouldn't qualify.

But what if the two murders—Joan's and Darren's—were somehow connected? Adam had benefited by Darren's death. Could Joan's be of some value to him? Lia didn't see it, but that didn't eliminate the possibility.

She doubted she'd get any insight into that from Eva, but the woman should at least have been aware of her husband's whereabouts on the night of Joan's murder. Lia scoured her thoughts for some way to bring that out.

Eva handed her the check and set Eloise on the floor, ready to leave. As Lia walked them to the door, she threw out the only thing that she'd managed to come up with. "Did you go to the show Saturday night at the community center? I heard it was pretty good."

"Saturday night? No, we had tickets for the Forrest in Philadelphia. A revival of *Chicago*."

"Nice! Did you and your husband enjoy it?"

"Adam couldn't go, he didn't feel well, so a friend of mine used his ticket. I had bought a dress specially to wear to it," she added, apparently pointing out the importance of not canceling altogether. "And I had a hair appointment in the city that afternoon I couldn't miss."

"Well then, it all worked out." And what had Adam been up to during all that? Since Eva scooped up Eloise and took off, Lia wasn't able to find out—at least not from either of them.

L ia called Tracy about the new commission, including whom it was for, since it was Tracy who had clued her in on Eva's background.

"So you managed to meet the Bearden heiress. What's she like?"

"Quite attractive, but, as you guessed, not exactly Mensa material. Rather self- and pet-absorbed."

"Where does the husband fit in?"

"I don't know. I'd love to meet him but haven't figured out how yet."

"Would he like an Ugly Christmas Sweater?" Tracy asked, which brought a laugh from Lia. "How are you doing, Lia?" Tracy asked. "Maureen said not to bother you, so I didn't. If you're taking knitting orders, maybe things are getting back to normal for you?"

"I've forgotten what normal is, actually. But I'm okay. Any discussion that involves knitting is a nice break from all the other stuff."

"The other stuff happens to be another murder, one that you discovered." Tracy's voice grew softer. "That's rough stuff, Lia. Maybe you should step away altogether. If the craft fair fails, we'll find another way to keep on knitting."

"It's not only that, though. There's Belinda. She's being unfairly dragged through the mud because of it."

"You're a good friend, Lia." There was a long pause. "Promise me you'll be careful?"

"I promise. Please don't worry."

"Hah!"

Lia smiled, appreciating the caring concern, and after ending the call saw that she had a text from Hayley.

Will be there 5-ish. OK?

Lia texted back that it was fine, then put down the phone. Her daughter had quit her first real job and was heading home, unemployed. On to the next worry.

Chapter 29

Lia put concerns about her daughter on the back burner for the time being. Worrisome as Hayley's job situation was, she wasn't in danger of being charged for murder, as Belinda was.

Mathis's name had come up as a possible murder suspect, at least for Darren. But Lia hadn't yet met the man face-to-face. It was time she did, and she'd thought of a way to do so that wouldn't broadcast her real motive.

She finished the breakfast that Eva's visit had interrupted, then changed from her at-home clothes to a more businesslike outfit of skirt and jacket. She had business to do, but not the ordinary kind. What she had in mind was a bit more devious.

Lia parked near the office building and sat in her car for several minutes, waiting. Her quarry was Charlotte Pratt, Mathis's assistant, whom she'd questioned earlier at the tennis courts. According to Brady, Charlotte often went to the coffee shop midmorning, and Lia wanted to catch her on her return. Knowing Charlotte disliked Adam Mathis and her job, Lia hoped that would work to her advantage.

She perked up as she spotted the woman approaching from the opposite direction, a large take-out coffee cup, likely meant for Mathis, in hand. Lia jumped out to meet up with the woman as she closed in on the building's entrance.

"Hello, Charlotte," Lia called out and saw puzzlement on the woman's face. "Lia Geiger. We met at last week's tennis lesson?"

Charlotte's face cleared. "Oh yes! Sorry, it took me a minute."

"I had the advantage. I saw you first. We both look different in our street clothes, don't we?"

"That's what threw me off—no tennis shoes. Nice to see you. You coming in?" Charlotte asked as she reached for the door.

"I am, and I'm heading to the same place you are," Lia said.

"My office?"

"Yes, and running into you could be very fortunate for me."

Charlotte shot her a questioning look as she stepped in, holding the door back for Lia.

"I want to speak to Mr. Mathis, and I don't have an appointment."

"Ah." Charlotte headed to the elevator and pressed the call button. They were alone in the small, faux-marble lobby. "What about?"

"The Schumacher barn." At Charlotte's look of surprise, she added, "But I mainly want to get an idea of what he's like."

"In that case, get him mad." The elevator doors opened, and they got in. "If he thinks you're of some use to him, he'll be all charm. Aggravate him and his true side will come out."

"I think I can manage that," Lia said. A small smile curled her lips, which Charlotte returned. When the elevator reached her floor, she exited into the hall and led the way to the office. Her glance back showed that smile was growing with each step.

"Give me a minute," she told Lia as they entered the waiting area. She knocked on an inner door, then took the coffee in, returning after a minute to say, "I gave you a small start on the aggravation." She slipped behind her desk. "The shop didn't have his usual. He has to make do with a lesser brand."

"Poor thing," Lia murmured back, bringing a low chuckle from Charlotte.

"I told him you had an appointment. He never checks the book."

"Great. Thanks." Lia picked up a magazine and paged through it, assuming Mathis would spend a few minutes on his coffee. The waiting area was pleasant, decorated in shades of gray and white, and the genuine leather chair she sat in was comfortable. The pictures on the wall were generic landscape scenes, the frames probably more valuable than the prints, but altogether, like in most waiting rooms, the décor was inoffensive.

A second woman sat at another desk, several feet to the right of Charlotte's and in front of a second office door, possibly Darren's. Though she seemed occupied, Lia wondered what she had to do with at least one boss no longer there. The thirty-something woman with long auburn hair glanced up and noticed Lia's gaze. Her brows pulled together in annoyance, and Lia looked down at her magazine. Apparently the stress in the office that Charlotte had previously described hadn't totally disappeared.

Charlotte continued to busy herself until she got the signal. She beckoned Lia and led her into the inner office. "Mrs. Geiger is here to see you, Mr. Mathis."

Mathis greeted Lia and held out his hand, which she shook before taking the chair he gestured toward. Possibly in his mid-fifties, he was not a tall man, perhaps only an inch or two over Lia's average height, which she judged while they were standing. Seated, however, she found herself having to look up to meet his eyes. An elevated chair?

She also noticed his thick mane of hair—a rich chestnut brown that was attractive but didn't quite match his middle-aged face with its share of sags and wrinkles. Hair dye? Not unusual, she knew, for men with much younger wives or who wanted to project youthful energy in the business world. She doubted it had ever crossed Tom's mind, but to each his own.

"What can I do for you, Mrs. Geiger?" Mathis asked, smiling broadly, his hands clasped before him on the desk.

"I happen to be a good friend of Belinda Peebles," Lia began and watched the smile fade. "Before Darren died, he intended to buy the Schumacher farm and tear the barn down. This would affect quite a few people negatively, but most of all Belinda, whose means of income would be taken away. As a vendor at the fair myself, I want to know what your plans for the barn are, Mr. Mathis. I hope you won't be following through on Darren's."

Mathis coughed and cleared his throat a few times, clearly not having expected this. Probably he'd assumed Lia had come with a pitch for a community fund-raiser.

"Mrs. Geiger," he finally said, "it's early days to be saying with any surety what I will or won't be doing on any of Darren's plans. I'm sure you can understand what a huge loss his death was to us, as well as a terrible shock. We're all still reeling from it."

Mathis didn't look particularly reeling, and Lia remembered Charlotte's description of the office doing business as usual at Mathis's direction, the day after the murder. But Lia nodded. "You have my sympathy, of course. And I am sorry to be bringing this up at a time like this. But I'm sure you can see that Darren was acting simply to hurt Belinda. Their divorce had been bitter. Any business decision made on that basis can't be a good one, can it?"

"Well—"

Lia decided to switch tactics, using honey rather than vinegar. "Belinda always said you were the savvier of the two." She watched one eyebrow go up on Mathis's face, but she caught a slight nod as he apparently agreed. "You must see how tearing down a historic barn would be very bad for your firm's image."

Mathis suddenly frowned. "Have you been talking to Martin Brewer?"

Uh-oh. Lia recalled a little too late how Brewer had caused a ruckus at that office more than once over the barn. But she could truthfully answer "no" without explaining that she'd listened to the man but had never spoken to him. "I'm just pointing out what you surely know already, that it's simply good business to avoid antagonizing future clients."

"Mrs. Geiger, my future clients are probably far more

interested in the affordable housing I can provide for them. But you may have a point. It's something to consider, at least, and I definitely will keep it in mind. Now, if you'll forgive me, I do have a busy schedule ahead of me." This from the man who never checked his day's appointments.

He stood, not having far to go from his already high seat, and held out his hand once again, bringing an end to the discussion. Since Lia had hoped for but not really expected more, she was able to smile as though satisfied.

"Thank you for seeing me, Mr. Mathis."

"My pleasure, Mrs. Geiger." He came out from behind his desk to escort her to the door. "It's always great to meet someone who cares about her friends and her community."

"And such a wonderful, and active, community, isn't it?" Lia smiled sweetly. "Just this last Saturday, they put together a terrific performance at the center, with all the proceeds going to rebuild the children's playground at Gunther Park. Did you happen to go?"

"Saturday? Uh, no. My wife and I had tickets to a show in Philadelphia."

"Oh! How lovely. What did you see?'

He paused—*Searching his memory?*—then brightened. *"Chicago."*

"Lucky you! I heard Renée Zellweger was wonderful reprising her role."

"Yes. Very good." He opened the door for Lia and pressed one hand on her back to ease her out.

The door closed behind her, and Charlotte looked up from her computer, eyebrows raised questioningly.

Lia waved for her to step out into the hallway.

"How did it go?" Charlotte asked.

"I didn't get him mad. At least I don't think so."

"How disappointing," Charlotte said with a wicked grin. "Ah well. Did you get what you wanted?"

"I learned one thing that might be important. But there's something else. Maybe you can tell me." Lia glanced back at the outer office. "Does Mathis have any connection to Joan Fowler?"

Charlotte's eyes widened at the question. "The artist who was killed yesterday?"

Lia nodded.

"I don't know." Charlotte hesitated. "But . . . there were several phone calls for Mr. Mathis lately. From a woman who wouldn't give her name."

"He took the calls?"

"Uh-huh. And they always put him in a horrible mood."

Chapter 30

Lia smiled as she saw her daughter's burgundy Nissan pull up in front of the house, and she hurried out to meet her.

"Hi, Mom!" Hayley called over the top of her car as she climbed out. She popped her trunk and reached in for a suitcase and duffel bag. "Sorry, I'm a little later than I said. I stopped at the alpaca farm."

Lia hugged her and took the duffel from her hand. "The alpaca farm?"

Hayley grinned sheepishly. "A sudden impulse. I just wanted to see those cuddly things again. They were so sweet the last time! I think I made a special friend this time. Rosie."

"Rosie?" Lia started toward the house.

"She's fawn colored and has the cutest white face. She wanted to go home with me. I had to explain how she wouldn't fit in my car."

"Yes, that would have been tricky. Not to mention what you'd do with her after that."

"Well, I'd have a steady supply of alpaca yarn for you, I guess."

Lia laughed. "Right, if it happened to drop off of Rosie all washed, spun, and ready to go!" She placed the duffel near the stairs as Daphne jumped down from the chair where she'd been dozing.

"Daphne!" Hayley bent down to ruffle the cat's fur. "Did you miss me?" Daphne circled Hayley, sniffing intensely. "Hah! I bet she smells Rosie. Don't worry, Daph, I didn't bring her with me. Oh, Mom! I got you something." She unzipped the duffel and pulled out a skein of alpaca yarn. "I saw you lingering over it when we were there," Hayley said. "I thought maybe you could make a scarf with it? It would go with your winter coat, wouldn't it?"

Lia took the supersoft yarn—a lovely periwinkle blue—touched, both by the unexpected gift and by the idea that Hayley had picked up on Lia's fondness for the yarn. The fact that she'd probably need a second skein for a decent-sized scarf didn't need to be mentioned. Lia pressed the yarn against her cheek, loving the feel of it, then hugged her daughter a second time. "Hungry?" she asked.

"Not really. But I'd love some coffee."

"Why don't you take your bags up to the spare room, and I'll get it ready." As Lia headed to the kitchen, she thought about how she hadn't referred to her guest room as Hayley's room, even though her daughter was the only one who'd ever used it, so far. Much as Lia would enjoy having Hayley with her, she knew it wouldn't be good to encourage that, except on a visiting basis. Hayley needed to be on her own, to have the satisfaction of being a responsible adult who could take care of herself. She'd been on the road to independence for the last few months, but the trip had taken a surprising detour.

Lia sighed and slipped the first pod into her coffee maker, then put crackers, cheese, and a few cookies on a plate for nibbling. She brewed a second mug for herself, then loaded it all on a tray to carry into her living room, giving a shout-out to Hayley that the coffee was ready.

Hayley tramped downstairs. She quickly stirred milk and sugar into her coffee, then took a long swallow. "Oh, that's good." She sat back and patted her lap as an invitation to Daphne. "So," she said as the cat jumped up. "Tell me what's happened since yesterday. No more bodies, I hope?"

Lia winced. "Two is enough." She set down her mug. "First, tell me what your plans are, now that you've left your nice-paying job."

Hayley grinned. "Don't worry, Mom. I'll be fine." She grabbed a chocolate chip cookie and bit into it. A fallen crumb caused Daphne to sniff at but then ignore it.

Lia said nothing and simply waited.

"Okay," Hayley said. "I have something in the works. But it's not definite yet, so I'm really not ready to talk about it."

"Something in Philadelphia?"

"Uh-uh. Not going to say. As soon as I start giving out small bits, I'll end up blurting out the whole thing. I just don't want to jinx it."

"It's something you're really happy about?"

Hayley smiled. "I am. And I feel it's right for me, where the other place wasn't. I think I know what I'm doing, so I hope you'll just trust me for a little while, okay, Mom?"

Lia relented. "Of course I will. I'm curious, but I can wait." *But, please, not too long.*

"So what's happened here since I called?"

Lia told Hayley about her separate meetings with Eva and Adam Mathis and gave her impressions of the two.

"Sounds like an odd pair."

"Definitely not your average couple—if there is such a thing. Belinda called Adam a snake, and she's known him much longer than my few minutes with him. But in that brief time, some of his shadiness came out." Lia shared how he'd lied about accompanying his wife to the Philadelphia theater.

"Then he has no alibi for Joan's murder?"

"None that I know of. But I haven't come up with a connection between the two, either." She told Hayley about the mysterious calls to Mathis that Charlotte said had agitated him. "But there's nothing to say that they came from Joan."

"Curiouser and curiouser." Hayley sipped more coffee. "You know her Facebook and Twitter accounts are gone, don't you?"

"Joan's? No, I never checked. When were they closed?"

"I don't know. I just saw last night that they weren't there."

"Maybe she had second thoughts about what she'd done?" Hayley shrugged. "Who knows?"

They both fell silent for some moments, thinking, until Lia said, "Annie."

"Huh?"

"Did I tell you about the fight Annie had with Joan? You remember Annie, don't you?"

"The potter? Sure. There was a fight?"

"On Saturday afternoon at the craft fair. They kept their voices down, but there was clearly something very heated going on between the two. By Sunday, Annie was still visibly upset over whatever it was about and refused to discuss it."

"Hmm. So what was *she* doing Saturday night?"

Lia sighed. "She'd probably say she was home with her family, but that doesn't mean much anymore." She told Hayley what she'd learned from Jen Beasley at the knitters meeting about Annie's late-night visits to the 7-Eleven. "Apparently it wasn't unusual for her to work on her pottery while everyone in her household was sleeping, and then to step out for a little break."

"Or a little murder."

"I hope not."

"Yeah, I know. It's hard not to feel bad about all she must be dealing with because of her husband's awful accident. But, Mom, even if Darren was responsible for that, it doesn't excuse murder."

"I know."

"And a second murder? That's going on a rampage!"

"Maybe it wasn't Annie," Lia said. "After all, we don't know the exact time of Joan's death. All I've heard so far is 'sometime Saturday night.' If the only time Annie could slip away unseen from her house was close to midnight, it doesn't make sense that Joan would open her door at that time, and especially for Annie."

"True." Hayley's eyes lit up. "Maybe I can find that out from Brady. I mean find out the time of death." She grabbed her phone and tapped at it, apparently sending a text message to him, and didn't have to wait long for a response. Hayley grinned. "He's on duty, but I can meet him in half an hour when he takes his break!" She downed the rest of her coffee, then trotted upstairs to freshen up, returning in a few minutes to double-check with Lia on the location of the café Brady had named.

"Sounds walkable," she proclaimed. "But I'd better start now. See you!"

Lia waved her off, then settled down to knit, expecting to have a good amount of free time ahead of her. But she'd done only a couple of rows when her phone rang. It was Belinda, who asked, "Did you eat yet?"

"No." Lia ran over what she'd planned to fix for Hayley and herself. She didn't know when or if Hayley would be back to actually eat it, but either way there was plenty. "Want to come over? I can put something together in a flash."

"Don't. I'm in the mood for Chinese. I'll pick that up. Okay?"

Chinese. Lia knew what that meant. Back in their single days, when Belinda was feeling particularly down and wanted to talk, it was always over Chinese food.

"That sounds good." Lia didn't bother giving Belinda her choice. It was always moo goo gai pan, which her friend would remember, just as Lia knew Belinda would pick General Tso's chicken.

"Be there in half an hour."

They hung up, and Lia stared at the phone, thinking. Her friend obviously needed at least a shoulder to lean on. In case there was anything more, Lia should be ready.

Chapter 31

At least Lia's table was ready when Belinda arrived. Holding a large brown bag that sent out amazing aromas, she bustled in, all business, and unpacked the white cartons briskly, apparently able to accurately tell what was in each by smell. Or was it simply luck? Either way, no time was wasted.

Lia poured green tea from the blue willow teapot her mother-in-law had gifted her with one Christmas, and within minutes they were digging into their dinners, Belinda using chopsticks and Lia sticking with a fork. Little was said beyond small talk concerning the restaurant that supplied the food, how long it took, or how good everything tasted.

When neither of them could eat a single bite more, Lia poured a second cup of tea for both, settled back in her chair, and waited.

Belinda took a sip and set her cup carefully onto its saucer. "I don't know how much longer I can do this."

Lia's stomach clenched. *Do what, exactly?* Surely not that she couldn't keep up a pretense anymore.

"My blood pressure is sky-high. I'm sleeping, like, ten minutes a day. And this"—Belinda waved toward the stacked cartons—"this is the most food I've managed in days."

Lia relaxed. These were normal problems. Her friend wasn't about to confess to two murders—not that Lia truly expected it. "I'm glad you came. Sitting home alone is not good for anyone in times like this."

"Lia, sometimes I feel I'm losing my mind. Can all of this actually be happening? All I wanted was to earn a decent living at what I do best—management. A reasonable goal, right? What everyone in the world wants. And maybe to settle down with a decent life partner. I couldn't even do that! Instead, I picked a rat, who I should have seen through from the beginning if I'd had my eyes open. Here I am, going along thinking I've got brains and a certain amount of common sense, willing to work hard, and this is what it's come to?"

Belinda dropped her face into her hands, her shoulders shaking. Lia scooted over to wrap her arms around her.

"Don't do this to yourself, Belinda. None of this is your fault! Yes, you're in a miserable situation right now, but not because of anything you've done. Someone out there is killing people, people who happen to have a connection to you. But whoever it is won't get away with it!"

Belinda looked up, wiping her face. "But they *are* getting away with it. The police are looking at me!"

"At you and probably many others. It's what they do, Belinda. But I've been looking around, too, you know, and I've turned a few things up." Lia described her visit with Adam Mathis and catching him in a lie about his whereabouts on Saturday night.

"Adam!" Belinda spat out the name. "He'd lie to his own grandmother about the time of day if he thought it worked for him. I'd love to see him finally caught on something. But I don't see that he'd have anything to do with Joan."

"His assistant told me about several phone calls he took from an unnamed woman that agitated him. Might it be Joan? Could she have had information on him that he needed to keep quiet?"

Belinda thought about that. "Joan was a troublemaker, that was true. But it always was about herself. She wasn't one to go poking into other people's business, mostly because she didn't care about other people. If they crossed her in some way, that was different."

"Okay, might Adam have crossed Joan? Maybe in a financial situation? Or, oh, I don't know, sexual?"

Belinda gave Lia a side-eye. "Joan? And Adam? You're kidding, right?"

"I'm just throwing out whatever I can. Think about it, okay? Maybe something will come to you."

Belinda nodded but looked less than hopeful. She sighed. "You know you're wrong about none of this being my fault. If I'd walked away after that first date with Darren, I wouldn't be in this mess."

"Belinda."

"No, it's true! I had reservations, right from the start. But I quashed them. It's not like I had guys beating down my door, you know." She smiled puckishly. "Unlike you."

Lia laughed. "What? You call two serious boyfriends before Tom a mob?"

"There were plenty others who wanted to ask you out but didn't think they had a chance. Don't deny it. But I scared off anyone who even glanced my way. That's probably what attracted me to Darren. He didn't scare easily. Not the best reason to marry someone, right?"

"I'm sure he did his best to convince you he was wonderful. He fooled a lot of people."

"But not you, right? Or Tom?"

Lia hesitated.

Belinda laughed. "Don't worry. I could tell. But I convinced myself for a long time that you just didn't see his positive side. Oh, the things we do to ourselves! I was really great at rationalizing."

"We all do it. It's human nature. The important thing is now you see it all clearly, right?"

"The rose-colored glasses turned gray a long time ago."

"Not gray. Clear. You won't make the same mistakes again."

"Took me long enough," Belinda grumbled.

"That doesn't matter. What matters is the here and now and the life you have ahead of you."

"As long as it's not spent in prison."

Lia shook her head. "It won't be. You know you're innocent. I know. We just have to find out who's guilty."

"Just?"

"We'll do it." Lia stood. "But first we have to clean this table up."

Belinda dragged herself up. "There's always a catch." But Lia saw the beginnings of a smile and knew she'd managed to buck up her friend—at least for the time being.

They were loading the dishwasher when Hayley returned and followed the clinking sounds to the kitchen.

"Hey, Miss Belinda! I thought that was your car outside. How are you?"

"Much better than I was a couple of hours ago." She set down a plate and stepped over to give Hayley a hearty hug.

"Did you eat?" Lia asked. "We had Chinese. There's plenty left."

"No, I'm good. Brady knows all the best fast-but-good-food places in town."

"Brady?" Belinda asked.

"My old friend from school." She heard a ping signaling a text. "Excuse me." Hayley left the kitchen to tend to it. Lia and Belinda finished their cleanup, and when they joined her in the living room, Hayley explained, "Brady just wanted to check I got home okay." She grinned. "Like there's anything to worry about in Crandalsburg?" She winced. "I meant, of course, regarding muggers, not, well, you know . . ."

"We know," Lia said. "Brady is a police officer," she told Belinda. "New to the force, but he's been able to help us a bit."

"Yeah," Hayley said. "Like, tonight he gave me Joan's time of death. But not that helpful, it turns out. He said because her body was found so late, the ME could only give a range of several hours: between eight p.m. Saturday and eight a.m. Sunday."

Lia grimaced. "That doesn't help us to eliminate anyone." She turned to Belinda. "What time did Joan call when she asked you to meet her at the coffee shop?"

Belinda looked surprised. "Did I say it was a call? Actually she texted. Twice. I showed them to the police. They were sent around seven thirty Saturday night."

"Can I see them?" Lia asked.

Belinda dug her phone out of her purse. She pulled up the texts and handed the phone to Lia.

"The texts just show a phone number, not her name," Lia said.

"But she identifies herself. People get new numbers sometimes. Or have second phones. And since the text was about the craft fair, I didn't question it." She looked worried. "Should I have?"

Lia and Hayley exchanged looks. "It probably was fake," Hayley said. "Someone wanted to lure you out around the time of Joan's murder. I think you got a text from the murderer."

Belinda grabbed her phone and stared at it in horror, as if the words on the screen had suddenly turned venomous, which in a way they had. She was seeing them for the first time for what they really were: an evil attempt to destroy her by a person who'd already destroyed two others. She threw the phone onto the sofa, causing Daphne, who'd been lying nearby, to jump.

"What monster is doing this?" she cried.

"Whoever it is won't be doing it much longer," Lia said. "That I guarantee," she added, though her words sounded much more confident than she felt.

Chapter 32

Lia tried to convince Belinda to stay with her and Hay-ley, at least for the night, but she refused. She seemed to have recovered from her shock over the text messages, though how much of that was bravado Lia couldn't tell. But she at least allowed Lia to pack up the leftover take-out food to take with her, along with a container of frozen meatballs in sauce, which made Lia feel a bit better. Belinda would probably be eating General Tso's chicken for breakfast the next day, but that was out of Lia's hands.

The next morning, as Hayley cleared away their break-fast dishes, Lia got a call from her craft fair neighbor Olivia.

"I meant to call earlier," she explained, "but Michael was down with a cold. Are you okay, Lia? It must have been so awful to find Joan like that."

"It shook me up," Lia admitted, "but I'm doing okay now. My daughter is here and will be with me for a while."

The thought came to her that when six-year-old Hayley had a cold, she didn't get 24/7 fussing from Lia. More like a box of tissues and maybe chicken soup out of a can. Had Lia been a negligent mother? Hayley did, after all, survive and even thrive. But Lia allowed that perhaps Olivia's son caught worse colds than Hayley's. And it was very nice of her to call—once Michael's sneezes apparently had lessened.

"It's terrible what happened to Joan," Olivia said. "Do you think . . . ?" Her voice trailed off.

"Do I think what?" Lia asked.

"Oh, I hate to say it, but do you think it could have been someone from the craft fair? I mean, Joan was always so horrible to everyone there. Except her customers, of course. And Ginny."

"Ginny?"

"Well, Ginny gets along with all the craft fair people, doesn't she? It's kind of like we're her family."

"Yes, sadly enough. I'm glad to know Joan treated her decently, though she obviously couldn't bring herself to do the same with Annie. I can't imagine what brought on that terrible fight between them on Saturday."

"Poor Annie," Olivia said, sighing. "To know that her last words ever with someone were angry ones."

Lia doubted Annie would be the only one, but she knew what Olivia meant. And she still would like to know what had brought it on.

"Well, I'd better go," Olivia said. "I've gotten behind on my herbal soaps. I'm glad you have someone with you. No one should be alone right now." On those words, intended to be comforting but inadvertently stirring Lia's worries about Belinda, she hung up.

To push back those worries, Lia focused on appreciating Olivia's call. She had said that the craft fair vendors were like family for Ginny, and they were becoming that for Lia, too, a fact that came to the forefront once again when she found Maggie on her doorstep a few minutes later, holding a gorgeous cake in her hands.

"I didn't make it," Maggie immediately said. "It's Carolyn Hanson's. She asked me to bring it for her when she knew I was coming by."

"How generous of her!" Lia said, knowing the baker's business had dropped off like everyone else's at the craft fair. "And of you to come by. Please come in and have some with me."

Maggie grinned. "I could be talked into that. But just a tiny piece." She followed Lia into the house, greeting Daphne along the way to the dining area with a cheery, "Hello, kitty."

"Look what we have," Lia called to Hayley, introducing her to Maggie when she leaned out of the kitchen.

"Oh wow!" Hayley cried, eyeing the cake.

Maggie once again gave Carolyn full credit for it. "I'm much better with a needle than I am in the kitchen," she said, then responded to Lia's beverage offer with, "Tea, please, with cream. Or milk. Whatever you have."

Within minutes Lia was slicing into the cake, which Maggie informed her was carrot cake, "with real buttercream frosting, of course. Carolyn doesn't skimp. She thought she remembered it was your favorite, Lia, but isn't it everyone's? She also sends her sympathy for what you went through on Monday."

"Everyone's being so thoughtful." Had they responded similarly to Belinda after Darren's murder? Lia wondered. The circumstances had, of course, been different, with the murder having shockingly occurred on the crafters' own premises. With Belinda immediately under suspicion, Lia feared no one besides herself had reached out to her. She passed the plates while Hayley brought in tea and coffee.

As they enjoyed their treat, Maggie chatted at some length about the quilt she was working on. Just as Hayley's eyes began to glaze, they snapped clear when Maggie brought up Martin Brewer.

"After you and I discussed the professor that time," Maggie said to Lia, "I got to thinking about him, and I've been much more aware of what he did—or didn't—do."

"Yes?" Lia asked as Hayley set her fork down.

"What he didn't do was show up at the community center Saturday night."

"He was supposed to?" Hayley asked.

"Yup. The drama club put on a play about Mary Todd Lincoln, during the days after the assassination. Martin was supposed to lead a discussion afterward, but he never showed."

"Really?" Lia took a sip of her coffee. "Was any reason given?"

"Just an apology from Nan Bergen, the director. And something about his being indisposed. A good number of us had waited after the final curtain because of him. Instead, the lead actors came out with the director and talked about the play and their roles."

"Perhaps he was," Lia said. "Indisposed, I mean."

"Could have been, of course."

"Mom!" Hayley cried. "You're too trusting. Don't you think the timing is the least bit suspicious?"

"Of course it's exactly when Joan was murdered. But what would Martin have to do with Joan? Darren, I can see. But Joan wasn't planning to demolish the craft fair barn or any other sites that Martin cares about."

"There might be other reasons we just don't know about," Hayley said.

"Very true." Lia turned to Maggie. "Anything you can think of?"

"Not a thing. But . . ." She paused, her eyebrows wiggling. "Turns out he was seen later that night, driving."

"There you are!" Hayley cried.

"What time?" Lia asked.

"Around eleven. Abby Williams's husband, Deshawn, was out walking their dog and saw him. Abby was highly annoyed to hear about it because she felt our professor had skipped out on us."

"He might have been picking up something from the drugstore, if he was ill," Lia said.

"Mom."

"It's possible," Lia said, looking at Hayley defensively.

"You can get things delivered," Hayley said. "And the timing is still suspicious. More so now that we know he was out and about."

"When you can come up with a reason for Martin Brewer to murder Joan, then I'll agree with you. Until then . . ."

"Okay, I'll get working on that!" Hayley grinned, obviously liking the challenge.

"Then you might start with Penn State," Maggie said. "It's where he taught. Maybe Joan was there at the same time to study art?"

"Good idea," Hayley said.

Lia remained skeptical but knew it wouldn't hurt to try. Martin, after all, was a confrontational person, as Joan had been. If they'd disagreed on something important to each of them, Lia had to admit it wouldn't have been easily settled. That "something," though, would need to be extremely important to end in murder.

Maggie scraped up the last crumbs of her cake and, having shared what she'd come to share about Martin, left it in Lia's and Hayley's hands to deal with. With a final pat on Daphne's head, she took off, wishing them luck.

Hayley immediately jumped online, and as she worked, Lia's thoughts turned in another direction. Talking about Martin had reminded her of her last sight of him, when he'd rushed into the sub shop and demanded instant service from Ginny. Olivia had mentioned Ginny as one of the few who got along reasonably well with Joan. Maybe Ginny had a few insights to offer?

"I'm going out," she informed Hayley, who, absorbed in her Internet searches, only grunted. "To Tibet," Lia added. "For a few spices and maybe a yak. I shouldn't be long."

Hayley, staring at her screen, wiggled a hand in farewell. Lia shook her head and left.

Chapter 33

After driving halfway to the sub shop, Lia realized she didn't know how early it opened or even if Ginny would be there. Who knew what her work schedule was? But the ride was a short one and worth taking the chance. If luck was with her on those first two points, it would probably be with her on a third: that Ginny wouldn't be terribly busy at that midmorning period and would be free to talk.

Lia pulled her car into a parking spot not far down from the shop, cheered to see the neon sign lit. She winced when she walked into the place and didn't see the familiar plumpish figure behind the counter. But then Ginny magically appeared, straightening from her crouch behind the counter.

"Oh!" she said. "It's you, Lia! I thought it was our delivery guy."

"Sorry," Lia said with a smile. "Just me. With nothing to deliver."

Ginny returned the smile. "That's fine. I'd rather have you. How've you been? You must have liked our sub since you're back so soon."

"It was delicious and just what I needed then. But I'm here for another reason today. Do you have a minute to talk? I'd hate to hold you up from your work."

"No problem. I'm just tidying after the breakfast rush," she said, then laughed. "I can walk and chew gum at the same time. What's up?"

"I'd like to understand Joan better, after what's happened to her. I've heard that you were one of the very few who got along with her. Is that right?"

Ginny grimaced. She picked up a cloth to gather up bits of food debris in the work area. "Reasonably well, I suppose. She never yelled or called me names, if that counts."

"With Joan, that seemed to count for a lot. Why do you suppose that was? How did you manage to get on her better side?" Lia knew Ginny didn't buy things at the craft fair, so Joan wouldn't have been treating her as a valued customer.

Ginny paused her wiping to think about that. "I don't know. Maybe because we both were on our own? Kindred spirits of a sort?"

"Did she talk about that? About any family?"

"It only came up once, when I mentioned my mother. It happened that Joan's mother and mine had the same name—Shirley. Hers passed away years before my mom."

"Did Joan grow up in Crandalsburg as you did? Are there siblings here?"

"I think there's a sister somewhere. But neither of us is from Crandalsburg, originally. Joan moved here from Pittsburgh."

"Oh? And where did you grow up?"

"Before we moved here, we lived in a small town you probably never heard of. Boggs Creek."

"You're right. I never heard of it," Lia said, adding with a smile, "But I've heard of Pittsburgh. So I'm guessing Joan wasn't close to her sister?"

Ginny shook her cloth out over the sink. "I got that strong impression. I commented once on one of her paintings, a winter scene of kids skating on a frozen pond with trees nearby. If you looked carefully you could make out that the center branches of one of the trees formed a face, an angry, distorted one. She said she must have been thinking of her sister when she painted it."

"Ouch!"

"I know, right?" Ginny shrugged. "I thought she was at least lucky to have a sister. I always wished I'd had one. Joan gave me one of her watercolors once. Not the skating scene. A different one."

"That was nice of her."

"Yeah. It was slightly damaged. She probably didn't think she could sell it. But I managed to fix it. You can hardly see the wrinkle."

"Good. Ginny, did Joan ever mention Martin Brewer?"

"The history guy? Not that I remember. Why?"

"I wondered if there had ever been a problem between them, or if they even knew each other."

Ginny barked out a laugh. "If they knew each other, there was probably a problem, knowing those two."

"You know Brewer?"

"Only from here at the sub shop, and I don't like him. I can't see Joan putting up with him, even as a customer."

"That's pretty much what I thought, but I wanted to

check." A phone rang somewhere in the back, and Ginny made a move toward it, then hesitated, looking at Lia. "Go ahead, please," Lia said. "And thanks. You've been very helpful."

Ginny smiled. "My pleasure. Good to see you!"

Lia left the sub shop and got into her car. Before starting it, she pulled out her phone and did a search, then studied the screen. After a minute, she pressed her ignition button and took off, turning after a couple of blocks in the direction opposite her house. She drove about a mile before finding what she was looking for, stopped and parked, then got out of the car and walked over to a particular house. She glanced around a bit, then got back into her car and headed home.

L ia was promptly met at the door by Hayley, who announced, "Internet's down."

"Shoot. Why?"

Hayley shrugged. "Probably a server problem, which means it'll be back by itself—eventually. I didn't find anything useful about Joan, by the way. No connection that I can find, so far, between her and Martin Brewer. I'll try again later. I'm going out."

Lia realized Hayley had changed to running clothes. "Good idea. Get some fresh air."

"I'll probably stop at the drugstore on my way back. Need anything?"

Whenever that question came up unexpectedly, Lia could never think of a thing, so she shook her head and stepped out of the way, knowing she'd probably remember an urgent need once it was too late. As she watched Hayley jog off, she got a call from Jen.

"Lia, we need to switch the knitters meeting to tonight, or we'll have to cancel this week. Can you make it?"

"What came up?"

"I had to schedule our living room rug to be picked up for a cleaning tomorrow. We want to get the last of Daphne's dander out of the house for Bob's allergy. It's the only date they had open. Our downstairs will be all discombobulated."

"I can imagine. If you're sure you don't need tonight to get ready, I can make it."

"Oh good! I hated to disrupt everyone's schedules, but it's working out. And, no, Bob and I have tomorrow morning to move all the small things. The rug people will handle the heavy stuff. Thank you so much, Lia."

"Anything to help Bob breathe better."

After disconnecting, Lia realized her phone battery charge was low, so she hooked it up to the nearest outlet. She'd intended to do an Internet search, but Hayley's unwelcome news that her server was down canceled using her laptop. She never liked using the phone for extended browsing, so she left it to charge in peace and went to fix herself lunch.

She had finished her sandwich and was reaching into the refrigerator for a bowl of grapes when the phone hanging on her kitchen wall rang. Grumbling that it probably was a robocall, since most of her friends called her cell, she nonetheless reached over to pick it up.

"Mrs. Geiger?" a voice asked.

"Yes?"

"Your daughter is Hayley Geiger?" The brisk, official-sounding tone along with the question started Lia's nerves jangling.

"Yes. Is something wrong? Who is this?"

"I'm calling from Carter Medical Center, ma'am. There's been an accident. Your daughter has been brought here."

Lia's heart dropped. "What happened? How badly is she hurt?"

"Sorry, ma'am, I don't have that information. You'll have to speak with the doctor about that."

"Yes, of course." Lia drew a breath to say more, but the caller had disconnected.

Panic threatened, but Lia hurried from the kitchen to grab her cell phone, yanking it from its outlet connection, and immediately called Hayley's number. She was startled to hear rings coming from upstairs and followed them to the second bedroom. There she found Hayley's phone sitting on the dresser, where she'd left it.

Lia quickly called her neighbor.

"Sharon! Hayley's been in an accident. They've taken her to a medical center. I think they said Carter. Is that the right name? I have to get there. I can't think straight to look up directions."

"Oh no! Yes, it's Carter. Lia, let me drive you. I know exactly where it is."

Lia paused. Sharon was right. Lia had never been to that hospital, never had a need to since she'd moved to Crandalsburg. In her present state of mind, even putting an address into her GPS felt beyond her. "All right. Thank you."

"I'll be right out," Sharon said.

Lia thought about her insurance card but remembered Hayley was on her own plan. She ran back upstairs and scrambled through Hayley's purse, which was sitting on the dresser next to the phone. She found the card and dashed down to meet Sharon.

Sharon ran out of her house at the same time as Lia

and waved Lia over to her blue Impala, unlocking the doors with her remote as they closed in on it. Lia hopped into the passenger seat and buckled herself in. How badly was Hayley hurt? At least she was alive! But Lia couldn't bear the thought of her beautiful daughter being possibly broken and in pain. How could that have happened? Terrible thoughts flooded through her, so much so that she could barely breathe.

Chapter 34

The ride to the hospital took only half an hour but seemed a lifetime to Lia. Sharon drove expertly while making statements intended to be calming, which Lia appreciated hugely, though her heartbeat barely slowed.

Memories came to her of the day she and Tom had rushed four-year-old Hayley to the hospital after their daughter's failed attempt to imitate Superman by flying off her backyard swing set. Hayley's wails as Lia held on to her as best she could through the blanket she'd wrapped tightly around her daughter before securing her in the car seat had added to Lia's distress and feelings of guilt. She couldn't stop chastising herself for not somehow preventing the accident, even though she'd checked on her daughter regularly and Hayley had never tried anything so foolish before.

Tom had been wonderful, Lia remembered. Though he surely was just as upset and worried, he managed to cover those feelings and project calm and comfort. Having him to hold on to after nurses rushed Hayley into the emergency room had kept Lia from totally falling apart.

Being a surgical nurse hadn't helped her at all. It had only pulled up all the horrible possibilities that the average person wouldn't think of and added to her agitation. Such feelings had never intruded when she was doing her job. Then, her training always kicked in, no matter what the seriousness of the case at hand. That training largely went out the window, it turned out, when it was your own child. Lia had clung tightly to Tom until they were informed that Hayley's injuries were limited to a broken arm and bruises. Bad, but so much better than what it might have been.

Lia never missed Tom as much as she did right then, though Sharon was wonderful to take her in hand. Lia wasn't sure how she would have managed without her. But she dearly wished she had Tom beside her once again to assure her everything would be all right.

The medical center loomed ahead. Thank God! Sharon drove into the campus and wove expertly through the maze of curving roads and buildings, following signs that Lia was sure she would have overlooked.

"I learned my way around when my mom had her cancer treatments here," Sharon explained. "The staff is top-notch. Hayley's in good hands." She pulled up to an entrance marked EMERGENCY. "Go on in," she told Lia. "I'll park and come find you."

Lia unbuckled and scrambled out, barely remembering to thank Sharon, and hurried through the automatic doors. She quickly spotted an information desk and rushed over to it, only to have to wait behind an elderly man speaking to the woman handling the desk. The gentleman apparently had a hearing problem, which prolonged the interaction, probably not more than a minute or two, but it felt like an eternity to Lia, who struggled to keep her composure. Finally they were done, and Lia stepped forward.

"My daughter, Hayley Geiger, was taken here. How do I find her?"

"One moment." The young black woman efficiently typed in Hayley's name, double-checking the spelling. She clicked several time with her mouse, frowning. After more clicks and a deeper frown, she turned to Lia. "G-e-i-g-e-r?"

"Yes! And Hayley, H-a-y-l-e-y."

The woman tried again. After several grueling moments she finally said, "I'm sorry, I'm not finding her. Are you sure she was brought to us?"

Was she sure? After hearing *accident* and *your daughter*, had she listened properly to the rest?

"The person on the phone said Carter, I'm pretty sure. Is there another hospital with a name close to Carter?"

"No, ma'am, not if we're talking about Pennsylvania, as far as I'm aware. Your daughter is in Pennsylvania?"

"Yes! She was in an accident in Crandalsburg. She has to be here. Please check again."

The young woman nodded, compassion on her face, but Lia also read certainty that she hadn't made a mistake, that she hadn't missed anything. But she must have! Others had begun lining up behind Lia, waiting as impatiently as she herself had. She didn't care. She needed to locate her daughter. But something was wrong!

"I'm sorry, ma'am. Hayley Geiger is not in our system. You might check with other hospitals. She could be at one of them."

Lia nodded numbly and stepped aside. She looked around blankly, unsure what to do next. It was some minutes before Sharon appeared, stepping through the doors. Lia raised a hand and Sharon veered over.

"Did you find her?"

Lia shook her head. "They say she's not here. I don't understand."

"Not here! That doesn't make any sense. She must be here. They don't take accident victims anywhere else." Sharon made a move toward the desk, but Lia stopped her. She'd been thinking.

"Wait. Let me try something." She pulled out her phone and made a call, listening to the rings. On the fourth ring it was answered.

"Hi, Mom!"

"Hayley! Where are you?"

"I just got home. Why? What's wrong? Where are you?"

Lia could have cried with relief. Hayley was fine. It had all been a terrible hoax.

"She's okay," she said to Sharon. She told Hayley about the call and why she was currently at a medical center half an hour away from home.

"That's bizarre, Mom! Who would do such a thing?"

"I don't know. But I'm going to think about it very carefully on the way home. Please stay there for now."

"Absolutely. And tell Sharon to drive carefully!"

Sharon did drive carefully, and she brushed away Lia's apologies for her wasted time. She also declined Lia's offer of coffee when she dropped her off, as well as some of Carolyn Hanson's carrot cake, saying she needed to get her slow-cooker dinner going. "After you called, I thought we'd be eating pizza tonight instead. But I'm so glad Hayley is okay and all is well." Lia wasn't so sure about the "all is well" part, but she gave Sharon a final hug and went indoors to find her daughter.

The sight of Hayley coming down the stairs was wonderful despite the raggedy robe she'd thrown on after a shower and the damp hair straggling over half her face. Lia held on to her, only releasing her when Hayley hinted softly with, "Mom?"

"Sorry," Lia said, stepping back. "It's just that less than an hour ago I was expecting to find you unconscious in a hospital bed."

"I know, and whoever played that trick on you is an awful human being. I called Brady and told him what happened. You said the call came to the landline, right?"

"Right."

"He'll have someone check with the phone company. Maybe they can track down the creep. I'm sorry I didn't have my phone with me. I usually take it when I run, especially in Philly, but the pants I wore today only have one of those small credit card pockets. I remember thinking there was nothing to worry about here in Crandalsburg."

"Accidents can happen anywhere," Lia said. "But I understand. Just please wear large-pocket clothes from now on, okay? Well! I'm bushed, and my head is aching. I need to lie down for a bit before the Ninth Street Knitters meeting. Jen Beasley moved it to tonight."

"You're going?"

"Why not?" Lia asked, surprised at Hayley's shocked reaction.

"Then I'm going with you. I don't think you should drive all the way to York on your own."

"Hayley . . . ," Lia began, ready to protest, but quickly realized her daughter had been more shaken up by what had happened than she'd let on. "It might be a little boring, but if you're sure you want to."

"It'll be nice to see everyone," Hayley insisted. Then she grinned. "And they bring great food, don't they?"

"That they do," Lia agreed. "Which reminds me, I was going to bake a batch of cheesy spinach balls to take along. Would you like to do that for me?"

Hayley readily agreed, and Lia went up to her room, knowing her daughter would have something calming to occupy her mind, while she herself took a badly needed break. As she lay down, Daphne surprised her by hopping up on the bed. Lia pulled the cat closer, greatly appreciating the added warmth and comfort as she closed her eyes.

Chapter 35

The Ninth Street Knitters helped themselves to the nibbles that were laid out in Jen's kitchen, including Hayley's nicely done spinach balls, and started to settle down. A couple of the women asked Hayley about her job. She gave polite but noninformative answers, and they didn't press further. Once everyone had taken out their knitting, Lia cleared her throat.

"I had a rather distressing experience today." She described what she'd gone through, beginning with the heart-stopping phone call and the anxiety-filled ride to the hospital with the full expectation of finding Hayley badly hurt in the ER. "Once I got there I learned I'd been set up. The phone call was totally fake," she said, producing shrieks of horror from the group.

"What an awful prank!" Diana cried.

"More than a prank," Maureen said. "It's criminal!"

"I agree and have reported it." Hayley took a bite of her cheese-topped cracker.

"Good," Jen said. "I hope they catch that awful person."

Tracy, who'd remained quiet until then, said, "You know it might have been the murderer you've been tracking, Lia."

"Oh my gosh, she's right!" Diana said.

Lia nodded. "I've considered that possibility, too."

"What did the voice sound like?" Jen asked. "A man or a woman?"

"I wish I could say, but it could have been either—not pitched particularly high or low. I was so shocked that all I could think about was Hayley."

"Exactly what that creep planned on," Jen said.

"If you can't identify the caller as either male or female, that means it could be any of the suspects you've come up with so far: Adam Mathis, Annie Bradburn, or Martin Brewer," Maureen said. She settled back in her chair, continuing to work on the blue baby cap she'd started the week before, which was taking shape nicely.

"Assuming you haven't missed someone," Diana pointed out.

"Oh lordy," Jen said. "I hope not. But are we looking for one person who committed both murders? Darren Peebles and the artist Joan Fowler?"

They looked toward Lia for an answer, all except Hayley, who had gone to the kitchen for more nibbles. But all Lia could say was, "I just don't know at this point. All three of those people had both motive and opportunity to kill Darren, and all three had an opportunity for Joan's murder. Unfortunately, Annie is the only one who I know might have something like a motive against Joan."

"Unfortunately?'" Jen asked.

"Mom feels the same way I do," Hayley said as she returned to her seat, munching on one of Maureen's mini-meatballs. "That Annie's family is already going through so much. She'd hate to see it get worse."

"But that wouldn't be your fault, Lia," Tracy said. "You'd only be exposing it. If Annie is responsible for this madness, she'll have brought it on herself and her family. She'll have to be stopped."

"You're right, of course," Lia agreed. "And I'm not scratching her off the list out of sympathy by any means. But I'd still regret to find anything that incriminates her."

"But I don't see Annie playing such a mean trick on you, Mom," Hayley said. "I mean, sending you running to the hospital like that? Getting you worried to death?"

"Annie hasn't been herself lately," Lia said. "Olivia, who's been blocked from setting up playdates for their sons, has noticed it. The entire craft fair has noticed it." She told the others about Annie's unusually bitter-sounding argument with Joan the day of Joan's murder.

After they'd mulled that over, Diana said, "I heard about how the body was left." Knitting needles paused motionless as the others waited to hear. "One of her paintings was pushed over her head."

"Oh," Maureen breathed. "Symbolic! Like the way Darren's body was left in the craft barn."

"But symbolic of what?" Jen asked.

"I don't know," Maureen said. "What was it a painting of?"

"A farm scene," Lia told her. "Barnyard animals." The women looked at each other, puzzled. "It could mean something to the murderer or nothing. The only thing it seems to indicate, at least to me, is personal anger on the part of the murderer. It wasn't enough to kill Joan. She had to be left looking ridiculous."

"Something a woman like Joan would have hated," Hayley put in. "Maybe more than being murdered. Well," she backtracked, "at least she would have hated it as much."

"Definitely personal," Tracy agreed. "I'd say that leaves out the professor, wouldn't you? He's all about preserving local history. You haven't discovered, oh, I don't know, that George Washington once stayed at Joan's house, and that she planned to let it be torn down and replaced by a McDonald's?"

"Wow!" Hayley said. "I didn't think of that angle."

"Hayley's been doing Internet searches for a way to connect Joan to Martin," Lia explained.

"But I've been focusing on their pasts. I need to check on current stuff."

"Actually," Lia said, "Adam Mathis owns a property that Martin considers historic enough to be preserved. Nothing that George Washington ever visited, but people such as the Vanderbilts might have stayed there during the late 1800s. Belinda and I came across plans for it to be demolished."

"But Joan, not Adam, was murdered," Jen pointed out.

"And let's hope Adam won't be next," Tracy said half seriously as she held up her knitting. "I've just started on this sweater for his wife's dog, and I don't want it canceled halfway through. Or would she do that?" she asked Lia. "I mean, would losing her husband upset Eva's world enough to draw her attention away from her pet?"

"Hard to say," Lia said dryly. "Particularly if she had been having an affair with Darren, something I'm not yet sure of. But if she was, and if Adam murdered Darren because of it—more for Eva's money than out of jealousy—then, no, her world wouldn't be any more upset than it had been after Darren's murder. By that I mean very little."

"Strange woman," Tracy said. "I'll have to keep in mind that I'm knitting for the dog and not for her. The dog is nice, right, Lia?"

Lia smiled. "It is." The nip at Lia's ankle had long been forgiven.

"Hmm," Diana said as she paused her work on the luscious raspberry-colored sweater. "Have you possibly overlooked Eva as a murder suspect, Lia?"

"Eva?"

"Maybe Darren was on the verge of dropping her, and she flew into a rage?"

Lia scrunched her face in doubt. "I can't see Eva getting worked into a rage over anything. Besides, Darren wasn't murdered in a fit of rage. It was clearly planned. That wouldn't fit Eva, either."

"I fear we're back to Annie," Jen said, and Lia sighed.

At that point Jen's husband, Bob, who'd apparently been eavesdropping from the kitchen, entered the room, one of Hayley's spinach balls in hand. "You're not going to eliminate her because she's a woman, are you?" he asked.

A chorus of protests answered him, but he stuck to his guns. "Maybe it was my imagination, but it seemed like you all are looking for reasons to pin it on the two men while coming up with excuses for why it couldn't be the women. I'm here to stand up for my gender." He popped the entire spinach ball into his mouth.

"Bob, dear, you have to admit men commit the majority of violent crimes," Jen said.

"Mere statistics," her husband responded, "which prove nothing. If men commit the majority, then women commit at least some of those crimes, not none. Annie could very well be one of those in the minority. I'm just saying she shouldn't be so easily overlooked, especially with what you know about her."

"Bob's right," Lia said, earning an acknowledging bow from him. "I mean about not being overly generous to our own gender. We can't let bias of any sort get in the way of our thinking. Facts are what are important. And, Bob, I promise you that's absolutely what I'm trying to work with."

And she meant it. She just needed a few more facts.

W̶ow, I didn't realize the Ninth Street Knitters were so involved with our Crandalsburg murders." Rain started to dot Hayley's windshield as she drove them home from York, and she clicked on her wipers. "I didn't know they cared so much about Belinda."

"They barely know her," Lia said. "But they know she's my friend and care about her being treated fairly. Plus, with rumors continuing to fly over the unsolved murders, attendance at the craft fair has been terrible. If the craft fair closes, there goes the perfect outlet for our knitting. It would, of course, be much worse for Belinda."

"I liked the way they tossed out different ideas," Hayley said.

"Yes, they've come up with information I might never have found on my own. Tracy told me about Eva Mathis's background, and Jen passed on the fact that Annie often goes out and about alone and late at night."

"And Mr. Beasley thinks Annie's our prime suspect."

"Well, I think he just didn't want us to dismiss her too easily."

"We won't. She'll stay on our radar," Hayley said. "But

I'll keep digging for something that connects Joan and the professor." She reached Lia's street and pulled into the space in front of the house. "Our Internet service is back," she said, turning to Lia. "Did I tell you?"

"No, but that's good to hear."

It was very good to hear, since Lia had a few searches of her own planned.

Chapter 36

The next morning, Hayley slept late, and Lia, who'd had her own breakfast and cleaned up after it, guessed she'd been working online until the wee hours. Lia had been online, too, in her own room, but had finished much earlier. Her searches were less broad ranging than Hayley's. They'd produced one or two interesting things, and her next quest would need to be done in person. She'd already made a call to set it up.

Lia originally intended to invite Hayley along with her but decided not to disturb her. What Lia planned could be handled just as easily on her own. She had just slipped on a light jacket when Hayley straggled down the stairs.

"You're going out?"

"I shouldn't be too long. Anything come up about Joan and Martin?"

"Uh-uh." Hayley rubbed at her sleepy eyes. "But I

learned a lot about Penn State. Did you know the school's stadium is the fourth largest in the world?"

"I didn't know that," Lia said with a smile. "There's plenty of eggs, by the way, if you want them. The milk is getting low, but there should be enough for cereal. I'll pick some up on my way back."

"Okay," Hayley said. "Thanks. Right now I just need something to wake me up." She shuffled off toward the kitchen with a "See you later," more focused on coffee than whatever Lia's errand might be.

Lia got into her car and entered an address into the GPS. Her destination drive time was given as forty-five minutes, surprisingly short, though it would largely be on high-speed roads. She put her car in gear and started off, many questions running through her head that she hoped to find answers for.

The house Lia pulled up to was modest, a one-story brick among blocks of other one-story bricks, possibly built in the seventies. They were differentiated mainly by door colors or shrubbery, many of which were either overgrown or tired-looking. The Nortons' front yard included a plastic duck with ducklings that had seen better days, but the garden they graced was colorful.

Lia's knock was answered by a silver-haired, rotund woman. Lia caught the resemblance immediately, and, although she had been prepared after what she'd found online, it shook her. "Mrs. Norton?" she asked.

Her hostess smiled with open excitement. "Marian Norton." She reached out to take Lia's hands in both of her own. "And you must be Lia! It's so nice of you to stop by." Her voice was soft and oddly high-pitched, almost childlike. "We're so happy to meet one of Ginny's friends."

"Thank you," Lia said and stepped in.

The small entryway led directly into the living room, where a gray-haired man struggled to get out of a recliner, its footrest apparently stuck. Lia begged him to stay put and shook his outstretched hand as Marian Norton introduced her husband, Frank. Marian then grabbed the TV remote and turned down the sound, leaving Judge Judy's face on the screen, presiding sternly but silently over her TV courtroom.

Lia took a seat on the brown tweed sofa as Marian twittered again about how pleased they were she'd stopped in. She disappeared into the kitchen and returned with coffee and cookies, which she pressed on Lia. Though it was normal hostess fussing, it only made Lia feel worse about intruding under somewhat false pretenses. Lia hoped that nothing would come out of her visit that would disrupt the couple's simple but apparently satisfying life, though she wasn't at all certain of that.

"So," Marian began in her unusual voice as she took a seat across from Lia, "you work at the Crandalsburg Craft Fair? Ginny told us about the fair."

"Did she? What has she said?"

Marian suddenly squirmed. "Oh," she said, "most of it was very, very good, wasn't it, Frank?" Frank nodded solemnly.

"But?" Lia prodded.

Marian first asked what Lia's position was at the craft fair. Reassured when she learned Lia ran a knitting booth, she said, "It was another vendor, a lady who sold her own paintings. Ginny didn't think she belonged there at all. She really didn't."

"And why was that?' Lia took a polite sip of her coffee. The Nortons didn't seem aware of either Joan Fowler's name or her murder.

"Well, Ginny has an eye for such things, of course, being an artist herself and all." Frank nodded several times over that.

"Ginny's an artist? I didn't know."

"You didn't? Well, maybe I shouldn't have said. She doesn't like the attention. It can be so distracting. But she's a wonderful artist! She's been making pictures since she was little and could barely hold a crayon, hasn't she, Frank?"

Frank agreed with a stream of enthusiastic *uh-huhs*.

The Norton's front doorknob rattled, and a woman of about forty shouldered her way in, a bag in each arm along with a tote in one hand. A loaf of Wonder bread poked out of the tote.

"Angie!" Marian said. "I forgot you were coming today." She got up to take one of the bags. "This is our other daughter, Angie, Ginny's sister," she explained to Lia as she turned toward the kitchen. "Angie, Lia Geiger is a friend of Ginny's!"

"A friend?" Angie's frowning look was very different from Mrs. Norton's excited greeting.

"Well, we've chatted several times," Lia said. She worked at keeping her voice level after having just found out Ginny had a sister. "At the craft fair. I'm a vendor there."

Angie nodded and continued on to the kitchen without comment.

"Angie does my shopping for me," Marian explained as she hurried back. Lia could hear bags rattling. "Angie!" Marian called. "Let that be for now. Come join us." She sat back down and said, "Now, tell me. How is Ginny doing? She must have lots of paintings ready by now!"

"Um," Lia said, "she's been working hard." As was Lia, who'd been struggling with Marian's string of surprising statements. "Have you seen her lately?"

"Oh no," Marian said solemnly. "A serious artist like her doesn't have much time to spare."

"And besides," Angie said as she came into the living room, "we don't know exactly where she is."

"You don't?"

"Well, she moves a lot," Marian explained in her childlike voice. "Trying to find the right light to work in, and all those kinds of things artists have to think about, you know. But she comes by when she can, doesn't she, Angie?"

"Right. Like, uh, last February?"

"Yes, on Daddy's birthday!" Mrs. Norton said, clapping her hands together. "It was such a lovely surprise."

"Lovely," Angie echoed.

"And so lucky that I happened to make that extra dish of macaroni and cheese. It was always Ginny's favorite," Marian said.

Lia noticed Angie's eyes move toward the ceiling whenever Ginny's name was mentioned.

"Would you like to see Ginny's work?" Angie asked Lia. "My parents have piles of her paintings. We should show them to her, Mom."

Marian looked conflicted. "Why, yes. I'd *love* to take you down there. Only, well, don't mention it to Ginny, okay? It should be fine, you being a friend of hers and all. And I can't tell you how many times I wanted to show somebody her pictures. But Ginny always said not to. Not yet."

"Why is that?"

Marian rocked her head back and forth, her eyes shining. "She's getting ready for a big show! In New York. She needs to keep it all under wraps until then. You probably know how it goes."

Lia didn't, but she managed a nod. "How nice." She rose and followed mother and daughter through the kitchen to a narrow back hallway. There, a door opened to the basement stairway. Lia could hear Judge Judy's voice berating a plaintiff as Frank apparently returned the sound to his TV.

The three clumped down the stairs to a pine-paneled room. It might once have been usable as a sitting room but now had a multitude of boxes taking up much of the space between the few pieces of worn furniture. Marian wound her way through it all to reach another door, Angie and Lia following. When Marian opened the door and clicked on the light, Lia was amazed to see rows and rows of unframed, paint-covered canvases filling the storage area, all sizes, some on shelves, others lined upright on the floor, and several canvases deep.

"My goodness!" Lia exclaimed. "There's quite a lot."

"Years and years' worth," Marian verified. "Starting from middle school."

"Really? Is that when Ginny began studying art?"

Marian threw Lia a look of pride. "Oh no. She didn't need to be taught. It all came to her naturally."

Lia gazed at the overwhelming array of color, only gradually able to focus on individual pieces. She moved into the storage room and picked up a small canvas to examine, along with the one next to it, both lake scenes, then set them back down to step back for a broader look.

She was about to ask if these were from that early, middle school period, when Marian helpfully said, "She left those two with us in February."

"Oh." Lia was at a loss for what to say. The paintings were . . . not very good. She remembered Hayley's efforts in middle school, which the art teacher had kindly described as "creative," obviously searching for something positive to say. Hayley had many talents, but she was not an artist. Neither, it was apparent to Lia, was Ginny. But from the look on her mother's face, she'd managed to convince her that she was. Angie looked less convinced, and Lia noticed she was watching her closely.

Just to be sure of her own opinion, Lia checked as many canvases as she could, flipping through the stacks and holding several up to the light. None were of an abstract contemporary style that Lia freely admitted she had no eye for. Ginny had stuck to a more realistic style, doing still lifes, landscapes, and a few portraits. She'd also attempted copies of well-known paintings that Lia recognized—or barely recognized. The attempts were increasingly painful to look at, one in particular being a reproduction of Winslow Homer's *Hauling Anchor*. Lia had viewed that painting at the National Gallery of Art and even owned a print, which she'd never gotten around to framing. Ginny's version of the watercolor depicting a sailboat off Key West looked more like a child's folded-paper boat manned by Fisher-Price toy people. She doubted that Hayley's art teacher would have been able to come up with something positive, considering they had been done by an adult and not an adolescent.

Lia knew the women were waiting for comments. What to say?

"Marian!" Frank Norton's voice bellowed down the stairs, the first complete word Lia had heard from him. "Telephone. Doctor's office."

"I'll be right there!" She turned apologetically to Lia. "I've been trying to reach them for hours."

She rushed off, and Angie switched off the storage room light. "Mom's got health problems. They both do, but Mom's worse."

"I'm sorry to hear that," Lia said. She moved into the center room as Angie began to close the door.

"Yeah. She doesn't always admit it, but she's not up to doing a lot of things she used to do. I help out. So what did you think of my sister's paintings?"

Lia had reached the staircase. Angie's sudden question caught her with a foot on the first step. "Oh, I'm really not a good judge of artwork," she hedged.

"Me neither," Angie said. "But even I can tell they're junk." She smiled at Lia's surprise. "Yeah, my folks have swallowed her line for years. I go along with it 'cause I don't want to hurt them. Not that they'd believe me, anyway."

"I'm sorry. That must be hard."

Angie shrugged. "I deal with it."

"Angie," Marian's voice sailed down from the kitchen. "Will you be able to take me to an appointment Saturday at two?"

"Sure, Mom."

Lia continued up the stairs and into the kitchen, where Marian was apparently finishing up her call. By the time she'd hung up, Lia had made her way to the front door. There, she thanked Marian profusely for her hospitality, while hinting at an appointment of her own she needed to hurry off to. She was eager to leave without further discussion of paintings.

Marian issued a flood of come-on-back-anytime invitations as Lia edged out the door and down the short walk, while Angie stood stolidly and silently behind her mother. Once inside her car, Lia waved a final good-bye to her watching hostess before driving off. But after a few blocks she pulled into an empty spot next to the curb to make an unobserved phone call.

"Belinda," she said when her call was picked up. "I have some questions for you."

Chapter 37

When Lia got home, she found a note from Hayley taped to the end of the stair banister.

Had to run out. Back soon.

Just as well, Lia decided. She needed quiet time to think. She grabbed a quick bite to eat, then carried a cup of tea to her knitting chair, where she pulled out Paulette's alpaca sweater to work on. The knitting began to work its magic, settling her mind, and as the needles flew, her thoughts slowly organized themselves. By the time she came to the end of one sleeve, Lia thought she could see the entire picture more clearly. Only one knotty problem remained.

Daphne, who'd been curled up nearby, suddenly lifted her head. Lia also heard the car door slam and knew that Hayley had returned. Lia set down her knitting.

"Hi, Mom!" Hayley bounced into the house in high

spirits, until she caught sight of Lia's face. "What's wrong? Are you okay?"

"I'm fine," Lia assured her. "But something important came up this morning that I want to tell you about. Are you hungry? This might take a while."

"No, I ate over at the—never mind. I'm good." Hayley sat on the sofa across from Lia.

Lia took a deep breath. "This morning I drove to Boggs Creek."

Hayley frowned. "Boggs Creek? Where is that? Why?"

"It's less than an hour's drive from here. Just far enough away for Ginny Norton to keep her family out of her life."

"Ginny Norton." Hayley pondered the name. "Is that the woman who's always wandering around the craft fair? Why does she want her family out of her life?"

"As best I can tell because she's created a fictional life for herself which she needs them to believe, and her parents clearly do, wholeheartedly. But if they saw her reality it would burst their bubble and maybe also burst hers."

"Mom, you're confusing me. Why did you go looking into Ginny Norton's apparently strange life?"

"Because she pointed out to me on Monday—before I mentioned it—that Joan Fowler hadn't shown up at the craft fair on Sunday."

"And?"

Lia looked at Hayley steadily. "Ginny wasn't there on Sunday either. For the first time in as long as I've been a vendor, Ginny Norton did not come to the craft fair. How did she know that Joan was a no-show?"

"Hmm."

"Right. It got me thinking, Hayley. Ginny once told me a sad story about having spent years caring for her ailing mother and of inheriting the home after the mother died.

I remembered a comment of hers, that the less-than-lovely view from her house was that of an auto repair shop, and decided to do a little online digging. I found that the only repair shop in Crandalsburg with residential houses across from it is on Glenwood Street. When I visited the block, I managed to pinpoint which address was hers—the only house across from the repair shop and with no evidence of small children—toys and such. Once I had the address, I was able to discover through public records that Ginny didn't own but was actually renting the place, and not from anyone with the last name of Norton. The Internet," she commented, "is a vast source of information."

"Sometimes," Hayley said with a rueful look, most likely thinking of her recent fruitless searches. "So Ginny lied about a dying mother? Is that mother actually living in Boggs Creek?"

"Alive and well," Lia said. "Other than some kind of health problems, that is. But the astonishing thing is that the mother—and father, also alive—have been storing piles of Ginny's attempts at artwork. Years' worth. She's convinced them that she's a self-taught genius artist who's been preparing for the right moment to present her work to the world."

"Wow. And I'm guessing she's not, huh? But can't they tell from her stuff?"

"Apparently not. They don't seem, uh, particularly knowledgeable about the subject. And it's possible that over the years Ginny fed them plenty of supposed praises from others that convinced them. The sister sees through it, but she grudgingly plays along for her parents' sake."

"Okay, so Ginny's been putting something over on her folks and maybe on herself. But where does that put us? I mean, does this have anything to do with the murders?"

Lia sighed. "I'm afraid it might. After I left the Nortons' house, I spoke with Belinda. I described what I saw of Ginny's paintings, and that jogged her memory. She had to check her records—she keeps track of all vendor applications—but she found it. Ginny had applied more than once for a booth at the craft fair to sell her paintings."

"Uh-oh. And if they're as bad as you say, that couldn't have gone well."

"Belinda turned her down each time, and, yes, knowing her lack of patience and tact, I doubt it was handled gently."

"And . . ." From the look on her face, Hayley was putting it all together as Lia had done, remembering previously overlooked things. "Ginny was the one who told you there was bad blood between Belinda and Joan!"

"Exactly. She pushed that idea at me more than once, and I'd guess I wasn't the only one."

"To make Belinda a prime suspect in Darren's and Joan's murders! The Facebook and Twitter posts! Mom, she could have done those, too! Anyone can set up fake accounts under any name. They all disappeared after you found Joan's body."

"She could also have sent the text to Belinda that drew her out Saturday night, thinking she was meeting Joan," Lia said.

"While Ginny was murdering Joan herself!" Hayley jumped up from her seat. "Mom, we have to report her. She's the murderer!"

"Hayley, we can't do that. Not yet. We have no proof."

"But, but, the lies! The text!"

"Conjecture. We don't *know* that she texted Belinda or that she pretended to be Joan posting on Facebook and Twitter. Or that she murdered Darren as well."

"But if she thinks she's this great artist, she has to hate Belinda for probably belittling her art. She must have been working ever since to destroy her by setting her up as a murderer! Wait—" Hayley sat back down, seemingly struck by something. "Why wouldn't she just kill Belinda? Why kill the others?" After some moments she cried, "Oh! Killing Belinda must not have been enough for her. She needed to see her suffer. It had to be a huge power trip—don't you think?—to set Belinda up to be falsely convicted and spend the rest of her life in prison. Ginny could gloat over it forever. That must be it. Mom, we have to go and tell the police right now."

Lia shook her head. "Not yet, Hayley. It's still conjecture. What if we're wrong? What would we be doing to Ginny if she's innocent? Yes, I know the police won't immediately drag her off to jail on circumstantial evidence, but word would get around. If she's simply a mixed-up woman trying to believe she's less pitiful than she really is, how can we destroy that?"

Hayley chewed at her lip for several moments. "What if we come up with something concrete?"

"That would make the difference, of course. But I haven't figured out how or where to get that yet."

"Okay, then let's think on it."

After a few moments of sitting silently, Hayley stood. "I'm going out for a run. I do my best thinking that way." Lia nodded.

"You have your cell phone?" Lia asked as Hayley returned from her room, where she'd changed into running clothes and jogging shoes.

Hayley patted a back pocket of her shorts. "Back soon," she said and took off.

Chapter 38

Fatigue washed over Lia after Hayley left. She hadn't slept well for several nights as thoughts of all the recent happenings ran continuously through her head. She also felt weighed down by the worrying of what needed to be done concerning Ginny. She considered fixing another cup of tea or maybe coffee to perk herself up but decided to give in and take a rest. A short nap was all she needed and would probably clear her head better than more caffeine.

Daphne, in her feline way, read Lia's mind and followed her up the stairs to snuggle cozily, and within moments Lia fell into an exhausted sleep. When she awoke, she was astonished to find she'd slept for more than two hours. She shook her head groggily as she sat on the side of her bed and had just slipped her feet back into her shoes when her phone rang. It was Jen Beasley.

"Lia, do you have a minute?"

"Sure, Jen. What's up?" Lia caught sight of her matted hair in the mirror and ran her fingers through it. Her eyes, she noted, looked half-asleep.

"I was talking to my neighbor Maddie. Remember her? Her sister-in-law works the late shift at the 7-Eleven?"

Lia snapped alert. This was the woman who had passed on the information about Annie's late-night shopping excursions. "Yes?"

"Maddie's sister-in-law—her name is Sara, by the way—told her that Annie had been in the store on Monday night."

"The day that news of Joan's murder came out."

"Right. She said Annie looked more disheveled than usual. She usually stopped in, you know, when she'd been working on her pottery, so she tended to be a bit of a mess anyway. But according to Sara this was much worse, and Annie seemed to have been drinking. Actually, Sara said she could smell alcohol on her."

Lia winced.

"Sara tried to be pleasant and make light conversation as Annie wandered dismally around the small store, but Sara's only other customer brought up the murder, saying what a shame that someone so talented had been lost. Annie reacted with, 'Are you kidding me?' and went on sort of a rant, using pretty colorful language to describe Joan. Sara and the other customer were shocked, especially when Annie claimed Joan deserved exactly what she got and more."

Lia groaned.

"I thought you should know that," Jen said. "And I'm sorry. I know you're sympathetic to Annie's struggles. I am, too, but, well, I don't know what this means. I just thought you'd want to know."

"Yes, thank you, Jen. It's painful to hear. I'm not sure what to do with it, either."

"Maybe speak to Annie?"

"Maybe." Lia looked at the clock. It was closing in on dinnertime. Not the best time to try to do that.

They ended their call, and Lia went downstairs, expecting to find Hayley back from her run. But the living room and kitchen were empty. Had she returned and gone out again? Lia thought Hayley might have left a note, as she'd done before, after the hospital incident, but a quick look around found none. Lia decided to text her.

Still running? she asked.

She sent it off and went into the kitchen to see about their dinner, expecting to hear the ding of an answering text. After she'd pulled out a few leftovers and stood thinking about what to do with them, she realized she hadn't heard back from Hayley. She waited a bit longer, then placed a call. It went to voice mail.

"Hayley, please let me know where you are." Lia heard the growing worry in her voice and didn't apologize. Perhaps it would bring a quick response.

A knock at her door startled her. Not Hayley, of course, who would simply walk in. Lia hurried to answer it.

"Mrs. Geiger! So glad to find you at home." A thin woman with a big smile stood on the doorstep, holding a clipboard. "I didn't catch you in the middle of dinner, I hope?"

"No, I—"

"I'm so glad." The woman held out her hand. "Tamara Harper. We met at one of the neighborhood get-togethers?"

Lia vaguely remembered, thinking it must have been weeks ago. She nodded.

"I won't take up your time," Tamara promised. "I

know you're probably busy, as we all are, right? But this is *so* important."

Lia looked over Tamara's shoulder to see Hayley's car parked where it had been earlier that afternoon. Wherever she'd gone, it had been on foot.

Tamara, she learned, was taking up a petition. Lia had trouble concentrating on exactly what it was for. Something about new street signs? Or was it fixing potholes? Tamara's explanation rambled—so much for not taking up time—and Lia's thoughts kept returning to Hayley. Finally she reached for the clipboard, startling Tamara.

"Where do I sign?"

"Right there underneath Mr. Whittle's signature. Unusual man," Tamara said as Lia scribbled her name. "Have you met him? He—"

Lia thrust the clipboard back, saying, "I think my phone is ringing. I'd better go."

"Oh! Of course. Thank you so much, Mrs. Geiger. It was so nice to—"

Lia didn't hear the rest as she closed the door. Her phone hadn't been ringing, but she might have missed a text. She checked and found nothing. No text. No missed call. This wasn't good. Lia couldn't simply wait and hope to hear from her daughter. She grabbed her keys and purse and headed out to her car. She was going to find her.

As Lia pulled up to the Crandalsburg Café, she still had some hope that she was overreacting. She wanted to find Hayley sitting at one of the café tables across from Brady, that they'd run into each other and she'd totally lost track of time. But a quick look inside erased that. No sign of Hayley. Lia checked with the hostess in case Hayley had been in earlier, describing her carefully.

"No, ma'am. I'm sorry."

Lia thanked the woman and hurried out. Other restaurants were nearby, and Lia went in and out of them, along with the few shops that were still open that might attract Hayley, growing more worried with each unsuccessful stop.

She returned to her car. Perhaps Hayley had taken a break earlier, then headed to the park to continue her run. Lia had checked her phone often, but she did it again. Finding nothing from Hayley, she shot off another text before starting her car. There were jogging trails in the park, separate from vehicle lanes but often paralleling them. She would scour the winding road slowly.

It was starting to get dark. As she entered the park, Lia wondered if she was wasting her time. Would Hayley be there on her own? She had scoffed once at Brady's concerns about her being out alone after dark, since she felt so much safer in small-town Crandalsburg than in the city. The odds might be better, but that didn't mean crime was nonexistent, something she should have realized by now. But Hayley was young, and she was impulsive.

Lia hit her brake, luckily being the only moving vehicle on that particular stretch of road. Yes, she told herself, Hayley *was* impulsive. Their last conversation had been about Ginny and how they needed concrete evidence about the woman before going to the police. Could that be what Hayley had gone to find?

Lia turned her car around and drove as fast as she dared on the narrow road. When she reached the park exit, she paused, visualizing the way to Glenwood Street. Then she took off.

Chapter 39

Lia pulled up to the house she'd driven to the day before, the one across from the auto repair shop that she'd described to Hayley. No car stood in front at the curb, and no light came from within. But Lia went up to the front door and knocked hard. Then knocked again, and again.

"I don't think she's home." Lia spun around to see a woman in gray sweats holding a frisky, midsized dog on a long leash. "I saw her go out a while ago."

"Was she alone?"

"No, there was a girl with her. I don't think she was well. Ginny had to help her into the car."

Lia froze. "A girl. You mean a young woman?"

"I guess. Coulda been."

The woman's dog ran toward Lia, its tail wagging. "Jasper!" his owner called, but he kept going. As Lia looked down at him, she caught sight of something.

"Jasper, come here!" The woman tugged at his leash, and as he returned Lia bent down to pick up what she'd seen in the grass. It was a woven bracelet. Hayley's bracelet. The one she'd bought at the alpaca farm along with a matching one for Lia.

The woman started to walk on with her dog, but Lia called out, "Wait! What kind of car does Ginny drive?"

The woman stared blankly. "Gray, some kind of sedan, I think. I don't really know cars." She looked like she wanted to ask why, but Lia had already punched 911 on her phone. Ginny had kidnapped Hayley and had taken her somewhere!

She reported what she knew to the 911 operator, which was frustratingly little. At the end, after answering several questions, she sobbed, "Please! This woman, Ginny Norton, kidnapped my daughter! You have to find her!"

But would they? Her heart pumping hard, Lia ran back to her car. She couldn't just stand and wait. She had to keep looking herself. Where would Ginny have taken Hayley? As she climbed into the driver's seat, a thought rushed at her. If there was one requirement for Ginny's crimes, it was that they needed to point to Belinda in some way. Lia could think of one strong possibility that fit that requirement. She started her car and squealed through a U-turn. She had to get there!

Lia raced through Crandalsburg. But after pulling onto the road leading out of the town, she slowed. She'd spotted a familiar figure: Brady, jogging, and obviously off duty. She screeched to a stop and waved him over.

"Brady!" she cried as he ran up and peered through her lowered window. "Come with me! Hayley's in trouble." Words that brought an instant response. He yanked open the door.

"What's happened?" he demanded as he jumped in.

Lia told him about finding Hayley's bracelet outside Ginny's house and what the neighbor had seen. "Ginny might have drugged Hayley in order to move her to another location. I think it's the craft fair barn."

"The Schumacher barn! Why there?"

"Because that's how her thinking works." Lia had her car back in gear and pressed on the gas as Brady quickly buckled up. "Ginny will want to pin it on Belinda." Lia's voice quavered at the thought of what "it" could be, and she gulped to clear it.

"She won't get to do anything, Mrs. Geiger," Brady said firmly. "We'll see to that. You called 911?"

"Yes, but not about the barn. That came to me afterward."

Brady reached for his phone and reported where they were heading and why. "They'll respond," he said, "but keep going. We can get there before they will."

Lia drove as fast as she dared on the two-lane country road, whipping around the few cars that appeared ahead of her and grateful for the minimal traffic. Would they get there in time? What would Ginny do? What had she already done?

The craft fair barn loomed ahead with the metal rooster atop lit this time by a full moon. Lia slowed and turned cautiously onto the long driveway. As they approached, she saw a single car parked at the side, an older model and possibly gray, though the deep shadows made it difficult to be sure.

"Stop here," Brady said when they were still several yards away. She did, and they eased out of the car to steal silently to the building. The side door was ajar, but as they peered in Lia saw no sign of movement in the main interior, which was dimly lit by the moonlight. Lia took a step forward, but Brady held her back, pointing to the faint light coming from a window at the rear of the barn.

Putting his fingers to his lips, he left her to slip noiselessly around the back corner, Lia barely breathing until he made his way back. "They're in there," he whispered.

"Is Hayley okay?"

"She's wrapped in some kind of quilt and tied into a chair. She looks drugged. The other woman is talking to her—or to herself—as she's pacing. We have to wait. She might come out."

What if she doesn't? Lia thought, but she nodded. At least Hayley was alive!

They didn't have to wait long. Within minutes they heard the office door open and footsteps head down the short walkway toward the central area lined with booths. Vendors with bulkier wares chose to leave them at the barn from week to week. Ginny headed toward those.

Lia muffled a cry. *She wants to pick out craft pieces as she did for Darren! She wants to surround—*

Brady tapped Lia's arm. "Go to Hayley," he whispered. "I'll look after this one." He tipped his head toward Ginny.

Lia crept into the barn, keeping an eye on Ginny, whose back was to her, until she reached the walled-off walkway. She hurried down it and to the office door, then slipped silently inside. The sight of Hayley, wrapped and tied, her head lolling to one side, was both shocking and wonderful. She was breathing. She was okay!

Lia began working at the ropes. Ginny had tied multiple knots tightly, and Lia's fingers fumbled in her haste until she forced herself to slow down. She got one knot loose and was working on another when she heard shouts coming from the vendors' area. Then the sound of broken glass. She froze. More shouts. Then a gunshot!

Lia leaped to the door and locked it. Realizing that might not be enough, she jammed the second office chair under the doorknob and wheeled Hayley's to a far corner. She didn't know what had happened out there, but Brady hadn't been carrying a gun. Had he been shot?! If so, how badly?

Agonizing minutes of silence followed. Lia managed to loosen the remaining knots binding Hayley to the chair and carefully slid her daughter to the floor. The knob of the office door rattled. Hayley moaned, and Lia clamped a hand over her mouth. She heard footsteps lead away. Was Ginny leaving?

Another long silence followed. Worried about Brady, Lia was about to get up when a bullet crashed through the office window. She threw herself over Hayley. A second bullet hit the wall above them. Then more agonizing silence—until Lia picked up the glorious sound of sirens in the distance!

Lia heard a car start and screech away. It had to be Ginny fleeing. After a brief internal struggle, Lia cautiously left the office—and Hayley. She had to check on Brady, who might need her more. She first verified that Ginny's car was indeed gone, then went searching for Brady. Lia found him, bleeding from a shoulder wound but still alive on the floor near Maggie's booth. She quickly grabbed one of her friend's beautiful quilts to press against Brady's wound.

"Hayley . . . ?" Brady mumbled.

"Hayley's fine. You will be, too, I promise!"

She worked to staunch the bleeding and was relieved to soon hear the sirens racing up the road to the barn. When voices called out, "Police!" she responded with

"Over here! An officer's been shot. My daughter needs help. We need ambulances!"

Two police officers rushed in and took over as Lia quickly filled them in on what had happened. "Ginny Norton shot him," she said. "And now she's on the run." She gave her bare-bones description of the car.

"Don't worry," one of the officers assured her grimly. "She won't get far."

When Lia hurried back to Hayley, she was relieved to see her eyes opened, though blearily.

"Mom?" Hayley tried to raise herself but flopped back. "Are you . . . ? Is she . . . ?"

"She's gone. Everything's okay," Lia said. Or it would be as soon as Hayley and Brady got to a hospital. But Hayley didn't need to hear about Brady's situation just yet. There was time for that—thank goodness.

Chapter 40

I'm so sorry," Belinda said for at least the twentieth time as they sat in Lia's living room the next day. "I shouldn't have gotten you into this."

"I got myself into it, remember?" Lia said.

"Yes, but I should have stopped you. I should have taken care of it myself."

Lia smiled to herself, knowing just how that would have gone, but said nothing.

Belinda had come to the hospital the previous night—the same one Lia had rushed to two days before—and stayed with her until they were assured Hayley would be fine. After catching a brief couple of hours of sleep, they'd returned to bring Hayley home, but not before she'd gone to visit Brady, whose recovery from shoulder surgery would be much longer than her own. Belinda continued to hover over both Lia and Hayley at Lia's place, although there was little she could find to do for them beyond offering food and bringing cups of coffee or tea.

More food arrived soon from next door as Sharon appeared with a casserole. She was followed within minutes by Jen Beasley, who came as the representative of the Ninth Street Knitters and loaded with goodies from them all.

"I suggested that the others wait a couple of days before dropping by, but they all send their love," Jen said.

"So thoughtful!" Lia said, bringing her in to join the other three as Hayley got up from the sofa to give Jen a hug and help carry her bags to the kitchen. Hayley had assured Sharon she was fine and now did the same for Jen, probably glad that the entire knitting group hadn't shown up to have her repeat her reassurances several more times. But she also looked touched—and much better than she had some hours ago.

"So, how is that young man doing?" Jen asked after they'd settled in the living room.

"Brady came through his surgery great," Hayley said. "And the doctors think there shouldn't be any permanent damage—thank God. I know how he loves being a police officer. I'd really hate to see that derailed because of that horrible woman."

"So was she the one who called you and claimed Hayley had been in an accident?" Sharon asked Lia.

"I'm sure she was. She must have picked up that I was starting to figure things out and thought that would distract me."

"The thing is," Hayley added, "Mom didn't have anything solid on her. If Ginny had just played it cool, she might have gotten away with everything."

"Would she?" Jen asked. "She must have been awfully

unstable to do what she did. I'd expect someone like that to give herself away eventually."

"Perhaps," Belinda said. "But what further damage might she have done in the meantime? Who else might have died?"

Hayley nodded vigorously, agreeing with Belinda. "If she didn't see you going off to prison after she'd killed Joan, I'm sure she would have tried something else."

"And that's why you went to see her?" Jen asked Hayley. "To force a confession?"

Hayley squirmed. "Kind of," she said. "I was just so mad to think she had done those awful things and nobody could prove it. I'm not sure exactly what I had in mind. Maybe I thought I could trip her up somehow. Instead she tripped me up, literally. I never knew what hit me. I just remember waking up on the floor, and she was urging me to swallow something, telling me it would help me feel better."

"They said at the hospital that Ginny got some kind of powerful prescription sleep aid into you," Belinda said. "After she conked you on the head."

"Yeah, my head hurt really bad, and I vaguely remember thinking she must be giving me aspirin or something like that. But I wasn't thinking too straight at the time. The next thing I knew I was waking up in your office, Belinda, totally confused and trying hard to keep my eyes open." Hayley turned to Lia. "I'm sorry, Mom. I ended up causing a lot of trouble."

Lia reached out to squeeze Hayley's hand while biting her tongue to keep from saying a lot of things that sprang to mind.

"*She* caused it," Belinda assured Hayley. "Ginny! And now she's been stopped because of you. No more murders, my reputation is cleared, and the craft fair will recover—at least I hope so."

"It will," Jen said. "It might take a while, but it'll come back, maybe stronger than ever." She turned to Lia. "I want to know about Annie. She seemed to be putting herself under grave suspicion by her recent actions."

Lia sighed. "I know. But I heard from Olivia this morning. She said she'd had a heart-to-heart with Annie, which both surprises and impresses me, since Olivia finds that sort of thing difficult. But perhaps the shocking news coming out about Ginny inspired both of them.

"It turns out that the bitter fight Annie had with Joan just hours before Joan's murder was over Annie's husband. Annie has been under increasing stress lately, and she had little patience left for Joan's constant complaints flowing from the booth next to hers, which in Annie's view were frivolous. Apparently she voiced her annoyances more and more until Joan, who wasn't known for holding back, had enough, and the two of them fought it out, verbally. Joan hit hard when she claimed that Annie used her husband as an excuse for her own shortcomings and expected everyone around her to kowtow to her—or something like that."

Hayley gasped.

"I know," Lia said. "Cruel. The shocking behavior of Annie's at the 7-Eleven the other night that you described, Jen, apparently came from caretaker fatigue and stress and her turning to Band-Aid solutions. Olivia may have convinced her she needed help and to look into either a support group or counseling."

"Good girl," Jen said.

Lia nodded. "I hope Annie will follow through on that."

"Well, I guess I can stop looking for something between Martin Brewer and Joan," Hayley said. "The professor is off the hook."

"As well as Darren's partner, Adam," Belinda said. "Unfortunately. Well," she said, "maybe we can catch him on something else."

"I have a feeling his wife will catch him on something, eventually," Lia said. "If Eva cares enough, that is. All those phone calls to his office from a mysterious woman, along with his general shiftiness about where he was or what he was doing, should start to add up."

"It would to the average person," Jen said. "Eva doesn't seem to fit that description. Well," she said, "whatever works for her."

Lia agreed. "She seems content with her somewhat narrow life," she said, then added with a smile, "And Tracy might get to knit a few more dog sweaters."

"What I want to know," Belinda said, "is how Ginny got Darren to the craft barn so late at night. And how she got in!"

"I'd like to know how she lured him there, too," Lia said, "and I hope it will come out during police questioning. But remember your missing key, Belinda? You told the police after we found Darren's body that it had been stolen."

"That's right! So she must have taken it. I wonder how she did it."

Lia shrugged. *One more detail that may or may not be explained.*

After picking over the subject until they'd exhausted it, Jen and Sharon took off, to be followed soon—at Lia's urging—by Belinda.

"You've been great," Lia told her. "But you need to

catch up on some of that sleep you lost while sitting at the hospital with me last night."

Lia had lost the same amount of sleep and could feel herself drooping. But a parade of well-wishers, neighbors, and fellow craft fair vendors continued to show up at her door, most carrying something edible in their hands. Finally Sharon, who'd observed it all from her window, called and offered to be a gatekeeper.

"Enough is enough," she declared. "I'll sit on your porch and express your regrets. And I promise not to eat anything that they leave with me. You need some peace."

"You're an angel," Lia declared.

Hayley was in better condition after resting at the hospital the entire night, and because of her own natural energy. But she appreciated the break for another reason. "I want to head over to the hospital tonight to see Brady."

"I'd wait until morning," Lia strongly advised. "He's had major surgery. But tomorrow he'll be much more responsive. You could take him one of the treats from our growing pile. There's far too much for us."

"Okay," Hayley agreed, though reluctantly.

She brightened when Lia suggested texts to him would be okay. "But don't be too surprised if he doesn't answer right away. Give him time."

The next day was Saturday. The craft fair had been closed—temporarily—and Lia was at home, waiting to hear Hayley's report on her trip to the hospital.

"Brady looks so much better!" Hayley said when she returned, clearly in high spirits. "It was scary how he looked the last time."

"People coming out of anesthesia are never at their best. I'm so glad he's improving," Lia said.

"We had a great talk. He told me about everything that had gone on while I was totally zonked. It really was a brave thing he did, wasn't it? I mean, closing in on Ginny like that. He said he needed to stop her when she started heading back to me. He didn't know she had a gun, but he had to consider it a possibility. Can you imagine?"

"He's a police officer," Lia said. "I don't want to say it's their job—even when they're off duty—but they've been highly trained, and as a whole they're the kind of people who run toward danger to protect others."

"And I'm ashamed to say I never thought about that. Or appreciated it. I certainly appreciate what he did that night! And what you did, Mom. And I wish like crazy I hadn't put you both in such danger!"

Lia reached out to hug Hayley. "You didn't know what she might do. And I think it's safe to say you've learned from it."

"Uh-huh," Hayley murmured, hugging back tightly. She stepped back and sniffled, then managed a smile. "I learned something else today, something you were wondering about."

"Oh?"

"A couple of Brady's police buddies showed up while I was there. Ginny's in custody, of course, with plenty of charges against her, and they think there shouldn't be any problem getting convictions. Along with a pile of other evidence, they said they found Ginny's burner phone at her house. It had the texts she'd exchanged with Darren Peebles that brought him to the craft fair barn that night. Apparently she convinced him she had damaging information about Annie's husband that she would hand over.

Something that would put an end to the lawsuit Annie and Ken had filed against him."

"Aha!"

"And that's not all, Mom. There was the text she sent to Belinda pretending to be Joan and arranging to meet her at the coffee shop that night. It also contained the fake email she'd used to set up the Facebook and Twitter accounts under Joan's name."

"I think Ginny must have felt a lot of resentment toward Joan," Lia said, "because of all the praise and attention she received for her paintings. It was probably one reason she chose Joan as her next victim in her drive to implicate Belinda. Ginny certainly worked hard at her crimes. Too bad she didn't just apply all that effort and cleverness to something legitimate and productive."

"Speaking of working . . . ," Hayley said, her eyes dancing.

"Yes?"

"I was going to tell you when you'd come back from that drive to Boggs Creek, but all that stuff that you found out from Ginny's family made me put my stuff on hold."

"And . . . ?"

"I got a job! And it's something I know I'm going to absolutely love!"

"How exciting!" Lia cried. "Please tell me more."

"It's at the alpaca farm." Hayley held up her hand. "Don't worry! I won't be mucking out stalls, though I wouldn't mind all that much. I'll be using my communications background to promote everything about the farm and help make it as successful as it can be."

"That's terrific, Hayley! But when did this all come about?"

"Remember I stopped at the farm on my way here from

Philly? It wasn't just to pet the alpacas again. I also talked with the Webers. They didn't know at that point that they needed someone like me, but I explained to them why they did," Hayley said, laughing. "They had to think it over, of course, so I didn't say anything to you right away. It might have come to nothing. But then they called me back for another discussion and said they thought having someone like me on their staff would be a very good thing."

Lia threw her hands into the air. "Yippee!"

"Mom, I'm so excited. I get to do the kind of work I studied four years to do, and I get to promote a business and a product that I'm so enthusiastic about. Everything I'll be saying about it will be one hundred percent genuine, unlike, well, never mind. And I'll be setting up special events and fun things. I can hardly wait! And on top of it, I'll get to be around Rosie."

"Rosie?"

"My special alpaca friend, remember? Now you won't have to adopt her and raise her in your backyard for me."

Lia laughed. "As if. But does that mean you'll be moving to Crandalsburg?"

"Gosh, I haven't really thought that far ahead. I can't stay in Philly, that's for sure. Commuting to the farm from Crandalsburg wouldn't be bad, but I'll have to see. Can I stay with you until I figure it out?"

"Of course, dear. As long as Rosie stays at the farm." Lia felt like dancing a jig, delighted as she was with the wonderful news and the thought of Hayley settling so much closer.

"I told Brady," Hayley said. "I hope you don't mind me telling him first?" When Lia laughed and flapped her hand, Hayley explained, "He asked me when I had to go back to Philly, and he was looking so down about it that I just blurted it all out. You would have thought I gave him tickets to the Super Bowl! He's so sweet. Now that I'll be around, and once his shoulder is back in shape, of course, I can help him work out to get the rest of him back in shape. You know, we really have a lot in common. We both like jogging and sports, and we both . . ."

Lia smiled as Hayley went on about things that Lia had already picked up on but never dared to voice. She didn't know where this budding relationship would go, but Hayley could do a lot worse than draw closer to a young man of obviously excellent character and intelligence, and who was clearly smitten. She felt a nudge at her ankle, and Lia looked down, her smile widening as she was reminded of the third occupant of the house who would also be delighted to see more of Brady. She reached down to ruffle her affectionate ragdoll's fur.

Lia was so proud that Hayley had taken her job situation in hand, decided what she really wanted, and gone for it. Salary hadn't been mentioned, but that was another thing that was Hayley's decision. Being able to look forward to each workday with excitement was worth a lot. And Lia suspected working at the alpaca farm would be just a start for Hayley. It would be a very enjoyable start, but there might be more opportunities presenting themselves along the way.

Lia suddenly grinned as she thought of one thing that surely hadn't figured in Hayley's job assessment but which held a definite upside for Lia: all the skeins of beautiful alpaca yarn that would be so much more available to her. And possibly at a discount!

With that thought, Lia settled into her knitting chair

and pulled out the sweater she'd been working on for Paulette. She ran her hand over the luxuriously soft yarn, looking forward to working once again on the intricate pattern. She was ready for her life to get back to normal. It was time to knit.

Acknowledgments

Many thanks to Linda and Mitchell Dickinson, from whom I learned so much about alpacas and their fibers. The Painted Sky Alpaca Farm in Maryland was a delight to visit as well as the inspiration for my fictional alpaca farm.

Our long-running critique group once again deserves my gratitude. Besides helping press my first-draft chapters into proper shape, Becky Hutchison, Debbi Mack, Sherriel Mattingly, Bonnie Settle, Marcia Talley, and Cathy Wiley continue to inspire me with their own writing. I'm especially grateful to Bonnie, whose knitting expertise saved me more than once from a blunder.

Jordan Hughes generously advised me on certain police-related protocols, which helped so much. Thanks, Jordan!

I'm very grateful to my editor, Sarah Blumenstock, and all the behind-the-scenes staff at Berkley, who worked so skillfully and patiently with me to make this the best book possible, and to my agent, James McGowan, who so ably got the ball rolling.

Top thanks go, as always, to my husband, Terry. His support and patience with my regularly appearing writing angst apparently has no limits. Let's hope the angst does.

Don't miss the next Craft Fair Knitters mystery

Stitched in Crime

Coming Winter 2021 from Berkley Prime Crime!

The next morning, Lia called Cori about her customer's request and arranged to drop off the photo he'd left with her. Hayley, true to her promise, had cleared several of her boxes from the living room, giving a little more breathing space to the area. The fundraising event she was working on was taking place in less than two weeks, when hopefully Lia's living room would look much less like a storage locker, though Lia knew many of Hayley's personal, boxed-up things would remain. At least the area around Lia's knitting chair had remained clear. Hayley understood that that space was sacrosanct and had so far avoided piling anything near it. So far.

Maybe Lia could pitch in on the search for an apartment for Hayley?

With that thought, she gathered up her keys, the dog photo, and the sheet of paper with Cori's address and headed out her door, noticing the fresh tidiness of her lawn as she did so. She smiled. There were definite advantages to having a housemate. That and the occasional gourmet dinner like the one Lia came home to the previous night. Maybe she wouldn't press too much on that apartment search. Her little house wasn't actually bursting . . . yet.

Lia soon discovered that Cori Littlefield's house was surprisingly large. Large, that is, for a single woman whose means of income, as far as Lia knew, was fairly modest. She double-checked the address to be sure she hadn't gotten it wrong, but it appeared to be correct. Spotting the beautiful crocheted wreath on the door convinced her, its multiple crocheted flowers picking up the bright blue color of the well-kept, century-old house's siding. Lia climbed the three steps to the wraparound porch and knocked on the door. Soon she heard locks turning, and the door opened a crack on its chain as Cori peered out.

"It's you!" Cori closed the door in order to slip the chain, then opened it wider to face Lia.

"Good morning," Lia said. "I hope I didn't disturb you." She started to reach into her purse for the photo, ready to slip it through the crack and leave, but Cori unexpectedly stepped back.

"No, it's fine. I was waiting." She smiled. "Want to come in?"

"Thank you. Just for a minute." Lia stepped into the small foyer and followed Cori's wave toward the living room on the right. It held an interesting mix of styles, hinting at having been furnished over several years. A sprinkling of antiques mingled with maple tables, and Lia wondered if the wall-to-wall carpeting hid a hardwood floor. As she sank onto the flower-printed sofa, she recognized the stained-glass Tiffany–style lamp beside it as similar to one she had coveted when she and Tom were first married.

"I have lemonade," Cori said, indicating a tray with glasses and a pitcher. "Would you like some?"

"How nice," Lia said, genuinely pleased. "What a lovely house you have," she said as Cori poured out two glasses. "I love houses with lots of character."

Cori handed Lia her lemonade, then sat on one of the side chairs. "It's my mom's," she said.

Lia nodded, wondering if Cori's mother would soon appear.

"I moved back about a month ago," Cori said. "I used to live in York."

"Did you? I lived in York for many years." Lia talked about the knitting group that she drove back to meet with once a week. "We started getting together years ago at one of the women's homes."

Cori seemed to be waiting for more, so Lia went on. "We all love to knit, but over time we began running out of people to knit *for*. So when the opportunity at the craft fair came up, we jumped at it. Now we can knit to our heart's content. The house we meet at, Jen Beasley's, is on Ninth Street in York. That's how my craft booth got its name: Ninth Street Knits."

Cori nodded. "I wondered about that." She smiled, but when she didn't offer anything about herself, Lia decided to ask.

"Did you sell your crocheted art when you were in York?"

"A little. There was a craft store that took things on consignment. At first, people that came there mostly wanted to try their own versions." She grinned. "Most of them found out it wasn't so easy."

"I'm sure they did!" Lia grinned back. "Oh, before I forget, let me give you the photo of the dog that this man hopes you can duplicate in yarn. His contact information is on the back." Lia got it out of her purse and handed it over.

"Cute dog," Cori said. She studied it for a few moments, then nodded. "I think I can do that."

"Great. You'll make his daughter very happy, I'm sure."

"Would you like to see some of the things I've been working on?" Cori asked.

"I'd love to." Lia set down her lemonade and followed Cori to the back of the house, where Cori's workroom was located. They passed through the kitchen, but no "Mom" was there, nor did Lia hear sounds of another person in the house.

Cori showed her around the workroom, which contained a dizzying array of crocheted angels, flowers, animals, and birds lined up on several tables.

"My goodness!" Lia exclaimed. "I guess you're ready for the next rush. These are wonderful!" She picked up one of the angels. "Do you follow patterns?" she asked.

"Sometimes," Cori said, clearly pleased to talk about her craft. "But I can figure out a lot of these on my own. After a while, you learn."

"How long have you done this?" Lia set down the angel and picked up one of the birds, a red cardinal.

"Oh, gosh! I started way back. My mom taught me how to crochet when I was little, and I liked it. It was relaxing."

The phone in the kitchen rang. Cori started. "Once I learned, I couldn't stop!" she said, glancing nervously back at the kitchen as the phone continued to ring. By the fourth ring she gave in. "I'd better get it. It might be important."

Lia smiled and nodded. While Cori dealt with the phone, Lia examined a bowl of crocheted carrots, peppers, and lettuce arranged prettily in a small basket. Behind that was a folded afghan. Lia lingered over the afghan, fingering it and admiring the color pattern, until something in the corner of the table caught her eye. It was a diorama of some sort in a three-sided shadow box, tucked in the back.

Lia reached over to carefully lift the box and bring it closer for examination. There was a sloping green crocheted hill and two crocheted figures, along with a scattering of flowers and a small bush. Studying it closely, Lia realized it depicted a nursery rhyme: *Jack and Jill went up the hill to fetch a pail of water. Jack fell down and broke his crown, and Jill came tumbling after.*

Except . . . something was wrong. Instead of Jack at the bottom of the hill, a female figure lay there, a small red bucket tipped on its side beside her. The male figure stood at the top, looking down at Jill. Though Lia told herself she was being silly, that a crocheted figure couldn't really show what he was thinking, his crocheted eyebrows looked menacing.

"This shouldn't be out!" Cori had returned. She rushed over and snatched it up.

"I'm so sorry," Lia said. "I wanted to see it better. I was very careful." She paused. "Is it supposed to be Jack and Jill?"

"Jessica! Not Jill, Jess—No! It's nothing! Just something I made up. It's stupid." She hurried the shadow box out of the room, and Lia heard her stomping up the stairs.

When Cori came back down, Lia had returned to the

living room, and she apologized once more. Cori waved it away, though she still seemed flustered. "I have to go," she said. "My phone call . . ." she added, vaguely implying something important about it.

"Of course," Lia said. "I didn't mean to stay this long. Thank you so much for the lemonade! I hope your special order works out."

"My . . . ? Oh, the dog. Yes. Thank you for bringing the photo."

Cori walked Lia to the door, where she politely but briskly said good-bye, and Lia left with a highly unsettled feeling. Something was wrong, but she had no idea what it was. Or what, if anything, she could do about it.

Ready to find
your next great read?

Let us help.

Visit prh.com/nextread